Holiday Heartwarmers

HOLIDAY HEARTWARMERS

Mimi Barbour

Sarna Publishing

Praise for Mimi Barbour

**Finalist in the Marge Wilson Contest
    **1st Place Winner for Chanticleer Clue Contest
    **USA Today Author (3 times)
    **New York Time Best-selling author

"As far as I know, I have read everything Mimi Barbour has published, and I bought most of them. I keep coming back because I love her sense of humor and style of writing and I always fall in love with her characters." ~ *Reviewed by A. Chambers*

"As a writer myself, I think that one of the true marks of an excellent author is solid, believable character development, and in my opinion, Mimi Barbour is the master of character development!" ~ *Reviewed by author Flo Barnett*

Dedication

This trilogy is dedicated to my Beta Readers who helped me ensure that the quality of the stories were there. Some assisted me in choose the names of the three novellas and others made suggestions to improve their quality.

Just know that you're truly appreciated.

Have a wonderful Christmas season and may it be filled with family, friends and fun.

XO

Mimi

Also author of...

She's Not You (Book 1)
Love Me Tender (Book 2)
***

Undercover FBI Series
— Popular & Compelling! —
Special Agent Francesca (Book 1)
Special Agent Finnegan (Book 2)
Special Agent Maximilian (Book 3)
Special Agent Kandice (Book 4 – to be released Winter 2015)
***

Holiday Heartwarmers Trilogy
— Truly a Christmas favorite! —
Please Keep Me (Book 1)
Snow Pup (Book 2)
Find Me a Home (Book 3)
Holiday Heartwarmers Trilogy Box Set
***

Other Titles
I'm No Angel
Hotshot Cowboy
Big Girls Don't Cry
Christmas Runaway
The Surrogate's Secret
Mimi's Mix (Box Set)
'Tis the Season (Box Set)
Hearts, Flowers & Romance (Box Set)
A Taste of Passion (Multi-Author Box Set)
Dangerous Encounters (Multi-author Box Set)
Ten Christmas Brides (Box Set with 9 other authors)
***

All Mimi's books can be found on her Amazon
Author Page:

http://bit.ly/MimiBarbourAmazon OR
Website: http://mimibarbour.com

Please Keep Me

Holiday Heartwarmers Trilogy
Book #1

Christmas is family time in Carlton Grove…

In this beautiful holiday love story, Belinda Page, a single mom of a very intelligent four-year-old daughter, is at her wits end trying to keep up with the baby genius. When the child throws herself into a lake to rescue a puppy, Belinda is frantic. Turning to the man who saves both babies, she seeks his support – until she finds out he's one of those hated Carltons. After all, it was at their home where she'd gone to a party, been drugged, raped and left to deal with the consequences.

Dr. Reed Carlton, an introvert who feels uncomfortable around most people, can't believe his luck. He's finally found Lindy; a girl from his past, a fond memory that has haunted him for over four years. Except that once this Lindy learns who he is, she hates him. What was that all about? At least her daughter and the puppy were on his side. But would their affection be enough for Lindy to accept him into her family's life.

Dedication

I want to dedicate this first novella, **Please Keep Me,** to Debbie Turner, the wonderful lady who came up with the title and got the **Holiday Heartwarmers** trilogy started.

Have a wonderful Christmas Season, my friend. May you be blessed with family, friends and lots of fun.

XO

Mimi

Prologue

Dark and frightening, the night sounds of busy birds, buzzing insects and muted traffic from the faraway streets created a surrounding racket that disturbed the terrified puppies. Rustling of the tree branches added to the discord, as did the wind sweeping up dry leaves and forcing them against solid objects where they splattered and crumbled.

The overwhelming, surrounding scents were tantalizing and yet not familiar and therefore, not comforting. Only the smell from the teats and the warmth of their mother's body was yearned for and missed.

Inside the cardboard box, the one female puppy communicated with her two brothers; *he's gone!*

Scampering to the corner of their flimsy prison, she thought back to the fight that had ensued between the man and her mistress before she and her brothers had been thrown here.

"Amelia, you kept those mutts? Before I left last week, I told you to get rid of them."

"But, Jimmy, they were too little to be weaned from

Bella. I was waiting until this weekend to try and sell them." Her mistress's lovely voice had sounded placating and miserable all at the same time.

"Who's going to buy these three? Their mom is a fat, ugly, overly-friendly lab with no guard skills; don't know why I let you talk me into keeping her. And that vicious Samoyed brute across the way, who's no doubt their father, is meaner than the devil who owns him."

"Jim, they're cute pups. I bet I can get a few dollars for them."

"Sure, and until then we have to listen to them kai-yiying all the time, clean up their messes and feed them. No more! I want them gone. It's bad enough we have to trip over that bag of bones without having to deal with her stupid offspring too. Never mind! Since you're as useless as a garden hose in a forest fire, I'll take care of this myself."

He yanked the three pups out from under the tummy of the keening dam where they'd burrowed in fear. Grabbing a nearby box, he hurled them inside. After a short drive in a car, he carried the carton for a few minutes and threw it down.

"Good riddance!" Those were the last words the puppies heard from him. The fading sounds as the man crunched away were terrifying.

Whimpering at the memory, after multiple tries, the female puppy bounced until her front paws gained purchase on the box's edge. Straining her neck, she peered out.

The moon, riding high in the starlit sky, provided illumination for the snoopy pup. *I think it`s a park*, she told the other two, whining, sharing her thoughts.

Chubbs, her roly-poly brother, subsided lazily in his corner, his furry body falling over and staying there. *What are we going to do?* Little beady black eyes watered as he howled pitifully.

Stop that caterwauling! It hurts my ears. His brother's normal cranky manner was evident in his insensitive attitude. *We'll sleep now, and in the morning, Sis can go and find us some help.*

Okay! That's a good idea, right, Sister? Chubbs yawned and curled up next to his brother. Both were asleep in seconds. Only their sister snoozed with one eye open, guarding their new dwelling.

In the morning, sounds of human voices woke the three. Again, the female bounced in the corner until she had her front paws clinging to the side of the carton. In the distance, she saw a lot of water. There were people running along its edge. To her left, there was a grassy field where humans were playing a game with a big brown ball.

Cranky wanted to see the world she was describing. When he got close, she used his butt as a ladder and worked her way up and over his head, landing ungraciously in a heap on the grass outside of their container.

Go, Sis. Find us help! Chubbs and the Cranky pup whined together.

Chapter One

Reed Carlton couldn't believe that his three brothers had talked him into a game of touch football, and on Thanksgiving yet. A day he'd normally be working. Or at home recuperating from too many shifts at the hospital where, as the youngest and easiest-going of the staff, he worked as a surgeon.

Since they'd recently opened the new surgical wing at the local clinic, he'd been playing catch-up with all the cases that had been put on hold for months. It seemed that everyone over the age of fifty and within a hundred mile radius had been waiting for some form of surgery. There were so many hip and knee replacements scheduled, it was a wonder anyone could still move around.

Carlton Grove, Washington, the small town where he'd grown up had become quite a thriving metropolis in the last decade and their hospital had had no choice but to expand and include facilities that the population demanded.

"Reed, throw it here." Gathering his drifting thoughts, he looked over at his youngest brother and grinned.

Harley was the most energetic and he normally managed to wear the rest of them out. Reed tossed the ball and watched as Harley, making a wily maneuver, snapped it from the air, dodged the three on the other team and headed for the goalpost. A line drawn in the dirt with a couple of branches planted at either end signified its importance.

In the next play, Reed received the ball and headed to the same goalpost, hoping to get in the clear so they could score again. This time, Harley, overly enthusiastic, heaved the ball way over Reed's head in the direction of the lake. Hurrying to retrieve the slippery object, Reed raced over the hill and his heart slammed into his throat at the scene playing out below him.

A furry white puppy ran to the top of the slope by the edge of the lake and had lost its footing. It slid and then rolled, ass over tea kettle, over the bank and into the water.

Meanwhile, a small child in jeans and a hoodie raced into the water with no hesitation, obviously intent on saving the puppy. As Reed watched, he could see they were both in trouble. One minute the little one was waist-high and reaching for the dog, and the next, he was in over his head struggling to find footing. And the pup, now in the kid's clutches, fought to free itself, which only made matters worse.

Oh-oh! Reed and everyone who had ever swum in that lake were aware that the shore was dangerously uneven. One minute you'd be safe walking on ground in low water, and the next step would take you down. Dead, rotting vegetation on the lake's bottom made it slimy and greasy in some places, dangerous in the extreme. Unable to balance, and with a wriggling puppy to contend with, the boy went under, taking the dog with him. Reed dropped the ball and ran faster than he ever had before.

Chapter Two

"Hollie?"

Belinda was furious at herself. One minute she'd played the polite stranger to tourists looking for the closest restaurant, and the next, was repaid by her naughty daughter taking off—God knew where.

The child was a terror, never listening to her, always thinking she could do as she pleased. A constant battle went on between the two. Only this morning, she'd been forced to bribe Hollie with a walk in the park if she'd go to her daycare after lunch and behave like the other children in her class.

Hollie had wrinkled her nose and looked disgusted. "The girls play with dolls and stuffed animals. And they giggle about everything. They're goofy, Mommy. And the boys fight over the same toys. Or whine. *Those* goofballs whine a lot."

"Hollie, baby, you're exaggerating. They're nice children. I spent my assigned afternoons helping out at the daycare, and I never saw a goofball in the crowd."

"*You* don't have to play with them. I don't want to. But

whenever I try and go off on my own to read, Miss Dummy makes me stay with the others."

"*Hollie!*" Belinda hid her smile and remonstrated with her daughter over the mispronunciation of her teacher's name. "You know darn well her name is Miss Dumry. Please don't make that mistake in school or she'll send you home again."

"I know." Hollie lowered her face, but not before Belinda had seen her tears. "She doesn't like me. I guess it's 'cause I don't like her neither."

"Of course she likes you, sweetheart. She's just very busy. There're so many children that she hasn't any time to pay special attention to just one."

"No! It's 'cause she's always checking her phone for messages and texting her boyfriend."

"I'm sorry, baby. Mommy's working really hard to try and save enough money to get you into a better school, one you'll love." Belinda was careful to call it school rather than daycare, knowing that would appeal to her disruptive little genius a lot more.

With an advanced curriculum, Hollie'd behave better. A grin broke through Belinda's worries. She decided she was probably the only parent who had a four-and-a-half-year-old child suspended from the relaxed, public daycare system.

Thank goodness, she'd managed to sweet-talk them into only making Hollie stay away for a week and not forever. They'd taken her daughter's disappearance on an unaccompanied walk in the empty grounds as a serious matter and used terms like 'uncontrollable' and 'single-minded'. This daycare had been the third placement Belinda had arranged for her high-strung little rebel and she'd begun to run out of options.

Hollie's problem was that she was just too intelligent. Bored easily, she found the other kids to be babyish and silly. Belinda felt heart-sick every time she thought of the private school she had in mind where the program included all kinds of activities that would appeal to her baby's cleverness. Stuff like painting with water colors rather than crayons, working in plaster making leaves and other realistic impressions, and not doodling with colored plasticine.

They taught them a lot more about the world around them and her baby would soak that all up and beg for more. Plus, the teachers were highly qualified and the class sizes realistic. Unfortunately, who had the kind of money to pay their ridiculous rates?

Lately, overwhelmed with the sole responsibility of Hollie's welfare, Belinda wondered if she'd done the right thing in choosing to keep her baby. Friends who'd strongly suggested an abortion were no longer people she hung around with. Her family, struggling to put her two older brothers through college, had no extra money to help. Instead, they'd advised her to go the adoption route.

She'd done neither. And now, she was pretty much on her own—same as always—and left to deal with the outcome of that choice.

"Hollie!" *Where was that child?*

A scream tore through her worry and Belinda stiffened with instant panic. The hairs on the back of her neck began doing that creepy thing they did when a person's instinct told them there was trouble. Her pulse tripled and distressing heart tremors quickly followed. Breathing normally became inefficient and she panted instead. *That was Hollie screaming.* Belinda, throat clogged with fear, began running. *Oh, Lord, what now?*

Chapter Three

Once Reed hit the water, he knew he had to get to the little guy. But since the puppy had wrenched away from the reaching arms, he figured the best way to gain control would be to grab the pup and take it along with him. Lunging for the animal, he hit a low spot and his feet lost purchase. One minute he was wading through the cold lake, and the next, he was in over his head.

Knowing it was too late to change his mind, he dove for the pup and grabbed its thrashing hind leg, and then turned for the boy. Except that the kid had somehow managed to snag his neck from the back and was choking him so hard that panic gripped Reed's senses.

Fighting to remain calm and not let go of the distraught pup, he tried to flip the boy onto his front where he could better control his movements, except the boy was having none of it. And instead, sensing that Reed was trying to dislodge him, he squeezed even harder. In trouble, Reed went under again. He swallowed a mouthful of water and came up choking.

Knowing he only had seconds to take control, he let go

of the pup and wrenched the little hands away from his neck. Once unlocked, he yarded the frenzied thrasher over his shoulder and hugged him close to his chest.

"Calm down, son. I have you. You're okay now. Stop fighting me."

Whether the kid heard him or not, Reed didn't know for sure. What he did know was that the boy had seen the pup on its own, and not understanding that animals could swim, he thrust away from Reed and threw himself toward the mutt yet again.

Bellowing so he'd be heard, Reed followed. "He's okay, boy. The dog can swim." Reed hauled the sopping wet little body back in his arms, only to have to physically subdue the child. "Listen to me." Reed shook the body to get his attention. "I'll get the puppy."

Finally having his feet on the ground where he could stand, he lifted the kid high over his shoulder. Then, to make sure there would be no further argument, he grabbed the bedraggled puppy, swimming for all he was worth in his free hand, and waded to shore where a group of people now waited.

Dripping with water and fury, Reed glared around him, hoping to see someone who would claim both daring little monsters.

The woman who ran forward, reaching for the mischief-maker, was reasonably rational, or so Reed thought until he saw the luminous terror glinting in her drenched brown eyes.

A feeling of déjà vu hit him like a sucker punch in the gut. *Lindy?* Before he could say a word, she'd wrenched the child out of his arms, lowered them both to a crouching position as if her knees didn't have the strength left to keep them upright and was kissing the tiny face nonstop, hugging the body and rocking them both from side to side.

Sobs broke from her, excruciating sounds of fear and self-reproach. "Baby, oh, Hollie. You scared Mommy so much. Never, ever wander away from me like that again."

"Mommy, I found a puppy. He's mine."

Reed, watching the two, felt a shifting in his heart region and unfamiliar soft emotions flooded.

Dazed and obviously half out of her mind, the woman he knew as Lindy agreed. "Yes, okay, honey. I love you, baby."

Since everyone's attention was on the re-joined family, the canine mischief-maker who'd started the whole spectacle shook herself hard to get rid of the water and fell over from the exertion. Then she wiggled her way to the woman's knees, scrambled between the clutching pair and jumped up to add her kisses too.

Both the woman and, as it turned out, little *girl*, opened their arms in welcome to include the canine into their circle of love. The pup craved the attention and squirmed so she could lather both their faces in a frenzy of adoration.

Just then, Reed's brother, Harley, approached. After making sure Reed hadn't suffered unduly, he commented, humoring everyone in the crowd, "It's just a mild case of puppy love, folks. Thanks to my brother, hero of the day, it looks like both babies are fine."

Chapter Four

Reed's middle brother, Terry, had had the forethought to fetch blankets from the car and appeared, passing the dry wraps to Reed.

"Thanks, bro." Reed took the blankets and approached the small family. He dropped the smallest cover over Hollie and Lindy made sure it enfolded the tiny body. She'd calmed somewhat and instead of kissing her baby, she now had the child by the arms and was doing what all mothers did in dangerously stressful moments; she was mothering.

With her expression full of tempered wrath, she wrenched the child away from her and shook the thin shoulders to get the attention she needed. Her eyes drilled the little girl's and the words she used would not be misunderstood. "Baby, what have I told you over and over? You left me. You must never do that. I need you to stay beside me all the time."

Pitifully, the little head hung from drooping shoulders. "I'm sorry, Mommy. I didn't know I went so far away. I only wanted to play with my puppy. But then he fell into the water and he needed me to help him." Her chubby hand reached forward and gently patted the woman's face, while big earnest melting brown eyes stared out from under a mass of curls that spiralled like a ginger halo around her little pink-cheeked face.

Lindy visibly melted and her control broke. Reed figured that her love and the recent worry for her daughter must have taken the starch out of her backbone. As if she needed some support, Lindy glanced up and caught his stare. "Tell her what she did wrong. I don't know how to make her understand."

As all eyes turned in his direction, Reed felt the onus shifting to his shoulders. Not knowing what the hell Lindy expected from him, nonetheless, he crouched down and faced the stubborn child still gripping the listless pup hanging over her arm.

Small but fierce, the kid looked defiant. Her bottom lip protruded and her brown eyes revealed anger and resentment. Yet he saw the fear she hadn't the ability to hide and that made the damn nervous tick explode in his right cheek. A warning bell clanged in his head. *Be Careful!*

The pup snapped out of her daze and took his measure also. The two stared at him. It was like nothing he'd ever faced before. Uneasy, he smiled at them and both pair of eyes looked wary, yet waited trustingly.

A second emotional deluge caught him unexpectedly. A mind that in a flash could answer any medical question put to him had nothing in its banks to deal with this dilemma.

What the hell did this woman expect of him? Given that he was the Carlton brother who never had much to say, the situation left him panicking. In fact, his family had often joked that their reserved brother had chosen the best possible route as a surgeon because most of the time his patients would be unconscious.

Without meaning to, he reached out and wiped away some drops of water from the child's face. They had escaped from the damp spiralled curls that bounced around as if they had a life of their own. Her eyes measured him, watchful, but she didn't flinch.

He heard the pup's pleading whine. Slowly, kindly, so as not to startle the little girl, he took the uncomfortable creature from her hurting grip and gently lowered her to his own knee. His big hand almost enveloped the small body as he petted the wet quivering animal. "You mustn't squeeze so tight. It hurts her."

When the first sob broke, not a sound could be heard. "I didn't mean to. I love her." As if she couldn't handle any more of the stressful situation she'd found herself in, the kid threw herself at Reed, her arms strangling as she blubbered her sorrow against his neck. "Don't be mad at me. I didn't mean to be a bad girl. But I had to help my puppy."

From the second he felt her tiny body melt against his, Reed's arms reacted. He hugged her to him, whispering brokenly, "Shush, sweetie. We're not mad. But you have to promise your mom not to ever run away from her again. Okay?"

"Okay." A reedy voice answered, but the arms still clung and the face still burrowed, seeking his warmth.

"Promise?"

"Okay."

"Uh, huh. You have to say the words. Then you have to mean them." Suddenly, a thought interrupted. Separating them, he watched her wary expression, "Do you understand what a promise means?"

"Yes." She tried to look away but he didn't allow it.

"What does it mean?"

"It means I'm going to be in a lot of trouble if I say those words."

Chapter Five

A lot calmer after she'd seen Reed laugh, Hollie left his arms and was now working on Belinda. "The puppy's mine, Mommy, she loves me."

The creature began to whine pitifully. First she stared at Belinda and then Hollie, her little black eyes full as if tears were brimming.

Look, she's begging. She's saying, please keep me."

As soon as Hollie had flung herself in those male arms, the pup, lowered to the ground to leave his hands free, had begun bouncing up and down, yipping her consolation. Now she was plastered against Hollie's side, gazing at her with pure worship.

Because of her daughter's pointing finger, automatically Belinda's glance fell on the now fluffed-out white canine, and dammed if those black eyes and grinning snout weren't beseeching her just like Hollie had said.

"No, baby, you can't keep the puppy. She must already have an owner." Hoping someone in the crowd would step forward, she deflated when no one did.

Belinda couldn't believe the manipulation her little

genius was working on her. And at a time like this when she was particularly vulnerable. Hollie had even added those magic words to include the puppy's make-believe appeals. *Please keep me! Really?* Weakness overcame her usual refusal. After all, she'd just watched her child survive a dangerous, near-death situation.

"She loves me, Mommy."

"No, Hollie. You know we can't look after her." Proud that she hadn't been swayed, Belinda recognized the hint of weakness in her tone and hoped her smart daughter hadn't caught it.

What made the situation worse was that this was a constant argument between them. Hollie had pleaded for a pet non-stop, and though Belinda would love to cave, she couldn't. So she always used the same argument. *"Not yet, honey. We can't look after a pet because we're never home. But one day, I promise."*

Belinda forced her eyes away from the entreaty in Hollie's, and noticed that most of the bystanders had faded from the scene. Only Belinda, Hollie and her savior were left to hear the puppy's heartrending whine.

Suddenly, the furry body scooted over to Belinda to snuggle as close as possible. Now it was two against one. *Oh, God!*

Belinda's heart dropped. First she looked at Hollie, and then at the puppy. Two pairs of eyes begged the impossible. She couldn't bear taking on any more responsibility. Her hands covered her mouth, but not before a moan broke loose.

"Sorry, sunshine. The pup belongs to me." The commanding male voice saved her ass and an overwhelming urge to do the same as her daughter had done just minutes earlier took hold. If only she could throw herself into his arms, wrap hers around his neck and sob with relief.

Instead, she shot him a look of gratitude and for the first time since the incident happened, she paid attention to Hollie's good-looking rescuer.

Short dark hair damply clinging to his head only created more focus on the soft brown eyes of the handsome devil. She recognized regret in his expressive face and knew he had stepped in to save her over the puppy—that he wasn't the real owner. *How sweet was that?*

Endearingly, he didn't try and hide his disgust at his lack of control. His stance revealed his annoyance. But when he saw her searching, he grinned lopsidedly and shrugged.

It was the grin that struck a chord. Memories long buried fought to be more than a fleeting vision, but faded almost as quickly as they started. One thing was for certain, she'd never met the man before because he wasn't someone any woman would be likely to forget.

Chapter Six

What the hell are you doing? His soft-hearted rescue, a position he'd never experienced before, had appeared and spoken before passing the words through his brain. And now that organ was laughing hysterically at his blunder. *Too late, you idiot! You can't take the words back. Look at Lindy's relief.*

It was true. Overwhelmed with gratitude, the woman wore a huge smile. "I'm sorry, baby. The dog belongs to this gentleman. You must give her back. And then thank him for rescuing you."

Hollie looked at her mom and then at Reed. Her wobbling lip almost unmanned him, but he waited to see what she would do. Shoulders again drooping, blanket now laying on the ground at her feet, she bent over and kissed the furry head. Then her little hands pushed the uncooperative dog toward him. "She's too little to know she's yours. Don't be mad at her. I guess she likes me." Sniffing audibly, she finally picked the puppy up and handed her over.

Reed looked at Lindy, whose eyes were still begging for support. He'd felt low before in his life but never like his belly was scraping the gravel. Still, the relief shining from his former one-night-fling's eyes couldn't be ignored. He had to carry on with the lie.

He took the beast from the little hands and held her against his chest, getting his chin bathed by the rough tongue and puppy breathe. "She doesn't recognize me yet because I just got her very recently. *Yeah, like a few seconds ago!* I'll have to train her to stay, ahhh... where I put her." Reed had no real intention of keeping the animal. As soon as he could escape from this awkward situation, he would find out if anyone knew where the pup came from. If not, he'd find a home for it. Someone among the staff at the hospital would take the little pain-in-the-ass off his hands.

"What's her name, sir?" Hollie couldn't seem to let go.

"I haven't named her yet. Without even pausing to consider the question, he asked, "What would you call her?"

"I'd call her Cloud."

No hesitation. Hollie answered and he had to ask. "Why Cloud?" The name surprised him. He'd expected Fluffy or Snowball, or something equally childish.

"Because she's white, soft and round like a cumulus cloud. I love clouds. Did you know there are a lot of different ones?"

Shocked stupid, Reed only nodded, his eyes flying to Lindy, who was trying not to let her pride be overcome by a smug grin. Intelligent beyond her years, the kid must be a handful.

Securing the blanket around her daughter yet again, Lindy picked her up and stood. She faced him as a stranger, a warm smile of appreciation lighting her beautiful face.

Reed, holding Cloud, got to his feet and waited, trying

to decide if he should remind her of their last meeting almost five years earlier, the weekend of his May 12th birthday. He watched her expression, peered into her oblivious gaze and decided she had no idea who he was. Strangely, that hurt. Made him decide the hell with reminding her of a night he'd spent years remembering.

Lindy smiled. "Please, what's your name? I want to thank you, and it seems too informal to call you sir like Hollie."

"I'm Reed Carlton. I work as a surgeon at the new hospital here at the Grove."

Lindy's expression closed and her smile faded. "You're a Carlton?"

"Yes." He'd never had to apologize for his antecedents before. But for the first time in his life, he felt compelled to say he was sorry. And if it would bring back the smiling girl from minutes earlier, he'd seriously consider changing his name to Wojciehowicz or Stubbs.

Stiff now, her previous warmth vanished, Lindy spoke in crisp tones, an order her daughter knew better than to ignore. "Hollie, thank Mr. Carlton for saving you today. He was very brave and we're both grateful." So saying, she forced her hand out to shake his. Pulling away as soon as his fingers closed around hers, she leaned her daughter closer and waited.

"Thank you, Mr. Reed. Me and Cloud are very happy you were there."

"Me too, sunshine. Be good and listen to your mom, okay?"

"Okay." Reaching with her small hand, he thought Hollie was aiming for the wriggling puppy. Not so. He felt her little fingers gently pat his cheek. "Be nice to Cloud. Maybe we can meet in the park, in the mornings on week-ends and I can play with her."

His eyes flew to meet Lindy's. She shook her head, the movement quick and furtive, her eyes now empty of their previous warmth.

Huh? What just happened? "That's a deal, honey. I'll watch out for you."

Chapter Seven

Of all the men in a city of over seventy thousand and rising, Belinda couldn't believe that Reed Carlton would be the one to save her baby. After all, the Grove was big enough that she'd gambled on never having to deal with a member of the family she'd detested for almost five years.

Maybe it wasn't fair of her to blame the entire Carlton clan for what had happened to her. But since her disgrace had occurred in their ostentatious home, and she had no idea of the actual culprit, it was just easier to condemn the host. Who, of course must have been a Carlton, maybe even Reed himself. Truthfully, she didn't know because she couldn't remember. How could she when she'd been drugged and virtually raped?

Just the thought of what had happened to her that May weekend was enough to make the sandwich she'd gulped down earlier feel like it would be making a re-appearance.

Stop thinking about it! You have to live here, there's no other choice.

Carlton Grove was where her family was and though they weren't able to help her financially, they did allow her to bring their grandchild to stay overnight when she had late shifts at the pub where she bartended. Without that second income, she doubted she could manage to bank even a penny of the wages from her other job.

Rushing now, Belinda zipped around their tiny apartment chosen because it was close to the park. Quickly, she bathed Hollie and made them both ready for the day.

Later, after listening to the little one chatting continuously about Cloud and Mr. Reed, pretending to pay attention with the occasional nod and hum of agreement, Belinda stopped her old beater and dropped her little monster munchkin off at the day-care.

"Hollie, remember your promise? We agreed that if I took you to the park this morning and we played on the swings, you would be a good girl this afternoon. Since it's your first day back, you must find a way to get along with Miss Dummy and behave..."

Giggling, her hands over her mouth as if to stop the laughter, Hollie scolded, "You mustn't call her that, Mommy. Remember? It's Miss *Dumry*."

Red-faced, trying to hide her own smile, Belinda glanced around to make sure she hadn't been overheard. "Sorry." She gently slapped her own mouth and said, "My bad! Miss Dum*ry* hopes to find more time to be with you, so be nice. Okay?"

"Mommy, if she'd put her phone... O-*kay*! I'll be good."

Belinda kissed her and watched as her little hellion ran off to join with a group of the others, mostly boys, and observed Hollie pushing her way in and then taking over the conversation. No doubt, by the end of the day, everyone would have heard about her morning's exploits.

This didn't bother Belinda near as much as what had happened earlier, while they were still at the apartment.

She'd left Hollie in the bath so she could call her mother to make arrangements to drop her daughter off after supper. She had her regular housekeeping job for the afternoon, had time to make them supper and then do a late shift at the pub.

Returning to the washroom, she'd spied her daughter in the mirror. Hollie had been rocking, hugging herself and crying softly, tears streaming from her sad eyes. Piled in front of her sat a mountain of soft white bubbles closely resembling a cloud.

Chapter Eight

Reed stood holding the crying puppy, soothing her as she wriggled to get down. Finally, he lowered the fluffy animal to the ground and then had to run and scoop her up again as she took off, following the woman and child now some way ahead.

"Oh, no, you don't! They can't take you, Trouble. Hey, settle down." The pup had a mind of her own and was frantic to get to the little girl who kept glancing back and waving sadly.

Finally, Reed had to wrap Cloud inside his blanket and turn the other way before the puppy stopped fighting him and relaxed with whine of dismay.

"Harley! Man, I'm glad you waited." Reed sloshed his way to where they'd parked, glad to see his brother leaning against the car, a cellphone held to his ear and a smile plastered over his face. As soon as he saw Reed, he shut down the conversation and stood. "Hey, bro, quite a morning you've had, super hero of little children and puppies."

"Zip it, dumbass! Here, take the mutt."

Harley stepped back and held his hands up in denial.

"Nope. I don't want the headache, man. It's all yours. Sure is a cutie though."

"Just hold her so I can get these wet clothes off me. I have a set of sweats in the car."

Shaking his head, vigorously, Harley laughed. "I ain't falling for that old trick. You've gotten away with it more times than I want to remember. That animal is all yours."

Pissed and showing it, Reed's voice deepened. "Did you by any chance see where it came from? Or notice anyone looking for her?"

Harley laughed out loud once more and shook his head, obviously enjoying his brother's predicament.

Sighing with disgust, Reed used the towel to make sure Cloud was dry, opened the rear door and shoved her carefully onto the seat. Then he closed it and went to the trunk. "Look, you're a cop, right? You're supposed to be so observant. Did you see anyone searching for a missing...? Stop grinning like an idiot and shaking your head. It's beginning to make me want to hurt you."

Harley cracked up. Not intimidated by his older brother's grouchy disposition, he finally straightened his face and solemnly answered. "I already told you. I didn't notice any unusual behaviour, but I can put an APB over the system to see if we can apprehend the nasty varmint who'd leave a teeny-weeny, adorable little puppy all alone in a park in the hope that some big-hearted, pea-brained shmuck would take pity on it."

"Jesus, man, with that smart mouth, I can't believe you passed the academy."

"And I can't believe you're a wealthy young surgeon who hangs out alone in a big old house, I might add, with a fenced-in yard, never goes anywhere and lives like a hermit. Guess it's your ugly face that's the problem. Must be why you never have any girlfriends."

"Yeah, right. At least I'm not a slut like you, always with a new chick on my arm, breaking their hearts every time you cut them off. Don't know how you sleep at night with all those rejected women calling you to reconsider."

Purposely, Reed used this example to get at the now straight-faced man glaring his way. One time Harley had left the speaker on his phone open and the whole family had overheard a female voice begging him to give her another chance. When he needed taking down a notch, they used this to tease the best-looker in the family of handsome boys.

Harley stiffened and straightened. His face lost its teasing look and his voice turned to steel. "That bitch did me wrong, not the other way around. And no one makes a fool of me and gets a second chance to do it again. And... in case you never figured it out, the females I spend my time with are all women who know the score. Until I meet 'the one', they're only pit stops on the course."

Knowing he'd overstepped the boundaries, Reed reached out and grabbed Harley's arm to shake it consolingly. "Sorry, man. That was shitty. I didn't mean it. Guess my temper's still working on high. I know you'll find your one and only. Hell, you've been talking about her as long as I can remember. But, I'm different. I'm a moody, introverted prick and I like my own space. Can't imagine any woman wanting to put up with the likes of me and wouldn't take the chance if I found one."

"Don't blame you. She'd obviously have mental issues to even consider taking you on." Harley, now visibly relaxed, patted his brother's hand before it disappeared. Reed didn't touch people often and when he did, it mattered. Being a smart man Harley apologized also. "I shouldn't have teased you, bro. Sometimes the devil gets into me and I can't resist. Look, I'll ask around and see if anyone knows anything about the pup. But my guess is that whoever dumped her here wanted her gone and couldn't be bothered to find it a home. My advice is to either take her to Mom or to the pound. She's cute. She'll be adopted."

"Yeah, well, I can't do that. I kind of promised the kid that I'd meet her in the park sometimes and let her walk Cloud. I can't go back on my word."

"Cloud?"

Reed shook his head. "It's a long story."

"So what were you planning to do if you'd have sucked me in to adopt the mutt?"

Reed grinned. "I'd have played uncle and taken the nuisance on outings, just like I expect you to do now."

"Yeah, like that's going to happen."

Chapter Nine

Mindlessly cleaning the house of her oldest client, Belinda tried to come up with some plan where she could somehow keep the little puppy and make her adored baby's dream come true. The image of Hollie sobbing into her hands had broken her heart, as it would any loving mother who knew the one thing her child most wanted, she'd just refused to give to her.

Plus, it had been obvious to anyone with eyes and a heart that the two little ones had bonded from the beginning. Belinda had heard Cloud whining after they'd walked away, and she seen Reed chasing the pup when she had tried to follow them.

But, no matter which way she jiggled her daily routine, there was no time in her busy schedule for the care of an active puppy. Especially one that looked like she'd be growing into a fairly large dog.

After all, not only would she need to be housebroken and have a fenced-in yard, she'd have to be fed, walked, groomed and trained. And... those things didn't happen in a few spare minutes. As it was, Belinda gave every bit of her free time to her daughter and those precious hours never felt sufficient.

Most days, guilt had her questioning all her decisions. *Does this laundry, baking, vacuuming... really need to be done, or should I use the precious time to play with Hollie?*

Also, the expense of taking on a pet just didn't fit into her overextended budget either. Already she did without a lot of ordinary comforts in order to save her pennies.

Completely lost in concentration, she knocked over a vase which brought her back to the present. The oil she'd been waxing into the antique furniture gave off fumes of cleanliness and old times that usually cheered her. But today, no matter how gleaming the tables looked, her heart was heavy with uncertainties.

Falling snow caught her attention. She straightened and stared out of the bay window at the luxurious gardens surrounding the older home. Because of the weirdly mild autumn, huge baskets of fall mums were still vying for attention. Now, all were slowly being buried under a white comforter.

"Belinda. You have sighed more than that old furnace does in the winter, and trust me, it's on its last legs and needs replacing. Can't you please tell me what's on your mind? If there's anything I can do to bring back your usual happy face, I'd like to help."

"So now you're telling me I sound like a crappy old furnace and look like a grinning computer icon. My day can't get much better." Laughing to take any sting from her words, Belinda went to her employer and, leaning over her wheelchair, she gave her a gentle hug.

Maeve Wakefield giggled, the sound brightening Belinda's spirit. "Put words in my mouth—go ahead—see if I care. But don't ever make light of how much I appreciate everything you do for me. It's because of you that I'm able to continue living here. Your help makes it possible."

"You pay me, Maeve." Belinda cut in softly.

"Not nearly enough. For one thing, I've never seen you just walk around here, you're usually moving at a sprinter's pace. And you know darn well I couldn't manage without you cleaning my house, doing my shopping and laundry, preparing a lot of my meals and even taking out the garbage. Those care-givers who come in and dress me and come back in the evening to put me to bed do help too. I appreciate you making those arrangements with them. You look after all those things, so do you see what I mean? It's only because of your constant attentiveness that I'm able to stay home."

"It's been my pleasure; you know it has, Maeve. I don't know what I'd do without you and this job."

"I just wish I could pay you more so you wouldn't have to take on the extra night work. Maybe I'm being silly hanging on to the old barn. I should probably sell and look for some place smaller?"

"Maeve, we're not getting into that nonsense again. I love helping you here at Cherrylane. If you moved away from your memories, you'd be sick at heart, and if you add that to the already weak valves you're living with, there's no telling what would happen."

The two laughed comfortably together and Belinda began sighing with relief for having gotten out of a tight spot. But... she should've known better. Previously having been a lawyer, and a damn good one, the seventy-eight-year-old hadn't forgotten the original thread that had started the conversation. "Sit down here and tell me what happened to give you such a pinched look and sad expression."

Taking a final glance at the shining room full of treasures, gilded mirrors and frightfully expensive keepsakes, then peeking at her watch and seeing she had a few minutes to spare, Belinda did just that.

"Hollie fell in love this morning." Telling a story to Maeve had to be done with drama. She wasn't the type who appreciated a boring tale.

"Aha! Well, I won't ask when the wedding is since I do believe Hollie graduating elementary and high-school is compulsory, but you can tell me about her new beau?"

Laughing, enjoying the discussion as much as she knew she would, Belinda played along. She smirked while answering, "The name is Cloud."

Maeve's eyes twinkled and her wrinkled hands folded together before she dropped them in her lap. "Very interesting! He's either a Native American, or quite possibly a Doberman pincher. Which is it?"

"Ha! You're so smart. And quite close. From the looks of his coloring, his beady little black eyes and grinning... ahhh...snout, I would say *she's* more likely to be a Samoyed puppy."

"How precious! I love that breed. They make wonderful family pets, especially the females. Can you bring Cloud to see me?"

Losing her grin, Belinda stared at her red, chapped hands. "We didn't keep her. She was wandering in the park this morning, slid down the embankment and went right into the lake. My impulsive and irrepressible Hollie happened to see this and went right in after her, thinking to save the pup. Instead, she lost her footing and took a header. I arrived in time to see a man rescuing them both. He ended up with Cloud."

"The dog was his?"

"Not really. I think she's a stray. Despite all the onlookers nearby who saw what happened, not one stepped forward to claim the animal. And Hollie was wearing me down with her begging. Then Mr. Carlton claimed her. I believe he lied to help me, though I begrudge having to accept this gesture. Quite possibly, if I'd known he was a Carlton I wouldn't have, but it's too late to back down now."

"I don't understand."

"Hollie made him agree to let her walk the puppy if we were able to meet in the park on weekend mornings." Belinda didn't hide her frustration fast enough. Wily Maeve had eyes like a hawk.

"And that's a problem, why?"

"Because I hate the Carltons—plain and simple. It's because of them that I had to change my life, give up my dreams of being a nurse and ended up as a single mom."

"My goodness, Lindy, what in the world did they do for you to feel such resentment?"

The nickname made Belinda hesitate. Maeve was the only person who called her that from time to time and, whenever she did, memories tried to break through which left Belinda feeling a strange yearning.

Shaking off her reaction, the overwhelming urge to tell her story took hold. Seeing Maeve waiting, and trusting her more than anyone else she knew, she finally decided her painful experience needed to be shared.

Plunging in before she changed her mind, she began. "When I was young and foolish, visiting my folks for the May weekend from college, I'd gone along with a group of friends to a party at the Carlton home. Normally, I didn't hang around with this group; they were wilder and way more unconventional than I was. But one of the girls who

I'd grown up with asked me to come with her. She'd invited me to go with her so many times that I felt bad for all the refusals.

When we arrived at this big house, there was a party in the wild stage; booze everywhere and couples were being far more than romantic—if you know what I mean. Not used to this kind of behaviour, I'd all but decided to leave when one of the cool girls I'd known in high school gave me a glass of beer and welcomed me so nicely that I decided I was being a prude. Then someone asked me to dance and, without a thought in the world, I left my drink on the table and didn't return to it for some time. When I did, I was so thirsty that I drank it and that's the last thing I remember. The next day, I felt achy and sore and had a hangover. Mainly, I was scared because I couldn't recall any events from the night before. My girlfriend told me I'd had a fabulous time, had flirted with all the guys and had even disappeared with someone. She thought it might have been one of the Carlton boys, but she wasn't sure."

"Oh, oh!"

"Yes! As you can imagine, I was very embarrassed. Then three months later, I was totally devastated."

"And Hollie was born Christmas Day."

" As you know she was premature."

"Goodness me, Lindy, I'm saddened by your story, but aren't you being rather harsh on this fellow who rescued Hollie today? After all, he could be her father."

Oh, my God...

Chapter Ten

Belinda held out the first weekend after the incident, refusing to go to the park. Instead, she took Hollie to her parents' home one afternoon for her mother's birthday party, and she arranged a movie the next day to take the pouting child's mind off where she yearned to be. But she just didn't have the stamina to withstand the barrage of 'please' that her determined little monster fired at her for the rest of the week. All she could do was pray that Reed Carlton didn't show up this morning.

Dressed warmly, Belinda followed her excited daughter along the walkways toward the lake and breathed a little easier when she didn't see any fluffy small white animals nearby.

Dancing along, excitement lighting her pink cheeks, Hollie wore a new red hat and matching sweater her mother had knitted for her to help pass the long lonely evenings watching romantic sitcoms on television.

All the snow was finally gone from the freak snowstorm they'd had the day after Hollie had fallen into the lake. The cold spell had given over again to warm weather, but the smells of winter close by made the day extra beautiful.

"Stop running to and fro, Hollie, you're making my neck sore trying to keep track of you. Let's give Mommy's tired legs a break, and sit here on the bench and I'll tell you a story."

Grudgingly, Hollie came and plopped down beside her mother and sulked. "Mr. Reed said he'd bring Cloud. He promised."

"No, baby, he didn't do any such thing. It was a casual 'maybe' and you know it."

"But he winked at me, Mommy, and that means a promise."

"Where in the world did you get such a goofy idea?"

Oh, no!

Bouncing with delight, Hollie took off at a mad dash to meet up with the yipping puppy who was in a panic to get to her. Their meeting in the grass brought tears to Belinda's eyes. Both canine and child were so delighted to be together again that the kisses and licks were all mixed together in a hugging frenzy of love.

Reed, holding an empty leash, approached and stood near the bench. "May I?" He gestured at the seat.

Rather than sit near him, she stood instead. "I was just going to walk. I-I need the exercise." *Liar!*

"You weren't here last weekend. I came both days."

"Are you accusing me of being a bad mother?"

He swung to face her. "What? Why in the hell would you think that? I just wanted Hollie to know that I hadn't broken my promise."

"Oh, you two. It's enough for me to try and control that little devil, and now I have you siding..."

"Hold it, Lindy. I wasn't accusing you of anything, or

trying to make you feel bad."

"What did you call me?" Furious beyond reason, she spat out words at the same time as she glared her anger.

He backed up a step. "Isn't your name Lindy?"

"My name is Belinda Page. No one calls me Lindy."

Awkwardly, Reed put his hands behind him. "I'm sorry. We met once a long time ago and you introduced yourself then as Lindy. I recognized you, but you didn't seem to remember me, so I never said anything."

Oh, my God! It's him! He must be Hollie's father.

A sickening feeling of dread overcame her and she was forced to sit down again on a different bench. Pain seared her temples, pressing relentlessly, pounding into her panic. Hugging herself to control vicious accusations from spewing, she bit her lip and hid her face.

"Lindy, here let me help you." He gently forced her head toward her knees and rubbed her back.

His touch soothed but she didn't want his hands on her. She couldn't look at him. *Oh, God!*

"Take deep breaths. That's good. Slowly."

She shied away from his hands. Her mind raced, thoughts fighting over each other to be heard, to make sense. Though she followed the instructions from the soft-spoken male voice, she tried to conceal her reactions to his touch. *I need to get away!*

"Mommy, what's wrong?" Both child and puppy had come running and were now fussing over Belinda. Hollie tried to hug her around her head and the pup whined pitifully. She heard the fear in her little girl's voice and that was enough to give her the strength she needed to snap out of her pity-party. Feeling the puppy's tongue on her cheek, giving her own brand of comfort, Belinda gave Cloud a cuddle and took the time to breathe deeply.

"I was a little dizzy, baby. But I'm fine now." She caressed Hollie's worry away from her face and held up the excited canine. "Cloud. You've grown." Gathering the quivering mutt close, she let the animal shower her with affection.

Hollie, obviously satisfied her mom was fine, turned to the hovering man. "Mr. Reed. You came like you promised."

"Of course! I think Cloud knew she would see you here. She pulled me so fast to the lake area; I had a heck of a time keeping up. I was worried the little monster would drag me along behind her if I fell."

Seeing her laugh at the mind-picture of the little puppy pulling along the big man, Hollie's giggles had him chuckling also.

Belinda, fearful of the child racing off again with her furry friend, rose carefully, steadying herself by holding onto the back of the seat and made a suggestion. "Let's take Cloud for a little walk now, because it'll soon be lunchtime and we'll have to go home to eat."

Hollie's demeanor changed instantly. Stiff with resentment, she appealed, "We can go on a *long* walk. I'm not hungry."

Belinda watched Reed hide his smile and turn away.

"Yes, baby, but little puppies tire very easily. Their legs are short and not as strong as a big girl like you. We'll go around the park and that should be enough for one day." Though her voice started out in a gentle humorous tone, it had changed by the end of her sentence. It became firm and meant business, and Hollie knew not to argue.

Reed attached the leash to the puppy's collar and handed it over to outstretched chubby hands. The two were off at a run.

"Hollie Page. You stay in my sight, you hear me?"

"Yes, ma'am." A grin and nod were shared, and then all her attention became focused on her furry companion.

Chapter Eleven

"Hollie's very good with the pup. And Cloud adores her." Reed knew he needed to fill in the silence. It was obvious that Lindy was still suffering from her earlier predicament. He just wished he knew what he'd said wrong.

Lindy's answer took time but she eventually replied, "It's all I've heard about for the last week: Mr. Reed this, and Cloud that. She was furious at me for not bringing her last weekend."

"Truthfully, I expected to see you. Even Cloud seemed disappointed when there was no sign of Hollie. She whined when I took her away and pulled so hard at the leash that I had to pick her up."

No way would Reed tell her how he'd dressed in a new outfit, groomed the pup for an hour and had even bought a chocolate-covered candy apple as a special treat for Hollie. Disappointment had ridden him for days and was most likely felt by anyone who had the misfortune of working in his surgeries.

He'd told himself he wouldn't come today. He'd work. But when the time came he'd booked the morning off, and here he was trying to understand why the woman he'd been so attracted to seemed to hate the very sight of him.

Since she didn't answer, he added, "I wasn't accusing you. Please don't think that—"

"No, don't apologize. It's me. I'm behaving badly."

She faced him, her cheeks still pale. Melted chocolate, her brown eyes highlighted by curled dark eyelashes didn't quite hide her raging emotions. Pink lips quivering slightly, lush and full, drew his attention. She'd changed in the last few years, filled out—seemed more mature and even more beautiful. "I have to ask you something. Did we meet at a party at your house five years ago?"

Reed studied her pallor and quickly put his hands behind him, stuffed them in his back pockets, a habit he had for self-protection. He stared at his shoes and took a minute to decide his answer.

Unsurprisingly, his mind raced into the past and he was reminded about an incident as a carefree young teen. When he'd impulsively reached out to a distressed girl, he'd gotten his face slapped and his heart broken. The girl he'd believed returned his affection hadn't had the finesse to deal with a boy's sensitive nature. Head over heels in love, he'd trusted that she'd cared about him in the same way. Not so. He'd learned a huge lesson that day: *don't ever open yourself to a female. More than likely, you'll live to regret it. Keep your walls up and stay behind them.*

She waited, staring, not moving. He sensed her anxiety and it made him ultra-nervous. *For pity's sake, just tell the truth.*

"Yes, we did. Look, I tried to find you again but you'd disappeared." Watching the varied emotions she couldn't hide, he stopped talking and waited. Didn't she remember the incredible night they'd spent together? She'd flirted

with him, come on to him but with a naiveté and sweetness that had hooked him big time.

Not one to party, that night he'd been celebrating the
end of his finals and had gone a bit crazy. When she'd
shown up, acting the sexy siren, she'd just been too damn
perfect to ignore.

And he hadn't regretted that decision. At first, when
he'd realized she'd never been with a man, he'd tried to
stop but she hadn't let him. He'd never been with a virgin
before, but she'd been sweet and giving, leaving him with
the feeling that he'd been special.

After they'd satisfied their hunger for each other, he'd
gone to get them some wine and a platter of goodies.
When he'd returned to his room, she'd disappeared. He'd
searched frantically, asked everyone if they knew her but
many had left and those still around had no idea who
he was talking about. In the end, all he'd had from their
encounter was the beautiful memory and her first name.

"What do you mean I disappeared? How did I do that?"

Feeling like he was walking through a live minefield,
Reed hesitated. Then he decided to speak truthfully.
"Lindy—it's what you asked me to call you—we hit it off
that night. Both of us were infatuated—"

"Mommy, you were right! Cloud is tired. She's whining for me to carry her. I guess we better rest for a while."

Reed couldn't decide if he welcomed the interruption
or not. Lindy's eyes were huge, watching his face closely. It
appeared as if she wasn't breathing, so enthralled was she
with his words.

The sigh she let escape ended in a tiny imperceptible
cry that shot straight to the muscles in his throat and made
swallowing impossible. He watched her struggle to shake
off the spell, but not before he recognized the frustration

she couldn't hide. With her hands gripping each other to still their trembling, she finally answered. "Yes, okay, sweetheart. Maybe it's time that Mr. Reed, I mean, Mr...."

"Please, just call me Reed."

She searched his eyes and then nodded. "...time for Reed to take Cloud home for her nap."

No! Clamouring in his head, the instinctive word made one thing very clear to him. He didn't want this meeting to end. "Look, we haven't had much time to be together. So, can I take you ladies for lunch? There's a restaurant just at the entrance to the park called Di's where the owner is crazy about Cloud and allows me to put her under the table while I eat. We can go there if you like?"

Watching the by-play between mother and daughter, he had no idea how she withstood her baby's arguments, enhanced by pleading eyes and trembling lips, for as long as she managed. He'd have been a goner after the first *I-promise-to-be-a-good-girl–forever* tearful plea.

Chapter Twelve

Sitting together in the booth at Di's, Belinda wasn't exactly sure how she got there. Certainly, Hollie had played a big part in making up her mind. Guilt had ridden her hard at how seldom she could afford to give her baby a meal in a restaurant. Plus, she knew how much it meant to the little girl to have more time with Cloud.

Once the waitress had fussed over the tired puppy and they'd settled her on the mat under the table, she'd taken their orders and left them to move on to the other customers. Hollie, sitting on the floor near Cloud, was happy in her own little world, and had left the two adults facing each other with just the well-washed table top between them.

Looking anywhere but at Reed, Belinda studied the cozy place and saw an atmosphere and faded furnishings that hadn't been updated in decades. It reminded her of the diner she'd practically lived at with her high school friends. The good food smells that attacked the minute they'd walked in were making her mouth water and she realized just what a treat it was to be waited on and having her meal served to her.

"I'm glad you came." His words seemed to surprise him, make him uncomfortable, as if they escaped his mouth before gaining his permission.

Speaking low, she shared, "Hollie doesn't get to eat out very often. It's a wonderful treat, so thank you for inviting us." Belinda stopped talking before she made a fool of herself. As much as she yearned to go back to their earlier subject, fear and shyness stopped her questions.

"My pleasure. Really!" He put his long-fingered hands on the table and stared at them in a funny way before he looked at her, his eyes full of warmth. "After you left the park that day, it took some time to settle Cloud. She fretted terribly for hours. Strange as it may seem, I think those two bonded... ahh, I'm not making much sense but you had to be there to see the little monster grieve. Finally, that night, I had to bring her into bed with me and hold her close so I could get some sleep. And trust me, if anyone would have told me I'd be doing anything so asinine, I'd have laughed and told them to get real."

Belinda saw his cheeks redden before he bent over to check under the table. It was as if his confession had escaped without him meaning to say anything. Sensing his discomfort and not being a person who liked to see others in distress, she quickly cut in, "I think that was sweet of you. Many would have shut her in a bathroom or the garage."

He straightened. "Only one person has ever accused me of being sweet." Their eyes met, and there was an emotion in his that had her breath catching and her heart beating so fast she swore the pulsing in her chest must be visible.

As if the words were forced, she admitted her own situation. "It was the same with Hollie, only she carried on for days. I have a strict rule that she must sleep in her own bed, but that night I had to share it with her, to soothe her. She refused to understand why we couldn't keep *her* puppy."

"You could have. You knew it wasn't mine."

"No. That's just it; we don't live that kind of a lifestyle. I work two jobs, and as much as I would have loved to have Cloud, I have no time left over to raise another baby."

Lost in his searching gaze, warmth and gentleness making the green hues in his brown eyes darker and more intense, she didn't notice when his hand enfolded her fingers to stop their unconscious fidgeting. It was the brush of something against her leg that dropped her back to earth with a thud. *Hollie!*

"We need to talk." A frantic urgency had entered his low voice, and she felt pulled between mothering her child and losing herself in the chaotic emotional whirlpool he created with every glance.

Ignoring his insistence, she pulled her hands from under his and reached down to her child. "Sweetie, come with Mommy now. Our food will be here soon and you need to wash your hands before you eat."

He leaned back, watchful, waiting for a response to his plea. Before she could whisk the child away, he tried again. "Lindy? Answer me. When can we meet?"

"No. I mean, not yet."

"When?" His right eyebrow rose and steel entered his voice.

"I don't know. Excuse me. We'll be right back."

By the time she'd returned with the munchkin, the hamburgers had been delivered, along with Hollie's strawberry milkshake and a huge basket of flavourful fries.

Being considerate, Reed had fetched a higher chair for

the little girl to sit in but when she spotted it, mutiny appeared and she crossed her arms, her mouth forming the stubborn pout that Belinda knew well.

Reed stepped forward. "Here we go, Sunshine. They have the special chairs for little girls to use. Let me help you." He reached to lift her and Hollie backed away.

"Those chairs are for babies."

Looking nonplussed, Reed nodded first. Within seconds, he realized his mistake and his head changed direction. "Not really. They're not *just* for babies; the owners have them for anyone who wants to... ahh, sit up higher." Looking for help, he glanced her way. Belinda quickly shook her head and grinned. Let him suffer his own folly. She'd experienced her daughter's displeasure often enough, she had battle scars no one saw—didn't mean they didn't exist.

"I'm bigger when I sit on my knees. They're strong and it's healthy exercise. I do yoga with Mommy and it's one of our poses. Right, Mommy?"

Her hands outstretched, Belinda shrugged at Reed and watched him surrender gracefully.

"Okay, swift, you got me there. A yoga chick; heck you must be older than I thought."

Giggling proudly, Hollie answered. "I'm five on Christmas Day. I'm just kinda short."

Chapter Thirteen

Right after they'd eaten, before Reed could pin Lindy down to a date and time for their next meeting, she'd rushed Hollie along and vanished.

Driving back to the hospital for his afternoon appointments, he remembered the little girl's proud statement: *I'm five on Christmas Day.*

Suddenly that fact hit him like a rock on the side of his head. He swerved, his foot ramming the brakes hard. Stunned, his brain opened an inner calculator and he quickly added the months from the night in May when they'd been together. A quick sigh of relief followed.

Thank God! Hollie couldn't be his.

Why sadness washed over him, he didn't know, but a faint inner glow faded and his heartbeats slowed. The brainy, curly-haired angel with dimples and the attitude of a little warrior wasn't his. He swallowed the sigh and pulled into his reserved slot. Gripping the steering wheel with both hands, he lowered his forehead and for just a few minutes he let himself wallow in unexpected desolation—*she wasn't his.*

Upon reaching his office, he spied his receptionist talking with his next patient, one of his favorites.

"Ah! Here's Dr. Carlton now."

"Maeve, my dear, how are you today?"

"Could be better, Dr. Darling. Could be better." Maeve coughed and the harshness in her voice deepened. "Now if you'd stop being so damn finicky and write me a large prescription for some of those pain-relieving narcotics you're hoarding, I'd be perfect."

Smiling at their nonsense, he answered. "Sweetheart, if you'd quit trafficking the ones I give you, they'd last longer. How many times have I told you to stop sitting on that street corner and selling the product?"

Giggling at their silliness, Maeve clapped her hands. "Okay, you got me there. I'll be good." She coughed again, and he helped her sit upright.

Wheeling her chair into his office, Reed proceeded to take her blood pressure and then he checked the information on his computer screen. "How's your breathing, darling? Is it getting difficult? Are you wheezing? Any chest pains? Having trouble sleeping?"

"Not really. But I'm tired all the time. My housekeeper has taken on all the chores for me because I'm pretty useless. She wants to hire someone to come and sleep in the house with me at night so I'm not alone, and I admit that I've given it some thought. I guess it's the stranger in the house aspect I'm not comfortable with. During the day, she's organized caregiver visits and an alarm button, but those dark hours can be lonely."

'I'm glad she's looking into it. You should have someone with you all the time now."

"Now? Okay, spill the beans. How long do I have, Dr. Carlton? I know you couldn't operate..."

"You mean you refused to let me."

"Yes, well, I didn't want to be any more of an invalid than I already am. I just wanted to live these last few months in as normal a way as possible, stay in my house and enjoy the life I have left. You said yourself that my ticker is wonky."

"Darling Maeve, I never said your *ticker* was *wonky*." Reed grinned. "I would never use medical jargon with a patient who wouldn't understand such technical terms. I remember distinctly using layman's words when I explained that you suffered from mild congestive heart failure. A heart attack was just a possibility. One I felt you had to be aware of. There were other procedures we talked about, such as radiation or chemical therapy that I thought might stave off the end, but you refused them all."

"Yes. I know. I'm a stubborn old wretch who's made up her mind. Rather than take any chances, no matter how slim, I wanted my last months to be special. And it's been wonderful. I've put all my finances in order, so I'm ready to go out of the world like I came in, kicking my legs and screeching like a banshee."

Reed laughed, couldn't help himself. The spritely lady sitting in front of him was a jewel and he would miss her terribly. But from the results of her latest scans and blood tests, she would begin fading more quickly now.

"I'm going to have a technician deliver an oxygen ventilator to you which you must begin to use constantly. You'll find it helpful for sleeping especially."

"Will it stop this infernal cough?"

"Sure, it'll soothe you and help your breathing ability a lot. I'm also giving you a different prescription for antibiotics and one for relaxation. You must take them as directed. Maeve, it's time for you to have someone with you during the day as well as the night, a person to help you with the new equipment. Do you have anyone you can ask?"

Maeve shook her head. "As you know, I never had any children and my sister died a few years ago, unfortunately preceded by her only daughter. So, no, there're no relatives. But I could ask my housekeeper to move in with me, I suppose. She's a lovely girl and has a small child of her own. Since I've willed everything to her, she might choose to move into the house anyway."

"Good. Ask her. It'll make all the difference to you in these last few months having someone to be with you. Otherwise, we'll have no choice but to bring you into hospital."

"Aha! You just let the cat out of the bag. I only have a matter of months now. Yes, I can see by your long face that the end is close. I'm not at all unhappy, Dr. Darling." Maeve reached out and took his hand, smiling as his warm fingers wrapped around her thin claw-like ones and squeezed. "You've been good to me, my friend. Please know how much I've appreciated having someone listen rather than just give orders. Bless you, Doctor, and thank you."

Chapter Fourteen

"Maeve, tell me again why your doctor won't operate." It was a question Belinda had asked before, and each time Maeve had looked away and made little of her response, putting Belinda off with a nonchalant shrug and a silly excuse. Furious that the medical community could be so uncaring with her precious friend's life, Belinda had been tempted to interfere. If Maeve's faculties were questionable, she would have. As it was, her friend was sharper than most her age.

Maeve shrugged. "Oh, you know, they have so many patients. I'm just one of hundreds. Besides, I have no complaints about my treatment. In fact, Dr. Darling has been wonderful. But he's insistent that I have someone live with me now or it'll be the hospital for me and I would hate that. So I'm asking if you and Hollie you can do it."

Belinda leaned over and gave her a gentle squeeze. A scent of roses wafted around her boss. Since the lotion had been one of Belinda's birthday presents to Maeve, the odor pleased her. "Of course we can move in here with you. Hollie will be ecstatic to be this close to special Auntie Maeve at Christmastime and she'll love having the yard to play in, especially if we're lucky enough to have snow this year. Plus, I'll feel a lot better being with you during the night, rather than constantly worrying when you're alone."

"It's settled them." Maeve slapped her knees and settled back in her chair. The white curls haloing her wrinkled face bounced with satisfaction.

"What about the evenings when I'm at work? There's a friend of Mom's, you've met her before, that lady called Freda who lives close by. She's babysat for me periodically when the family were away and she's strapped for cash most months. She might like to earn a few extra dollars to come and stay with you and Hollie during those hours. Should I ask her? She wouldn't charge much so I can probably pay her from my tips."

"I'll pay her, you mean. After all, you'll be changing your life for me."

"We'll work it out." Belinda had noticed the ventilator resting on wheels over in the corner and decided to take the plunge. "So, Miss Maeve, suppose you tell me about that contraption over there and how it works."

"Oh, we'll let my doctor explain. He's promised to come over tomorrow afternoon so he could explain everything. I couldn't make any sense of what the delivery fellow said. Spanish accents and my ears just don't go together. Guess I'm too old."

Belinda smiled. "Your Dr. Darling does house calls?"

"For me he does."

"That's wonderful. I'll be here. I can't wait to meet him." She turned away, hiding the determination from

Maeve to give the idiot a piece of her mind for not taking better care of her friend.

Too many patients... bah!

Chapter Fifteen

Belinda wiped the counter and settled back to washing glasses. It was quiet tonight in the bar area; most folks were in the dining room having a meal. Other than taking the occasional wine orders, she had the time to scan the room, see that the few regulars were settled and happily occupied with filled glasses. She let her mind wander.

Modern, yet warm and inviting, the wooden booths and tables scattered around the fair-sized room were tidied and waiting for the customers she knew would eventually appear. The greens, grays and blues used in decorating the walls and light fixtures presented the low-lit room with a convivial and inviting atmosphere.

Modern music played in the background, kept low for her own enjoyment and it wouldn't be turned up to fight with the noise of people having a good time until later when no one cared.

Having left Maeve's house to pick up Hollie and deliver her to her parent's home, she'd explained that it would likely be the last time the little girl would be overnighting with her grandparents for a while. Smiling at the memory of Hollie's glee, she allowed the satisfaction to take hold.

"Auntie Maeve wants us to live with her? In her house? Even me?"

"Yes, for the third time, she wants both us of us to live with her."

"I'll be a good girl, Mommy. I won't run around or yell very much. Maybe we could get Mr. Reed to bring Cloud over to see where we live and meet Auntie Maeve. She'd like that, wouldn't she? Then I could play with my puppy in the yard."

Belinda sighed over Hollie's noticeable use of the pronoun 'my'. "We'll see. I can't make any promises, munchkin. You do know that Auntie Maeve isn't well, I've explained this to you before, remember? She'll need a lot of sleep and then one day she won't wake up. Do you understand?"

The silence trembled. A sigh escaped the little girl, one of acceptance. "Yes, she told me she can't wait to go to sleep because soon she'll get to live with the angels. She's lucky. I wish I could see the angels."

Belinda smiled, swallowing the instant shot of dismay those words evoked. "One day you will, baby, but for now, you need to stay and look after Mommy."

Lost in her own world, reliving earlier moments, Belinda didn't see the man who approached the black granite counter and took a seat at the end of the bar until he lifted the menu.

Shock had her hesitating, but his welcoming grin started her feet moving forward. "Hi, Lindy."

"How did you know I worked here?"

"Hollie told me while you were in the ladies' room after lunch."

She tried to hide her smile and knew she'd failed when he returned it. Cheekily, she added, "How did you know I'd be here tonight?"

"I didn't." His playful wink had her raising an eyebrow and trying to suppress her pleasure. "I've checked in every night for a drink and figured I'd catch you sooner or later."

"You lucked out tonight. I'm only here for a short shift to cover for a friend. If you'd been a half an hour later, you'd have missed me."

His satisfaction was obvious. "Good. Then you'll be free for dinner."

"I wasn't angling for an invitation—"

"I know that. I never believed you were. But I want to get to know you and you don't really give a guy a chance to make that happen. You haven't returned my calls, and I know I used the right number because I heard your voice message."

Sheepishly, she looked down at her hands locked in a tight grip, one thumb peeling the nail polish off the other. "I didn't know there were messages. It's a new cell phone and the girl where I bought it set up voice mail. I've forgotten her instructions on how to recover calls."

His face lit up and the smile he sent her way had her knees knocking. My goodness, the man had charisma. When he looked into her eyes, she felt herself drowning in twin sensations of lust and – could it be – hope?

A server called her name and broke into their moment. Quickly, she filled the order, moving briskly and efficiently. Then she called to Reed and got his preference for a beer and the brand. While filling the mug, she glanced quickly in the mirror and felt thankful she'd changed earlier into her favorite soft blue sweater and the slacks that showed off her long legs and flat tummy.

Because she was only twenty-seven and lived alone, she'd spent way too many lonely nights working out, stifling frustration by doing exercise and yoga.

Be glad, girl. It's paid off.

He'd picked up his beer and brought it closer to where she'd gone back to washing glasses. "Lindy, *will* you have supper with me tonight?" Mistaking her hesitation, he added. "We can stay here, if you prefer. Most nights I eat alone so you would be doing me a huge favor if you'd have a meal with me. We could share our stories and bring each other up to date. Besides, it'll stop me from being bored with my own company and passing out with my face in the spaghetti."

Laughing at that mind picture, she studied him and saw the exhaustion the poor man suffered. "It might be best if you ordered take-out and got an early night."

Chuckling, he shook his head. "Trust me, that's my customary pattern. Sharing a meal and conversation with a woman not connected to the hospital would be a treat beyond anything you could imagine."

"Then, since Hollie is at my parent's house tonight, I'd like that." With her heart beating to where she thought she could pass out, where it made breathing difficult, she hoped he hadn't taken her explanation about Hollie's whereabouts as being a hint she expected more than dinner. Feeling absurdly tongue-tied, her usual state around men, Belinda held her breath.

"Great!" Waving his phone and grabbing his beer, he grinned like a man feeling happy. "I'll let you work while I go and answer some e-mails in the booth over there, until you're ready."

While she worked, her mind travelled back in time. Understanding clearly that her theories about being drugged and raped didn't make sense with a man like Reed Carlton, Belinda knew she needed to rethink her story. What had happened to her on that May weekend when she'd conceived their precious daughter?

Chapter Sixteen

They'd decided to move into the dining room where it was less noisy and designed for couples to enjoy an intimate meal. Now waiting for their seafood choices, Reed tried small talk to help Belinda to relax. He'd never known a woman so nervous and yet alluring.

Her appeal today re-sparked his hunger for her body. This girl had lingered in his memory, an ideal for his other partners to surpass. And it hadn't happened. She'd come between him and romance too many times.

Remembering her beguiling smile, the one she'd given him as he'd entered her body, the sweet caresses on his face and chest while they'd been attached, moving together as one to reach their climax, came to him both in dreams and moments like this when he'd relax his guard.

Lindy had made him feel like a star that night and he'd never forgotten her magic. No other woman had ever given as much, loved as sweetly or lived in his head, as she had.

Since she'd been on edge from the moment they'd sat down in their booth, Reed decided to clear the air. Acting like a person with a secret, one that didn't make her happy, she'd looked everywhere but at him. Her flyaway auburn hair was being sifted and tugged at continuously and the trembling in her hands was obvious, no matter how much she moved them. He couldn't stand the building tension a moment longer. "You wanted to talk."

Her eyes flew to his, wide, distracted and filled with dismay. She started to rise. "I think this is a mistake."

Reacting quickly, he rose and blocked her way, his body touching hers. "Please don't. I have no idea what's wrong, but I'd like to try and work things out." She'd stopped and was listening. Aching to touch her, yet afraid of her reaction, he leaned slightly closer and whispered, "I lost you once and I don't know why. We were beautiful together and you left me, ran away. I can't lose you again." Electricity speared between them, he felt the air sizzle and knew she felt it also. Her breath caught and the fact that she leaned against him, letting him support the weight of her body, letting his hand creep around her waist to give her his gentleness, he just knew she'd once again connected to him with that strange vibe they seemed able to generate whenever they were together.

He leaned his face against her neck, his breath disturbing the wisps of hair and she trembled, a small moan escaping. Careful not to make her feel he was in any way overriding her wishes; he slowly guided her back to the booth and then slid in next to her.

Taking her hand, he placed a kiss on the palm, folded her fingers over it and said, "Lindy, I'm not a romantic man. I work too hard and I'm lousy with people unless I like them. But when I care for someone, it never goes away. That night long ago, you made me care about you. Why did you disappear after what we'd shared?"

Tears emerged, filling, overflowing, and she looked at him, casting her spell once again with those incredible eyes. The rest of the world receded leaving only the two of them lost in their discovery of passion. Hands gripping, needing the touch, the connection, they basked in their joy of finding the other.

He leaned toward her and she met him. They kissed; drawing sustenance, then pulled back and again searched each other's souls. Incredible thrills worked throughout him until his mind spun crazily.

Food, heavenly smells of garlic mixed with seafood being placed on the table in front of them, brought him back to earth with a thump. Unwanted separation irritated Reed, driving him insane. He waited impatiently while the waiter poured the wine and fussed with the meal. Biting his tongue to stop himself from telling the idiot to bugger off, he hid his frustration.

Finally they were alone once again. He looked at her and saw her paleness. Reaching for his wine, he lifted it and motioned for her to do likewise. "To our future."

She clinked her long-stemmed glass against his and looked into his eyes. "Yes, to the future."

They drank a sip and he spoke in a quiet intimate tone. "Lindy, let's enjoy our first meal together and leave the 'talk' for after. We've plenty of time and I'd love to know more about you and Hollie. Would that be okay?"

Chapter Seventeen

Belinda felt a gigantic weight lift off her shoulders when Reed requested they get on with their meal and leave their talk for later.

"I'd really like that, actually. I'm starving and these shrimp look fabulous. I know the customers rave over them, but it's the first time I've ever had the good fortune to eat here."

"What? You don't get to eat where you work?"

"Some of us do. But we still have to pay a discounted price and so I bring sandwiches from home."

"You must be on a tight budget." Reed's eyes had narrowed and his interest was sparked. He was a man listening and she felt relaxed enough to openly share.

"Well, that's not unusual for a single mom. My expenses often exceed my budget. You know how it is. Besides, Hollie hates the local play school where she goes and I'm saving to put her in a private school that caters to children who are more advanced."

Reed smiled. Teasingly he replied, "And which parent doesn't think their child is the next Einstein just because she can count to a hundred?"

"True, but Hollie can do it backwards from a thousand." Smirking at his astonishment, Belinda added, "She can name most types of clouds because she watched a show on T.V. She also knows the differences between the dinosaurs and what they eat. The stars and planets are another area she's partial to. Should I go on?"

"Okay, wow! I see what you mean. She's gifted all right."

"Yes, she is. I did fairly well in school but never scored higher than average. Neither did anyone else in my family. Therefore it's hard for us to deal with a mind like hers."

"My parents felt the same way about me. I was advanced for my age, not exactly like Hollie, but I got bored very quickly with regular classes and was thrilled when I reached the higher grades and was more challenged."

Swallowing her glee to finally have answers to questions she'd had to put aside, Belinda said, "Then you'd understand why I think it's so important to get her into this special school."

Reed nodded and asked a lot more questions until, with a shock, she realized they'd not only finished dinner but were at the coffee stage and the restaurant section was closing.

Reed picked up on her astonishment. "They want us to leave. We could go back into the bar, if you want? We never did have that talk and I think we need to as soon as possible, don't you?"

She made up her mind. "Yes, we should." She wasn't quite ready to tell him that Hollie was his child but she did want answers to other questions and after tonight, she didn't want to wait any longer. The noise level streaming out of the bar helped in her decision. "Maybe we can go to my place for coffee? The bar's kind of busy."

"Nothing I'd like better."

"For coffee."

He winked and agreed, "For coffee."

***

"I'm sorry the place is so small but it has everything we need." Seeing Reed move around her tiny apartment brought it home to Belinda just how little room she and Hollie really had. Moving into the kitchen, she waved him to a stool across the counter and began the preparations for their drinks.

"It's cozy and familiar. Looks like the place I lived in off campus while taking residency. Only my rooms were never this tidy."

"I bet. I have brothers and if you're anything like them, well, let's just say my mother would throw her hands up in disgust." She laughed, remembering how many times she'd tidied up after them so there'd be peace in the house.

"Yep. That was me."

Picking up the plate of homemade cookies along with her tea, Belinda carried it into the other room and placed it gingerly on the coffee table. She sat on the end of the couch, hoping Reed would choose the chair next to her. Instead he sat beside her, leaned back and took a sip from his cup. "Hmm... good. I'm a coffee freak so I know when it's bad."

"I'm a tea granny; otherwise I'm up half the night." Realizing their conversation was absurd, she slapped her tea down in front of her and clasped her hands. "I want to talk about the night we met."

"Sure."

"About what happened."

"You mean when we hooked up?"

"Yes. How did we get to be together?"

"Don't you remember?" Reed placed his mug on the table, his movements slow and precise. There was a note in his voice that caught her attention. Her news had made his features tighten and he looked incredulous. "You don't remember anything at all. How we met? And danced?"

Realizing this news had gotten to him, she spoke softly, explaining. "No I don't. I was drugged."

"What?" He swung her way, anger filling the grooves in his face, replacing the smiling man who'd looked so comfortable just minutes before. "You were taking drugs?"

Shaking her head, she stammered. "No! No, they weren't m-mine. They were put in my drink. Look, when I got there, a girl I knew handed me a beer and being shy and out of place, I drank it. Next thing I remember is dancing wildly with a bunch of people and then nothing until I woke up in a bed alone, naked and terrified. I got dressed and left."

During her explanation, Reed awkwardly put his coffee onto the table. With his face turned to stone, only his eyes showed emotion and they were furious. "You were drugged at my house... in my home? Is that what you're telling me?"

Inching away from the angry man, Belinda nodded. "There's no other explanation." Staring him in the eye, she let him read the truth. "I've gone over it a million times. I always thought that the person who slept with me had to be the one who'd drugged me. And I could never forgive such behavior."

"I didn't drug you, Lindy. Believe me. I would never

stoop so low to get a girl into my bed."

She reached out tentatively, touching his arm for only seconds before shooting her hand back into her lap. "I know that now; now that I've met you. I can't figure out why it was my drink someone messed with, unless it was meant for another girl. My memory's vague about that whole night. All I remember is how packed the rooms were and the loud music, so many kids all milling around, laughing, drinking, dancing—it was crazy."

"Yes, it was crazy. And you were beautiful, you know, wild and having so much fun. I couldn't take my eyes off you. We danced together, a lot. Then you came on to me and I couldn't keep my hands off you. You were hot for me too and I figured you knew the score, knew what you wanted. Lindy, if I'd known you weren't yourself, I'd never have touched you."

"You couldn't tell I was intoxicated?"

He closed his eyes for a minute and travelled back in time. But soon he shook his head, his voice sincere. "No. I was celebrating that night for having passed the finals. And you were so full of fun, carrying on a bit wildly, but I figured you were as hot for me as I was for you. God, I'm sorry but I was cooked myself. I hadn't had a good night's sleep for months and the booze hit me big time."

She concealed her face, embarrassed by his description. Then he started talking again and she listened to every word, her breath suspended.

"I did try and find you, Lindy. You fascinated me and I was obsessed. The memories still haunt me. You were a virgin and so beautiful. You wanted me and I couldn't say no. Now that I think about it, it must have been Ecstasy that you took"

"Please tell me I wasn't performing for everyone?"

"Nope, just for me."

"I can't imagine."

"You were beautiful."

"You already said that. I must have been acting like a slut."

His hand slashed the air and he pointed toward her. "Don't ever say that." Anger sliced through his words and made her stare in astonishment. "You were soft and loving, as if it really meant something to you being with me. There was no... sluttiness whatsoever. Shit, Lindy, I'm not good with pretty words, I get all twisted up when I have to think of the right things to say." He reached for her hands and cradled them in his. Then he placed his forehead against hers. "I promise. It was beautiful. We were... good together." He leaned back to stare into her eyes and she felt herself drawn into his magic. She couldn't look away when he moved closer. "Like this."

Chapter Eighteen

His lips touched hers gently, questioning, getting permission, begging, and Belinda couldn't refuse his request, didn't want to. She'd kept her eyes open, as had he, and they looked at one another for as long as possible until passion ignited.

Lost in the excitement of the moment, she opened to him. Desire like none she had ever known sprang between them. Floating above her normal world of worry, she just let herself feel and– oh, God– it felt so right.

Her body reacted, craving what only he could provide. Panting, breath catching, passion took over and every logical reason she should stop this craziness from happening fled.

"Reed..."

"Lindy, I need..."

"Oh, God, yes..."

They began tearing at each other's clothes, ripping, pulling, working to get shed of anything that kept them apart.

Breathing harshly, kisses not nearly enough to slake their thirst, they stroked and caressed, writhing to get closer. Rubbing against each other, he caressed and squeezed her breasts until she cried out.

"Yes! That feels wonderful. Yes!"

"You're so beautiful, Lindy. I could never forget you, ever. You're like a drug in my blood, keeping me from caring about any other woman. It's always been you."

"I need you, Reed, need this. My God, it's been forever. Hurry!"

Totally naked now, Reed laid her back and covered her body with his, entering the wet haven waiting, throbbing, craving for his specialness. "Oh, God, sweetheart! I've missed you."

She lovingly caressed his face, kissing him everywhere, clinging, giving, loving. A climax began to build, slowly at first, and then, with every kiss and caress, every thrust he made, it doubled in strength. She panted each moan until she couldn't wait another second. "Reed!"

"I'm here. It's good, baby. I'm here." He moved faster, lifting her higher and then he gave one last heave and she exploded—flashing, igniting, bursting, sensations rioting, her body pulsating, clenching. Writhing in joy, she clung.

Inside her, wrapped around her, he buried himself deeply, arched and shuddered.

Together, they both reached heaven.

***

Satiated, they relaxed. He waited for her to speak. Having no words, other than his favorite which pounded in his brain: *beautiful!* Together, they were beautiful.

Is she crying? He'd moved away from her so he could gather her close to cuddle and stroke. Glancing down, he saw that her eyes were closed and her lips trembling. He couldn't stand it if she regretted what to him had been so bea... perfect. Leaning over, he kissed her lips to stop the wobbling and then he kissed her closed eyes to coax them to open.

It paid off. She looked at him, so open in her honesty, so bewildered in her behavior.

"See, I told you. We're beautiful together." He hadn't know what words he'd say until they came out of his mouth and made her eyes fill up. Her smile brought instant relief.

"I see what you mean. We're a little like tinder and sparks."

He grinned. "Okay, I might be tinder, dry and thirsty. But, baby, you're all sparks. You incited me just like you did the first time. Now do you understand?"

Staring into his eyes, she playfully blinked her long lashes. "Do you think I could do it again? Her smile invited."

"Oh, baby, you already have." He leaned in for a kiss, his rekindled tinder nudging her stomach.

She giggled for a few seconds and then stopped....

Chapter Nineteen

The next day, Belinda decided to pack some of her belongings to start the move over to Maeve's house. Hollie, her little chatterbox, hadn't stopped talking from the minute her grandfather had dropped her off.

"It's my day to go with you to Auntie Maeve's, isn't it, Mommy?"

"Yes, munchkin. While I'm working, you can visit her a little and then you can help me unpack. Hurry, because we need to get there a bit earlier than usual."

"Why?"

"Why? Because Maeve's doctor will be there to pass on some instructions for her care." *And I'm going to give the idiot a piece of my mind. How can a doctor, sworn to save lives, be so incompetent?*

Finally to get some peace, some alone time so she could revisit the night before, Belinda set Hollie to packing her own belongings. Giving her a box and instructions, which she knew would never be followed, she left her daughter busy and happy.

Soon she started gathering her own belongings and stopped when she reached for the pillow on the sofa. Lifting it to her face, she smelled Reed's cologne, closed her eyes and returned to the wonders of the night and the man who attracted her more than anyone else she'd ever met.

Making love with him had been beyond satisfying an urge, more like feeding a craving. As if her body had remembered his, they'd been good together, perfect... in his words... beautiful.

Eventually, they'd ended up in her bed until early in the morning, when he'd reluctantly left to go back to his own house for a shower and to get ready for the hospital and morning surgery.

Before he'd left, he'd forced a promise that they'd be together again soon. Unaware of why she'd agreed, he'd left in a bubble of happy anticipation, whereas she only dreaded their next date. Knowing how important it was that she tell him the truth, she groaned and again buried her face in the pillow. No doubt, as soon as she told him he was Hollie's daddy, the man would back off and it would be him not answering *her* messages.

She stopped dead. The pillow fell from her hand. Thinking of daddies reminded her they hadn't used any protection last night. *Oh, no! Not again!* Her knees gave out completely and she sank to the floor.

She couldn't be that unlucky, could she? Her brain kicked in and a thought popped up. They had a test now that would reveal the truth within twenty-four hours.

Okay, a stop at the local drugstore had to be made before she could go on to Maeve's. Premonitions swamped her mind, memories of another time when her prayers *hadn't* been answered. A sick feeling began attacking her stomach until she was forced to take deep breaths so she wouldn't lose her lunch. *Give me a break this time. Please...!*

Chapter Twenty

"Maeve, has Dr. Darling been here already?" Belinda arrived expecting to see a strange car in the driveway. "I wanted to have a word with him."

"He called to say he'd be a little late due to an emergency. He knew I wouldn't mind. He's a very busy man, works far too hard and has saved a lot of lives since he came home to practise here in Carlton Grove. He's the best of the Carl... Oh, there's the bell now, Lindy. Would you mind letting him in while I say hello to my favorite playmate?" Maeve patted her knee and beckoned to the child to climb aboard. "Come sit with me, Hollie."

Having been tutored by her mother to take care, Hollie gingerly lifted herself onto Maeve's knee and cuddled close. "Hi, Auntie Maeve. Mommy says we're going to live with you from now on."

"Would you like that? It's going to be Christmas soon. We can find a nice big tree for the living room and decorate it together."

"And I'll be spending the night with you, right?"

"That's right."

Clapping her hands, giddy and excited, Hollie hugged the older woman, careful not to squeeze too tightly. "I'm so glad. Maybe we can go shopping and you can help me buy Mommy's Christmas present."

"Of course I will. We'll have such fun."

***

First, Belinda stopped at the hallway mirror, ran her hands through her hair and checked that her lipstick was still noticeable. She wanted to look presentable to the jerk who she had full intentions of berating.

She opened the door and the handsome man who looked up from his phone seemed just as shocked as she felt.

"Reed!"

"Lindy. Why you must be the person who takes such good care of Maeve. The one she brags about all the time. She calls you her sweet housekeeper." He smiled, delighted with his conclusions. "I fully get it now."

"She told me her doctor's name was Dr. Darling." Belinda's feet seemed glued to the floor and she held onto the door, not opening it far enough to allow him entry.

He chuckled. "That spritely gal does have a way with nicknames, doesn't she? That's an old joke. You see I've always called her darling when I tried to talk her into certain... ahh, procedures. Her usual retort is... don't you darling me, and now she calls me Dr. Darling in retaliation."

He stepped forward, expecting her to let him in but she couldn't move. For too long she'd held a grudge against the idiot who she'd decided hadn't given proper care to Maeve. Now to find out that the idiot was none other than the man she'd slept with last night was more than she could handle.

Weak-kneed, tears close, she tried to make some sense

of the confusion drumming in her head. "I don't understand." She turned away and moved quickly to sit down.
"Maeve's doctor is an old fool. It can't be you." Tongue
loosened by shock, she blabbered the thoughts that had
free range in her head. "I was going to give him – you —
a good talking to. For not operating. For giving up on her.
Lung cancer can be managed with surgery. Yet you aren't
doing any. She's dying and you aren't trying to save her."

"Darling—"

"Don't you darling me either! I'm not an old woman
who you can manipulate. I want answers."

Reed stiffened. "I can't talk about my patient with you,
Lindy. You know I can't."

"But I can." Maeve wheeled into the room and stopped
next to Reed. She slid her hand into his and clung. "Hollie
is fetching me some water so we don't have a lot of time."

"I'm sorry, Maeve." Belinda didn't know what else to
say. She'd been caught messing in the other woman's
affairs, but she just couldn't stand by and see such an
injustice.

"Lindy, Dr. Carlton, who has always been a darling
and patient man, tried continuously to talk me into
surgery. He thought I had a good chance of surviving for
longer but he couldn't guarantee what level of functional-
ity I'd be left with. You see, I'm also in the beginning stages
of congestive heart failure which means that any operation
is doubly dangerous. So it was my decision to enjoy the
months I had left, be able to live them as normally as possible, and let the cancer eventually take me when my time
came."

Belinda stifled a cry but not before it was heard by the
others. Reed hurried to her side and sat next to her as if
shielding her from the pain of Maeve's words.

Maeve wheeled closer and reached out her hand to her. "Please don't cry. I've had a wonderful life, especially since you and Hollie came into it four years ago. You've been like a daughter to me and Hollie is as sweet a grandchild any old woman could have. With you moving in to help me, it will make it possible for me to spend the last of my days in my own home, and I can't tell you how happy that makes me."

Hollie sped around the corner, carefully holding a tall glass only half filled with water. "Here's your water, Auntie.... Reed!" Hollie quickly passed over the glass and then ran, leaping into Reed's open arms. She hugged him, exuberance spilling out—happiness lighting her pretty features.

"Hi, sunshine. So you're the little angel that Maeve keeps talking about. Now I see the resemblance."

Hollie laughed. "I don't look like Auntie Maeve."

"No. I was talking about the pretty angel I saw in a book recently. All you need are the wings."

Giggling, Hollie gave him another hug. That's when she noticed her mother's face and saw the tears. "Mommy? Are you alright?" She wiggled away from Reed and ran to Belinda. "Mommy?" Fear rang in her voice and was just the strengthening agent Belinda needed.

"Yes, munchkin. I'm just happy that Reed is Maeve's doctor and he'll be helping us look after her." Belinda patted Hollie's arms and ruffled her hair.

"Can he help us get a Christmas tree too?"

Chapter Twenty-one

It took some time for Belinda to wrap her head around the fact that Reed was Maeve's doctor. For so long, she'd held a grudge against the unknown physician that it took a lot of head-straightening to let go of her resentment.

Understanding that Maeve would not be having surgery hit her hard, took away her last hope. At most, her friend would live a few more months and Belinda would be left alone to parent Hollie. Never again could she bring those silly worries or proud accomplishments to Maeve. The ones most parents shared. The older woman's simple logic had soothed her many times when she couldn't see things clearly herself.

Working away like a zombie, cleaning out the upstairs bedrooms Maeve had designated for her and Hollie, Belinda's mind teemed with everything that needed to get done.

She'd settled Maeve for her nap and had left Hollie happily working away in her new Christmas coloring book they'd picked up at the drugstore this morning....

Drugstore! How the heck could I forget?

Her hand dove into a pocket and found the three packages of different brands of pregnancy sticks she'd wasted money on. But she had to know. Would last night's uncontrollable desires kick her in the ass again this time? Would she have to pay for the rest of her life for a night of enjoyment? It had been spectacular, mind-blowing, but...

She dropped the dust cloth and sped into the bathroom. Sitting on the edge of the bathtub, she stared into the mirror across the room. Slowly she approached and looked into her eyes.

What will you do if it shows positive? What – will – you – do?

She closed her eyes and thought back to the first moments she had found out about Hollie. How terrified she'd been, alone, and questioning everything she believed in. She remembered the litany. *This was her baby. Hers! No father in the picture. She was alone.*

Could she do it?

Would she do it?

A little baby...

The answer had come over her like a rush of knowing. She wasn't a child herself this time—and she had skills. Life promised challenges but then hadn't she always thrived on them?

Shaking herself away from the past, she lifted the first stick and unwrapped it. By golly, if she had another hardship to face, there'd be no negativity. Emotions flooded inside, love and gladness. If she was pregnant— right from the beginning—this baby would only know how much it was wanted.

Chapter
Twenty-two

Reed woke up on Christmas morning, ruffled Cloud's silvery softness and let the daydreams roll before starting the day.

The last few weeks had been hectic as hell and the night before weariness had caught up and slammed into him like a knockout punch from Mohammed Ali. Tuckered, he'd hit the sack and felt a lot better for the full eight hours he'd gotten.

Thinking back over the last couple of weeks, astonished at the amount they'd accomplished, satisfaction flooded in when he thought about how settled Lindy and Hollie now were with Maeve. They'd worked hard to set up Christmas for the old lady and her little sidekick, and last night, before he'd kissed Lindy good-night at the door, he'd taken one last look around and felt great.

The tree they'd bought from a farm on the outskirts of town sat in the corner beautifully decorated and glowed with Maeve's old-fashioned twinkle-lights and the many ornaments she'd squirrelled away over her years of being a Christmas freak.

More twinkle lights had been intertwined with the garlands that were plastered in the main room and hallway, making a surprising display that had turned out rather classy and not the overkill he'd expected.

Hollie, vibrating with happiness, had made the work fun. He'd never wanted to please anyone as much as he'd found himself wanting to please the little dynamo. Free with her hugs, he'd cherished every moment her arms had wrapped around his neck and she'd squeezed him with affection.

Even Maeve had dug her way further into his heart and the hours they'd spent together gave him a huge amount of satisfaction. Remembering made him smile. The Sunday before, when they'd all worked together to get the outside of Maeve's house looking as fancy as the inside, had been a blast. Snow falling added the perfect touch and Hollie had glowed. Hitting him in the face with a snowball, her crowning achievement, the munchkin's giggles had infected them all.

"Why, you little monster, who taught you to throw snowballs like that?" He'd picked her up and heaved her over his shoulder, pretending to smack her well-padded bottom.

"My mommy. She can hit anything so you'd better duck." Before he could, another snowball had smacked him in the back of his head. As soon as he'd released her, Hollie had ended up rolling in the snow, laughter convulsing her little body and Cloud hysterically licking her face which only added to her merriment.

He'd turned to face the attacker. "Why, you monster's mommy, it's more than past time to teach you a lesson."

He'd chased Lindy, thrown her over his shoulder and play-smacked her bottom as well. And she'd giggled in the same way as Hollie had.

Thinking back, Reed realized that those special moments were what he'd been missing from his whole, boring, predictable life.

He pictured Lindy, the girl, who'd burrowed her way inside him years earlier. Now, Lindy the woman had become as necessary to him as the food he ate or the air he breathed. Glowing, the center and essence for everyone around her, she lured him back day after day. He couldn't stay away from her magic.

Smiling, happily knowing that he'd wormed his way into their circle, he decided the first step had come when he'd made her accept help for their move from him and his two brothers.

It turned out to be a wonderful day and it had solved one mystery they'd all pondered over. Harley, his younger brother, had shared some great news. He'd recently met the woman who owned Cloud's mother. Long story short, the lady's crazy brother had taken a dislike to the puppies. Against her wishes, he'd thrown them in a cardboard box and abandoned them in the park.

At first, Belinda had worried that she might demand the return of Cloud but Harley calmed her fears.

"Amelia's fine about Reed adopting the little monster mutt. I told her how he spoils Cloud, buys her the best puppy chow from the vets and even lets her sleep with him, the big softie." He'd grinned at Reed's discomfiture, looking happy that he'd put the spotlight on his older brother.

"She won't insist that Reed return Cloud?" Reed heard the worry Lindy couldn't hide.

"Nope. Don't you worry; she's just glad that the puppy has found a good home."

When she'd leaned over and loudly whispered to Harley, he'd found himself grinning like a besotted fool. "The man dotes on her, you know. Even bought her a pink rhinestone collar and had her name etched on the fancy dangling bone. You'd think he'd bought it for Hollie, she was that pleased."

Watching his girl charm his favorite brother, having them bond to gang up on him, had made the day better.

His plan of bombarding her with his presence; wiggling his way into her life, seemed to be working. She began including him with everything they planned.

A movie night, a dinner date, even evenings spent watching television, they'd done it all, but he hadn't talked his way back into her bed. No matter how hard he tried to beguile her, work his charm, she'd held him off—gently but firmly.

His disgruntled sigh woke the puppy, who yawned and wriggled then came searching for her morning rub. While satisfying Cloud's needs, Reed thought of his own. Something stood in their way, stopped his and Lindy's romance from moving forward. A few times he'd sensed she had a secret to share, but the time had never seemed right the moment had always been lost.

Thank God, each night she'd come to the door with him and say good-bye. Their only intimacy was when she'd see him out. Those brief moments were his favorite time of the day. She'd let him hold her in his arms, but her kisses were chaste and not in any way an invitation to take more than she offered. Every time he'd tried to open a conversation about the situation, she shut him down, gently but firmly.

He didn't know how much longer he could stand it. Every time she sat near him, his heartbeats revved up and his hands itched to touch. Memories of their encounter rode him, making him remember. Being a man in love...

He shot up in bed unexpectedly and the unprepared puppy, now scrambling on the floor, whined and shook off the shock.

In love?

Chapter
Twenty-three

Belinda moved over to the window side of the bed and turned in the direction where she could see the dark being gradually invading by the soft glow of the morning sun. She stretched and then snuggled under the warmth; better take these quiet minutes to snooze. Soon Hollie would wake up and then Christmas would officially begin.

Over the last few days, she'd made up her mind: this was the day she had to let Reed go free. Pain radiated, driving her into a fetal position. Just the thought of losing him slashed a wound through her heart she didn't think would ever be repaired. But she couldn't keep him. It wasn't fair to tie a man down with responsibilities he hadn't asked for nor wanted.

It would have been better to end it earlier but she couldn't break Hollie's heart before Christmas. Both her baby and Maeve had built up such a hullabaloo for the holiday that she couldn't darken the mood, not for them, and especially not for her.

Therefore, the moments she spent with Reed were bittersweet and to be stored for the future. Through his actions, the special smiles, the soft touches, him trying to get her alone, she sensed he wanted more but instead, she kept him at arm's length. How could she lead him on when she knew their time was limited?

The squeaking door warned her someone was pushing it open slowly. Whispering, Hollie called out, "It's Christmas, Mommy. Can I come in?"

"Of course. Merry Christmas, baby. Come and snuggle under the covers with me. It's a bit too early to wake Maeve, and we promised Reed we'd wait until he arrives before we open our gifts."

Hollie leapt into the bed and wriggled her cold little body into Belinda's waiting arms, her icy feet landing on Belinda's legs. "Hollie Page, where are your slippers?" Belinda reached down to scoop Hollie's feet into her warm hands for a rub.

"I forgot. Mommy, I peeked downstairs to see if Santa had come, and he did. Oh, Mommy, there're scads of presents everywhere."

"Baby, I asked you to wait. Did you go all the way into the room?"

"No. Just to the doorway and then I came to get you. You know Santa ate his cookies and the milk glass was empty. I told you we had to leave him a lot. He gets hungry carrying so many parcels."

Belinda swooped in for a hug. "I guess you were right, sweetie. I bet he enjoyed them." She ruffled Hollie's snarled curls and started to finger-comb them into some semblance of order.

Thinking back to the night before, after Maeve and Hollie had both gone to bed, Reed had helped her assemble Hollie's new purple bicycle. Afterward, he'd scoffed down the majority of the shortbread, commenting how much he liked the red sprinkles and green icing.

Seeing as how Hollie had been the decorator, which he couldn't help but notice from the uneven mess, she'd grinned and whipped away two for herself. She remembered how he leaned in to lick the crumbs from her mouth and they'd ended up kissing hungrily, before she'd firmly pushed him away.

Hollie patted her face to get her attention. "Mommy? Do you think Reed will like my present?" The question had been asked and answered at least a dozen times.

The little artist had diligently painted him a special picture and had spent quite some time choosing the perfect frame. She'd drawn the whole family, including Maeve in her wheelchair, herself being held up in the arms of a really tall, dark-haired man who wore the largest smile, and of course Cloud, who sat proudly in front of Belinda.

Answering yet again, Belinda kissed her cheek. "He'll love it, munchkin. I wish I had one too. It's so beautiful." Belinda meant that sincerely. It was a five-year-old's rendition of love and a happy family, a treasure to keep forever.

Together with Hollie, Belinda had shopped for Maeve, Reed and her parents by going to a studio to have her and Hollie's portrait professionally taken. Since Maeve had offered her frames from the stack of old ones she had stored away, one expense had covered all her gifts.

Hollie twisted in her arms, grinning at her mom. "Santa *might* bring you a surprise too you know? But only if you've been a good girl."

"Cheeky monster. You know mommies are always good girls." Belinda tickled her before lifting her high, crawling from the bed and heading for the bathroom.

"Let's get washed, brush our teeth and see if Maeve is ready to get up in case Reed comes early."

Chapter Twenty-four

Belinda had never experienced such a lovely Christmas Day. Not only did they have a blast unwrapping their presents together, Hollie, excited about her new bike, had thanked her mother with so many hugs and kisses that she'd made Belinda glad she'd dipped into their savings and spent the money.

Once the child found the big, beautifully wrapped box from Reed, her eyes had grown huge with childish delight. While he placed it in front of her, she'd clapped her hands and danced on the spot.

"Since you made me such a wonderful present, I hope you like the one I found for you."

"For me?"

"Yes, it's all yours, Sunshine."

"Can I unwrap it?"

"Of course."

"Mommy?"

"Go ahead, Munchkin."

Saving the elaborate bow first, Hollie tore off the pink, shiny tinsel paper and suddenly plopped her butt on the floor. Her hands cradled her cheeks while tears gathered and the wails began.

"It's a dollhouse. Reed bought me a dollhouse"

Belinda bit her lip, terrified that her daughter would hate this symbol of what little girls were supposed to like.

Throwing herself into his arms, Hollie hugged him hard. "You bought me a dollhouse... *to build*."

Reed had looked beseechingly to her for help, but Belinda didn't know what had gotten a hold of Hollie so she couldn't save him this time.

"I hoped we could build it together, little Darlin'. Would you like that?"

Planting kisses all over his cheeks, Hollie resolved their worry instantly. "I love this. I love you, Reed." More kisses. "Can we start now?"

"No Sunshine, it'll have to wait for another day. Let's let your mommy unwrap her gift now, okay?" He handed Hollie a small box and motioned for her to pass it to Belinda.

Not sure what to expect, Belinda found her hands shaking when she unwrapped the exquisitely decorated jewellers box. Nesting inside on white velvet sat a delicate silver bracelet; one heart dangled with one word etched into it... *beautiful*.

Hardly able to breathe, Belinda shyly thanked him with words but her eyes let him know that she'd gotten the message and was touched.

***

While Maeve had a nap in the afternoon, Reed invited her and Hollie to Carlton House where they would meet his relatives and his cousin's children.

"But, Reed, we can't just show up. Goodness, your parents aren't expecting us. It'll be too much of an inconvenience."

"More like a shock," he said, laughter lighting up his features. "They'll be over the moon to finally meet you. I guess the word got out that I was seeing someone and they've been hinting for days about how nice it would be to spend some time together on Christmas Day. I believe my mother even bought Hollie a small gift for a just-in-case. She phoned me this morning to add more pressure."

His spontaneous hug, plus Hollie's enthusiastic pleading finally won her over. "Just for a short visit. We still have to get home to prepare our turkey dinner. Auntie Maeve will be expecting us."

Reed wrapped an arm around both girls to lead them to the closet for coats and boots. "I already told her I was kidnapping you both for a few hours and she was delighted. Now hurry up, or I might have to get my revenge on you two sassy snowballers since there's more snow coming down now."

Sure enough, the snow had increased to where it was hard to see the streets. Soft, thick flakes dropped non-stop and were an invitation to play, make a snowman, maybe snow angels. Belinda saw the glee on her child's face and lifted her away from temptation. Watching Cloud drill her nose through the snowbanks and then roll her furry mass in the white softness had all three of them laughing. Reed grabbed the frenzied pup and put her on the back seat of the car while Belinda coaxed the frown off Hollie's face. "Tomorrow, munchkin, we'll play then."

On the way to his parent's house, Belinda, sitting in the front of the car with Reed, caught him smiling at her. When she smiled back, he reached for her hand. Impossible to ignore or refuse his gesture, they locked fingers. His were warm and cradled hers gently.

Emotions passed between them, travelling through the link where their bodies touched, making normal breathing difficult. The effect the man had on her startled her silly.

Thoughts of what she'd planned for later froze the joy and replaced it with so much sadness that tears formed. Pulling away, she pretended to search for a tissue to wipe her sniffles, only secretly, she used it to dab at her eyes too.

When they arrived, he went around the car, opened her door and reached in for her. Affection lit his brown eyes to melted chocolate. Her knees weakened, making her stumble and he swept her close, hugging her to his body while he whispered in her ear, "You look so beautiful."

Stunned silent, she let him help Hollie from her car seat, pick up the happy puppy and escort them all to the front door of the house that she'd always thought looked like a mansion.

Unnaturally shy, sitting on her mom's lap while Cloud nestled in hers, it only took a lovely book about a lost little puppy from Reed's mother and a few invitations from the other kids before they swept Hollie and Cloud into their circle. Meanwhile, the adults treated Belinda with a kindness she never expected and it worked to put her at ease.

Soon she found herself in the kitchen with his petite, stylish mom, helping her to restock dessert trays. "You know, you're the first female Reed has brought to the house since a teenage fling broke up with him. It devastated him, changed him from being a happy, daredevil teen to a more studious, serious person. Don't get me wrong, he's always made us proud, working like a dog to get through medical school. But I have to tell you, I've missed his teasing, his stupid jokes and him laughing just because."

Belinda found herself hungry to learn more. "Some guys are very sensitive during those years. I remember my brother had a similar experience, only he ended up winning the girl back and they're married today."

"I'm glad that didn't happen for Reed. I doubt he'd be a doctor now and the last time I saw her, she had four kids and big hips to show for them"

Laughing together, Belinda felt her heart melt when his mother, Stacy, had wrapped her arms around her and given her a squeeze. "I like you, Lindy. You and Hollie are welcome in my home anytime."

Following the lady into the family room, a heaping tray loaded with goodies, Belinda's stomach felt like a pile of smoldering cinders were stored there, waiting to combust. Panic cracked her calm and she began to tremble from pure wretchedness. Today she had to give all this up. Let Reed go.

How the hell was she going to survive?

Chapter
Twenty-five

Soon, dinner was over, the dishes done and both a very tired Hollie and an equally exhausted Maeve were in bed. The time had come—zero hour. Belinda couldn't put it off any longer.

Returning to the family room where Reed lounged, cuddling a sleepy puppy, she dithered. Glasses of wine poured and ready for them to enjoy told her he expected time alone with her. He'd turned on the showy electric fireplace, had tidied the room and, other than the Christmas lights twinkling everywhere, the dim shadows lent a romantic element she wished she could shut off but didn't have the heart to. Left with no more excuses, she approached and sat down where he patted the couch next to him.

If only she could use her pounding headache as a legitimate reason to put this torture off for another day. But by delaying the inevitable, the stress would most like have her in a psych ward. This situation needed to get taken care of

– now.

"I thought you'd never quit fussing and join me. You need to relax, baby. You're wound up tighter than what's good for you." He slid the sleepy pup on the other side of him and reached toward her. "Here, let me rub your shoulders—"

"No!" Belinda slid further away from his hands. "Don't touch me. If you do, I'll make a fool out of myself and you'll never be able to walk away without having me clinging and begging."

Her words made him smile; the honesty she didn't even think to hide must have gotten to him. "What's wrong, baby? Whatever you have to tell me we'll deal with. Then we can move on."

"That's just it. There's no 'we'. No 'we're moving on'. There's only you walking out. And me making do."

"Never going to happen. You know I'm crazy about you. And Hollie."

"Good, because she's your child too, so there." A deep breath stopped her from passing out and sliding to the shaggy rug at his feet.

"I know. Isn't it wonderful? I love—"

"You know? *You know?* Why didn't I know you knew? How could you keep it from me? Why didn't you tell me—"

"Wait – shouldn't that be my line?"

She glared her mommy signal that he better not mess around, and he answered quickly.

"At first, I thought it couldn't be. You know, because of her birthday being on Christmas. Then earlier today, when I wondered where her other birthday presents were, she told me she'd been born a really tiny baby in an *incubatery*, her word, and that you couldn't bring her home until Valentine's Day. So you celebrated her birthday then. In her little old-lady, Maeve-like way, she thought it *marvelous* because she could have separate special days. I thought it was a marvelous too. Both her birthday being special and her being mine—ours."

Chapter Twenty-six

Reed's hands cupped her face so he could look into her concealed tawny eyes. When she refused him access, his heartbeats accelerated and he felt bile rising, making his stomach clench, tight, hard—sickeningly.

Earlier, when he'd learned her secret about Hollie, he'd felt a deluge of relief. So this was what had been making her act strange the last few weeks. Why she'd held him at a distance. Understanding had swept over him and he'd breathed easy for the first time since he'd met her. Once she understood just how delighted he was, there'd be no more obstacles to their becoming a couple.

He slid his hands under her gorgeous silky, auburn mass and caressed her scalp, wanting to help her relax. Even without a doctor's degree, he'd have known she had a headache. Periodically, for the last few hours, he'd watched her kneading her temple. Massaging gently, he tried to coax away her pain.

He might not be a born lover, had little experience

in the ways of females, but even he accepted that there was still something eating away at her. All day, watching her chew her lip and fidget with her hands, it had taken a lot out of him not to drag her in a corner and tell her he knew about Hollie, put her out of her misery. Explain how incredibly happy he'd been realizing the little angel he loved was his own flesh and blood.

Now he had to accept that she'd held something else back. What if this mystery turned out to be the clincher? The one he'd need to walk away from. Did he really want to know?

"Lindy, don't tell me anything that makes you feel so scared. Nothing matters. I don't care what you've done; it won't change the way I feel."

"It's not what I've done."

"Then for sure it doesn't matter."

"It's what *you've* done"

God no! Memories of another conversation intruded and panic, like a spear in his chest, drove deep. As a teen, he hadn't understood the jealousy in a young girl's character. The degree of intolerance, or for that matter, the degree of mean-spiritness either. Being a friendly sort of a chap hadn't gone over well with his girlfriend and him smiling at other girls wasn't to be tolerated.

Never again had he let someone have that much control—until now. Why would he let another get close enough to hurt him, to devastate him? His self-protective nature tried to get him to stand, leave, walk away from the pain. Only this time, he couldn't. She was the mother of his child. He loved them both—so much.

"Whatever it is that I've done, I'm sorry."

"You don't understand. You need to know. I have to...." She covered her face, tears seeping through her fingers.

"Please don't be angry."

"For God's sake, tell me. Let me make it better. I'll apologise, promise to never do it again, whatever it was that I did.... Are you giggling?"

"I am. I think I'm hysterical. But what you said about never doing it again was completely the wrong thing for you to say."

Flabbergasted, he held out his hands, palms up and smiled just a little. "Belinda Page. If you don't put me out of my misery right now, I'll be forced to kiss you until you do. I mean it."

Smiling, her tear-drenched face lifted and she leaned forward until her forehead met his. "You've gone and done it again."

"I have?"

"Oh, yes, you did it really good this time."

"I did? Can you just give me a little hint of what it was that I'm supposed to have done?"

"It'll be twins this time."

"Twins!" The shock took some time to catch up with his brain, but when it hit, he didn't miss a beat. "Two more like our Hollie?"

She'd stiffened, seemingly afraid to see his face, watch the blow—be disappointed at his reaction. He sensed her waiting, not breathing...

"Oh, baby, how can one man get so dammed lucky?"

Snow Pup

Holiday Heartwarmers Trilogy
Book #2

In this delightful Christmas love story, Deputy Shawna Mallory finds Billy McCrae – a runaway boy sleeping in a mound of snow with an anxious puppy guarding him. He's a sad child surviving a terrible existence until she puts a stop to it and becomes his foster parent. She's drawn to the snarky kid and just wants his life to be happier, his and the stray mutt who won't leave his side. Not that the boy cares about the dog... or her. Then she meets his father, the one who abandoned the boy when he was five.

John Reid McCrae wants only one thing in his life to make it worth living. Years ago he'd lost his son to a bitter wife and now his goal is to get Billy back. He'll do whatever it takes, no matter who gets hurt. Until he meets the town's stunning deputy. Can he put his needs ahead of her happiness?

Dedication

I wanted to dedicate this book to Peggy Roberson. She helped me come up with the title of **Snow Pup** and as soon as I heard it, the story seemed to spin itself.

Have a wonderful Christmas Season, my friend. May you be blessed with family, friends and lots of fun.

XO

Mimi

Prologue

Dark and frightening, the night sounds of busy birds, buzzing insects and muted traffic from the faraway streets created a racket that disturbed the terrified puppies. The rustling of the tree branches added to the discord, as did the wind sweeping up dry leaves and forcing them against solid objects where they splattered and crumbled.

The overwhelming, surrounding scents were tantalizing, yet not familiar and, therefore, not comforting. Only the smell from the teats and the warmth of their mother's body was yearned for by the pups and missed.

Inside the cardboard box, the one female puppy communicated with her two brothers; *he's gone!*

Scampering to the corner of their flimsy prison, she thought back to the fight that had ensued between the man and her mistress before she and her brothers had been thrown here.

"Amelia, you kept those mutts? Before I left last week, I told you to get rid of them."

"But, Jimmy, they were too little to be weaned from Bella. I was waiting until this weekend to try and sell them." Her mistress's lovely voice had sounded placating and miserable all at the same time.

"Who's going to buy these three? Their mom is a fat, ugly, overly-friendly lab with no guard skills; don't know why I let you talk me into keeping her. And that vicious Samoyed brute across the way, who's no doubt their father, is meaner than the devil who owns him."

"Jim, they're cute pups. I bet I can get a few dollars for them."

"Sure, and until then we have to listen to them kai-yiying all the time, clean up their messes and feed them. No more! I want them gone. It's bad enough we have to trip over that bag of bones without having to deal with her stupid offspring too. Never mind! Since you're as useless as a garden hose in a forest fire, I'll take care of this myself."

He yanked the three pups out from under the tummy of the keening dam where they'd burrowed in fear. Grabbing a nearby box, he hurled them inside. After a short drive in a car, he carried the carton for a few minutes and threw it down.

"Good riddance!" Those were the last words the puppies heard from him. The fading sounds as the man crunched away were terrifying.

Whimpering at the memory, after multiple tries, the female puppy bounced until her front paws gained purchase on the box's edge. Straining her neck, she peered out.

The moon, riding high in the starlit sky, provided illumination for the snoopy pup. *I think it's a park*, she told the other two, whining, sharing her thoughts.

Chubbs, her roly-poly brother, subsided lazily into his corner, his furry body falling over and staying there. *What are we going to do?* Little beady black eyes watered as he howled pitifully.

Stop that caterwauling! It hurts my ears. His brother's normal cranky manner was evident in his insensitive attitude. *We'll sleep now, and in the morning, Sis can go and find us some help.*

Okay! That's a good idea, right, Sister? Chubbs yawned and curled up next to his brother. Both were asleep in seconds. Only their sister snoozed with one eye open, guarding their new dwelling.

In the morning, sounds of human voices woke the three. Again, the female bounced in the corner until she had her front paws clinging to the side of the carton. In the distance, she saw a lot of water. There were people running along its edge. To her left, there was a grassy field where humans were playing a game with a big brown ball.

Cranky wanted to see the world she was describing. When he got close, she used his butt as a ladder and worked her way up and over his head, landing ungraciously in a heap on the grass outside of their container.

Go, Sis. Find us help! Chubbs and Cranky whined together.

***

When Sis didn't return, it was hunger that eventually drove Chubbs from the box. Irritation had made him leave his cranky brother who'd nipped him in the flank and then ignored him when he'd wanted to play. But once ouside, it was curiosity that led him to the mound of snow that covered a body. Once he'd dug a little nest, there was warmth and the irrational need to stay close, to protect, to wait until someone came and then sound the alarm for help.

Chapter One

So far, Deputy Shawna Mallory had searched everywhere kids tended to hang out in town and without any luck. The runaway, twelve-year-old Billy McCrae was nowhere to be found. Frustrated, she stopped driving and pulled the car into the lot closest to the park where the town's families spent a good deal of their spare time.

The tennis courts were closed due to the unusual snowfall. Normally they were full and had been until last night when the previous good weather had taken a turn for the worse. The soccer and football fields were empty too and even the lake looked deserted, whereas on normal days, there were always people running, walking, kayaking... Heck, you name it; the people of Carlton Grove did it.

Deciding to stretch her legs, Shawna circled the far side of the lake, keeping her eyes open in case she lucked out and saw Billy McCrae wandering around. She'd been looking for the youngster since early morning when his foster mother had called in that he'd gone missing.

Whipping out her cellphone, she let the precinct know

where she was and about her plans to explore the park just in case the boy had hidden there. She'd already been to see his teacher, only to find out that the kid hadn't shown up yesterday either and had a tendency to use the school as a place to sleep rather than learn. After questioning the rest of the kids, she'd found that he had no friends and that unfortunate situation was solely his decision. He pushed everyone away who tried to get close.

Striding, long legs eating up the yards, she kept moving, her eyes searching, listening. Circling around some bushes, a yapping puppy obviously in a snit about something ran towards her. It was the cutest thing she'd ever seen. Fluffy silvery-white fur puffed out, which made its little black eyes and snout seem oddly abnormal against the white furry background. The mutt tried hard to converse, get her attention, rotating, then running over to a snow pile and back again. She chuckled at his antics.

"Hey, cutie? You look like a snowball yourself. Are you lost? Come and see Shawna." She held out her hand, knelt down and coaxed. "Come, Snow Pup. Come here."

Frantic, the dog ignored her hand and plowed into her knees, jumping to her face, nudging her and then running back to the snow mound that suddenly looked suspicious. Not waiting for her to explore, the pup began digging at the pile and suddenly a plaid blanket came into view.

Holy Moly, there was a body under there.

Chapter Two

Shawna ran to uncover the curled-up figure and search for a pulse. *Billie McCrae! He's alive. Thank God!* She pulled off her outer jacket and gloves, lifted the boy onto her lap and covered him as best she could. Then whipping out her phone, first she called 911, and next she alerted the sheriff about what she'd found.

"Is he breathing?"

"Yeah, but his pulse is slow. He'd curled up under a blanket which probably saved him from a really bad case of frostbite and hypothermia."

"Is he conscious?"

"No. But his puppy stayed with him. It was the dog that got my attention and made me look under the pile of snow. From the amount heaped over top of him, I'd say he's probably been here most of the night."

Just then, two attendants carrying equipment and a stretcher came into view from the far side of the lake and put an end to her conversation.

"Here come the paramedics. I'll get back to you."

"Good. In the meantime, I'll pay a visit and alert the

foster family and also Child Services that he's been found. Good work, Shawna."

"Thanks, boss. See you soon." Thankful she worked for a kind, good-hearted man, Shawna knew she could stay with the boy, ride with him to the hospital and make sure he got the best of care.

Poor little mite. When she'd uncovered his face, long lashes had hidden his eyes and cold-reddened cheeks highlighted the pallor of his complexion. She'd rubbed them gently, trying to shield him from the wind.

The snow pup, seeing his mate, tried to help by using his tongue to lick away the falling snow from Billy's face. Rather than fighting the furry miracle-worker off, Shawna coaxed him to come and lie down near the boy's chest, hoping the warmth from his little body would keep out the bitter cold. She could smell the ice on his coat as the fur rubbed against her face.

Suddenly Billy opened his eyes—big, blue-gray and full of questions. He stared for long seconds and then smiled in such a heartrending manner that she flinched from the way her insides reacted. Instincts awoke inside her that hadn't been allowed to surface since she'd lost her beloved younger brother years before. The need to protect shot to first place followed closely by a strange warmth that saturated her heart.

"Did I die? Are you my angel?"

"No, babe, I'm Deputy Shawna Mallory and you're safe now. Don't worry. We'll get you to the hospital and you'll be just fine."

The smile faded, to be replaced with a fierce hardness he shouldn't be able to draw on, never mind share, Experiences beyond his years had created that look. "I won't go back."

Sensing the boy's angst, the pup tried to assuage Billy's anxiety with loving ministrations from his busy tongue only to be pushed aside as if Billy knew nothing about the pooch.

Shawna's tender heart double-timed and she realized that whatever she had to say would matter deeply to the boy. Circled like a ball in her arms, his watchful gaze not releasing her so she could invent some stupid story adults tended to feed young kids, Billy stared and waited. His obstinate mouth closed firmly, showing his distrust, while his eyes drilled into hers. This boy's awareness didn't belong to his size. He knew too much.

No lies. No BS. She needed to treat him right or he'd turn away and any hope of saving him, stopping him from running again, would be canceled. "You don't like your home?"

"I hate it. They're assholes, mean ones. I won't go back."

"Fine. Then you won't go back. You'll come home with me."

Chapter Three

"What the hell were you thinking, Shawna?" Her kind boss acted like a stranger in front of her eyes. He pushed himself away from his cluttered desk, got up and strode over to where she leaned against his office door. He had a gray mustache and hair that matched, which looked rumpled from him running his hands through it as a way to alleviate anxiety. "You can't make promises like that. Child Services won't just give you the boy."

"Why not? Last month when they were short of homes, they tried to pressure me into taking a few of the teens they couldn't place. Said that since I spend so much time at the center, they'd be willing to waive the paperwork and let me unofficially babysit just to get the kids off the streets until they could make arrangements. What's so different about me offering my home to Billy?"

She picked up the whining puppy leaning against her leg and cradled him in her arms. "Stop yelling, you're scaring him."

Annoyance lit her boss's rugged features until exasperation took over. "I thought you were going to take that damn mutt to the Humane Society."

"How can I do that?" As if the pup knew Shawna had saved him from a bad fate, he stretched, wriggled and washed her face before she'd had the chance to angle away.

"Oh, for heaven's sake, he's nothing but a stray."

"He's adorable and must belong to the boy. Ed, you should have seen how protective the pup was when the paramedics were trying to get the kid onto the stretcher. He kept trying to get on board and they kept pushing him away until I finally had to pick him up. He was frantic. Weren't you, mister?" She lowered her chin and rubbed it along the pup's neck.

"So you're gonna keep the puppy too?"

"Don't have much of a choice now, do I?"

"Oh, sugar, for anyone else, there'd be all kinds of solutions. For you and your soft heart, probably not."

She shrugged in agreement. "What happened when you went to the foster home? You've been quiet about them. I told you he won't go back there, right? There must be a reason for that."

"Tell you the truth, the woman met me at the door and wouldn't let me in. Said her husband had been out all night searching and had finally gotten to sleep."

"That sounds good."

"Might have been, until the husband yelled and told his wife to get her fat ass back in the house and close the door because she was letting in the cold."

"Oh-kay! Doesn't sound to me like a man who cares much, does it?"

"Nope. I called Gerda at Child Services, described the meeting and she offered to go back there this afternoon for a surprise visit. Said it's been a while since she pulled one and had meant for it to happen a few weeks ago."

"I think I'll call and see if she objects to me tagging along. Do you mind if I take the time?"

"Not if it gets that furry monster out of here. He was chewing my shoes laces, bugging the hell out of me a few minutes before you got here."

"Right! Guess your rubbing his tummy is a good indication of how much you dislike him."

"Go." Ed pointed to the door and then turned his back on her, but not before she saw his grin.

Chapter Four

Shawna knocked on Gerda's open door and walked into the middle of an argument.

"He's my boy. I can prove it. I'll pay for a paternity test, or DNA, whatever it takes for you to let me have custody." The tall man leaning over the desk seemed unaware that he had stepped over the line. Frustration was apparent in his attitude and the way he'd become tense when Gerda had shaken her head. His claim obviously meant more than his manners.

Shawna waited by the door, held back by Gerda's nod indicating she was up to handling the situation. Shawna took stock of the angry male trying to intimidate this woman who had no fear. Gerda had spent years fighting for the youngsters of Carlton Grove, would do anything for them. Unfortunately, her staff was small, her hours included a lot of overtime and her tired face showed a lack of sleep.

"Sir—"

"McCrae. My name is John Reid McCrae."

"Yes. Mr. McCrae. Look, you can't barge in here out of

the blue and demand I hand over a youngster to you before we go through the proper channels. You must understand that we have the welfare of the child to think about."

"I've explained the reason I wasn't here. I've been overseas for the last six years. I just returned because I heard from an old friend, who told me that Billy's mother had passed on months ago and that the boy had been put into the foster system. I came as quickly as I could."

"And why didn't you keep in touch with Billy's mother before so your name would have shown up in Billy's records and we could have notified you?"

"Because his mother hated me. I left to work in Chile and she never forgave me for going. When I got offered the construction job in Antofagasta, I begged her to go with me and bring our boy, but she wouldn't listen. Kicked me out, tore up my pictures and cut all ties. The letters I sent to Billy were returned. The only thing she kept was the alimony that'd been organized through lawyers."

Shawna sauntered around the room to slouch against the wall behind Gerda. She wanted to see the man's eyes, watch his reactions and assess his character. He glanced up for a second and she saw that they were gray—no blue and full of appeal, as if his pleas were too important for outright anger to be allowed. Blond, sharp features—she saw the boy in the man and believed Mr. McCrae's story instantly.

He glanced at her, looked away and then immediately swung back. Narrowed, his eyes tried reading hers to see whether she was friend or foe. But Shawna had too much experience as a deputy to let anyone see beyond what she wanted them to, and her brief nod was returned before he went back to work on Gerda.

"My wife kept my boy away from me for all the years I

was in Chile, even got a restraining order after I tried to get visitation rights when I came back each year for vacations. The last time I held him, he was still five, little more than a baby. Look, I'm back for good now and I want to give him a home. Doesn't that count for anything?"

"Of course it does. And we'll do everything we can to make it happen. But I have necessary procedures to follow on behalf of my client. There're a lot of forms you'll have to fill in and information we'll need to know before things can be changed."

"How long will all this take?"

"Why? Aren't you living here again?"

"I am now. I hadn't decided on where to settle, but you've helped make up my mind. I'll be here until I have my boy back with me where he belongs."

"Good. Make an appointment with my secretary on your way out and we'll get the ball rolling. The faster we settle the paperwork, the sooner we can make it happen."

Tall, slender in build, the man reached over to shake Gerda's hand. Then he made a surprise move that stiffened Shawna's back and made her stand at attention. He came to stand in front of her and held out his hand.

"Hello. I'm John McCrae."

Uncomfortable and not understanding why, she let her hand rest in his for a few gentle shakes before snatching it away. Tingles attacked and traveled up her arm, eventually landing smack-dab in her rioting stomach. *Oh!Oh!* Aroused, chemistry working, she forced her eyes away from his searching gaze.

What was she supposed to say? "Welcome to Carlton Grove."

Understanding that she'd said everything she intended to, he hesitated and then smiled. "Thank you."

He left behind a tense silence. Either the man was a magician, or extremely sensitive, she didn't know which. But one thing was for sure; he'd recognized her interest and he'd signaled his encouragement.

Chapter Five

A little later, when she and Gerda pulled up in front of the foster home, Shawna noticed the closed drapes and the conspicuous lack of anything remotely inviting about the gray house. If the snow hadn't softened its edges, there wouldn't have been any redeeming features at all.

Approaching the front steps, they heard screams, a voice in pain, suffering and not holding back. Shawna didn't hesitate for a second. Breaking in through the front door, she pulled her baton and ran into the far kitchen where the beating was taking place.

"You whore. Didn't I tell you I hate cold tea? How many times does it take for your stupid brain to learn that one small detail?" Mr. Vole, the foster father, had his wife by the hair and was yanking her across the floor.

"Stop it! Now! Let her go." Shawna's advancing didn't affect him until he saw the weapon she was prepared to use. That worked. He pushed his wife away and backed up.

"How the hell did you get into my house? You can't just walk into a man's home."

"I can when he's breaking the law."

Posturing like an idiot, he swelled to fill not only his five feet ten inches but also his fat gut. Both hands landed on his hips. "I never broke a law in my life."

"I guess beating a woman half your size is legitimate in your book, but it sure as hell isn't in the eyes of the court. How about you, Gerda? Is this kind of behavior acceptable for a foster father?"

Gerda, her bulk stretched to stand tall, rage battling with disgust, advanced on the man with her finger out first and her body following. "If I find one mark on Billy body, one scar or scrape, you will be charged, and if at all possible, jailed. And since the courts tend to rule in favor of Child Services, I will personally see to it that you are prosecuted to the full extent of the law, Mr. Vole. I'll see to it."

Shrinking, losing his bully-like demeanor, spit flying from his mouth, he sounded just like a growling dog. "The little shit asks for it. Never does what he's told, blasted brat. My wife has to discipline him, or I'd have taken over. And let me tell you, I'd teach him a thing or two."

But Gerda wasn't about to back down. "You sick fool. I placed that boy with you to protect, feed and love him. Not to abuse him."

Her words seemed to act like a trigger to a man unable to use control; his fist lifted and connected with Gerda's face. Shawna, lightning-fast, used her baton on his arm to stop him getting in another hit. When he looked like he would turn on her, she drove it into his gut. That message got through to him. She was serious and could hold her own. With him weak and doubled over, she cuffed him and pushed him into the chair by the table.

Throughout the battle, Shawna had kept her eye on the swollen-eyed little woman who'd remained cowering on the floor. Giving Gerda the once over to be sure her feelings were hurt worse that her face, she breathed a sigh of relief. She looked bruised but not beaten.

Shawna's voice, hard and serious, cut through the silence. "Okay! Who's willing to press charges?"

Two women's voices sang a duet. "I will."

Chapter Six

"You mean it? I don't have to go back there?" Billy's elated reaction shocked Shawna and drove home like nothing else could have, that the boy meant business. "I'd have run away again, you know." When he sat up against the pillows, the loose hospital nightgown slid off his thin shoulder, leaving his bruised skin visible.

His longish blond hair spiked out everywhere from his head, as if whoever had taken the scissors to it had meant to make him look foolish, or more than likely, they hadn't cared. Except it didn't—make him look foolish. Instead, it made him look endearing and turned his grey-blue eyes into pools of liquid mercury.

"I know, Billy, and that won't happen, right? I told you I would take care of it and I did. Mr. Vole's in jail on assault charges so he won't be able to hurt anyone else for some time."

"Oh, him! He was a big shit, but Mama Vole—she made me call her that—she was the worst."

Stiffening, Shawna countered. "She hit you?"

"All the time. Said if she didn't, he'd be after me with

his belt, and that I wouldn't want that to happen. Made no sense to me. Why would he beat on me when he had her to slap around?"

"Billy, I think you've got that wrong. She was as much a victim as you. He was the creep."

"If you say so." Billy closed his eyes as if he'd had enough of adult stupidity.

Shawna read the signs and couldn't let it go. "So, let me get this straight. She beat you to save you from him."

Disgusted with her inability to see clearly, Billy's expression showed his disdain. "Nah! She hit me 'cause she liked it. Gave her someone to take her own mad out on." He sniffed and looked away. "I don't want to talk about this anymore."

Shawna sat down on the bed beside him and waited until he turned back to her. Though his eyes were watery and his lip still trembled, he'd gained control and just looked fed up with the stupidity of grown-ups who refused to see clearly. "If I promise never to hit you, Billy, would you like to come and stay with me?"

His unwavering stare searched her face until her smile faded. Softness, reflecting the sincerity in her heart, replaced it and she opened up to let him see her seriousness. She wanted this boy, wanted to prove to him that not all people were scum, some could be trusted. She could be trusted. Not like before...

Once he got a hint of her gentleness, he sneered and turned away. "I don't care. As long as I don't have to go back to the Voles' madhouse, I just don't give a shit." Condemnation visible in his response, he rolled over, shut his eyes and ignored her.

Shawna knew he'd cussed on purpose to see her reaction. She also knew they had to start as they meant to go on. She bent over, rubbed his back and said, "You can swear with your friends and you can cuss all you want when you're alone, but the next time you use that language in front of me, I'll be thinking of chores for you to do to pay off the buck you'll owe me every time you forget." She leaned closer and dropped a kiss on the side of his forehead. He stiffened but didn't stop her. His sigh followed her to the door and melted her heart. He'd liked her touching him.

Chapter Seven

Just as Shawna approached Doc Brown, a man charged out of the hospital elevator and skidded to a stop in front of her. John McCrae looked like he'd been blindsided, shocked; a man on the edge.

"Gerda Ward, Billy's social worker, told me that he'd been brought to the hospital. I want to see him."

The doctor answered before Shawna could think of a reply. "No, she actually told you that wouldn't be possible at this time. She called me when you hung up on her." The doctor spoke with a deadly seriousness. He meant what he'd said.

"He's my son. I have a right—"

"No, you don't. You gave up that right when you abandoned your family." Old Doc Brown wasn't budging.

Indignant, John McCrae's voice rose. "I never abandoned *anyone*. There was no work here and we needed the money. I had to take the job overseas to provide for my family. My *wife*..." He spat the word out with sarcasm exposing his obvious distaste "...refused to accompany me. Look, I sent money every month, money she used. But she lied and told the courts I'd disappeared. They gave her full custody of Billy and refused to give me visitation. I'm his father. I love my son. God, why doesn't someone believe me?"

Shawna put her hand on his arm. "Please, Mr. McCrae. You're making a scene and that won't work in your favor. The doctor has no choice but to follow the rules. I'm sure Gerda will work hard to make things right for you. But at this moment, you need to back off."

He looked at her, his face losing the paleness from dreading the worst. "He's okay then, he's—unhurt?"

Her heart squeezed with pity. He didn't know. She spoke softly. "He's fine, right, Dr. Brown?" She and John McCrae turned to face the weary physician holding a chart.

"Yes. The night he spent in the snow didn't harm him as much as I feared. Looks like the dog's body warmth along with the blanket made the difference. But his ankle will take a week or so to heal. It's sprained pretty badly so he'll need crutches for the next few days. After that, he'll be no worse for wear."

"His ankle?" Shawna hadn't realized Billy'd been injured when she'd found him, or even when she'd visited him earlier. *Poor kid.* "Will he be able to go to school?"

"Sure, just as long as he has a ride there and back for a while, Shawna, he'll be just fine." Dr. Brown, a kind older man who she'd known for years, and joined forces with many times while on the job, answered with a wink. "Gerda said you'll be taking him home with you tomorrow?"

She nodded and felt John McCrae stiffen. "Yes. Billy's agreeable. I'll take good care of him." Shawna wasn't sure why she'd added the last sentence, but it seemed to satisfy

the father hovering behind. She sensed his anxiety less-
ening which, for some strange reason, gave her a sense of
relief that she'd chosen to say something.

"Look, young lady, don't overdo things. You have a
day job where you never put in regular hours. And there's
the teen center that takes a lot out of you. It's past time
you backed off a little. It wouldn't hurt you to go on a
date with one of those young men who swarm around you
like bees looking for a honey." A chuckle broke loose and
Doc Brown grinned, showing charisma that had probably
worked well for him in his youth. "Take one of them out of
their misery why don't you." The twinkle in Dr. Brown's
eyes brought a smile to her face. This was the litany she
heard from him every time they were together.

The doctor's son, being one of the bees, was the sole
reason he chided her. She knew he'd like nothing better
than to see them as a couple, but Shawna had no intentions of leading anyone on unless she couldn't live without them. Unfortunately, there wasn't anyone in her circle
of friends who matched her rather high expectations.

During their conversation, John McCrae had stepped
back but was still waiting. As soon as Dr. Brown squeezed
her arm and left in a flurry of white coat and Old Spice
aftershave, he moved closer. "Officer, can I invite you for a
cup of coffee? I'd really like to talk to you."

"No, I don't think that's a good idea." Shawna used her
special deputy stare when she gave her answer. Unwavering, it meant business; she meant business. There was no
way in hell that she wanted to be alone with a man who
had this kind of effect on her body's reactions. An overwhelming urge to turn into his arms, be sheltered by his
warmth and share her horror at the viciousness of some
people appeared for an instant, which she quickly

squashed.

Something inside her recognized he would accept her overture. How she could be so certain, she didn't know, but this man exuded such an aura of tenderness that she felt drawn to him.

"I've got to go."

"Please, I need to know how he is? Can't you understand?"

Stopping dead in her tracks, she turned McCrae's way and bumped right into his outstretched hand. Without conscious thought, her own hand accepted his and squeezed gently. "Mr. McCrae, he's an angry, unhappy boy who needs to be seen, listened to and loved. I can take care of the first couple of items on that list and hopefully soon, you can look after the last one. Now if you'll excuse me, I have a spare bedroom that needs to be cleaned out."

Chapter Eight

With regret, John McCrae watched as the tall, auburn-haired beauty walked away. Strange how her deputy's uniform flattered her, the dark slacks highlighted her compact ass, and her longish hair, wound into a knot at her neck, softened her features. A small dark mole high on her left cheek had delighted him, an enticement for hungry lips.

It had been a long time since he'd noticed any woman's attributes and it posed a problem that the deputy had to be the one to pull him from the blanket of celibacy he'd been hiding under for years. After all, the last woman he'd trusted had turned out to be a horrible human being, hadn't she?

His wife, Billie's mother Ada, vindictive to the end, had made it clear that since he'd overridden her wishes and left her to find work in Chile, she'd make him pay.

That last conversation, replayed many times in his head, flooded back yet again. He remembered the roses he'd brought Ada and his excitement after finding a really well-paying, long-term job, one that would use all of his skills as a construction engineer. Knowing her dislike of traveling, he'd approached the subject with caution, yet full of excited pride.

"Ada, I've been offered a position that's perfect for me. It's like they'd written the job description exactly to fit my skills. And the generous wages will pay off all our bills." He'd been referring to the foolish, extravagant charges she'd run up, without a thought to where the money would come from to pay for them.

She'd danced with excitement and run to throw her arms around him, certainly not her usual behavior. In fact, she seldom initiated any type of affection, rather leaving that kind of foolishness to him. "I knew you'd find something with your credentials, Johnny. See—you kept saying jobs were few and far between. But with your degree and experience, it just had to happen."

"Well, you were right. We'll be set from now on. This job will last for at the very least ten years and the wages are unbelievably generous."

She'd pulled away and stiffened. "Then why aren't you happy? What's wrong?"

He knew she'd sensed him holding back. Now came the hard part. "The job is to build a mine in Chile, a place in the northern part of the country called Antofagasta. The climate's very warm and dry, and there're a lot of Canadian and American expat families working there for the company—"

That was the point where she'd shoved him away and started to protest. "There isn't a hope in hell that I'll leave my home, take a small child and move to the ends of the earth to live in some strange, third-world country. How in the name of all that's holy can you even ask me to do so?"

"Sweetheart, it isn't like that. Chile is a lovely, peaceful place, and the city where we'd be living is modern and cosmopolitan. They have all the amenities we have here in Carlton Grove, in fact, a lot more. You can come for a visit and see for yourself."

Ignoring his pleading, she spat words out that drove fear into his heart. "So you lied to me when you said you were in San Francisco. You son-of-a-bitchin' liar, you went to Chile."

"Yes. I didn't want to get your hopes up and then disappoint you. The only job they're offering is overseas." He'd tried to take her hand then and had been slapped across the face for his effort. Lord, but it had been hard to continue. However, there had been too much at stake to give up. "Look, it doesn't have to take us away forever. We can come home a couple of times a year for vacations." He'd all but gotten on his knees at this point.

She'd crossed her arms and moved out of his reach. "You bastard! Going behind my back..." Face purple with righteous indignation, she'd sneered her answer. "Do I look that stupid to you?"

He remembered thinking that stupid wouldn't have been the word he'd have used. Mean, hateful, even childish would have been more in keeping with her attitude.

"I need to work, Ada. There's nothing for me here. You know how long I've been trying to get decent employment. Construction Engineering is scarce in all the states right now and our bills are piling up. We're getting desperate, for God's sake. Do you want them to foreclose on the house you're so damn proud of? If we take this job, we can keep it."

"No. I'm not listening."

So had started the worst period of his life—the unending arguments and her vindictive, hateful actions. They'd finally agreed that he would go alone, send her his wages and they'd revisit the discussion in three months when he got his first trip home. Except, by the time he returned, she'd decided that having his money more than compensated for not having him around.

She'd shut him out, pressed him to take all his gear and enforced the rules that grew worse as time went on. A year later, using his money, she'd gotten a divorce lawyer, full custody of Billy, and he'd been refused access to his own child. Even his promise to come back home and live with them had been laughed *at. Her retort, made with amused, pitying disgust, had been flung with reckless disregard for his feelings.* "No man leaves me and gets to come back. If you try and make life difficult for me, your kid will hate you as much as I do by the time I'm through with him, and there's not a thing you can do about it. So go back to your stupid job you wanted so badly, leave us alone and just make sure you keep my alimony coming. If you dare to try and cut me off, I will take my anger out on your son, see if I don't."

The intercom, calling for Dr. Brown, snapped him from out of the past with a jolt. He found himself in the hospital elevator, the doors opening on the first floor. Way ahead, he spotted the deputy leaving through the main lobby and he hurried to catch up. Why did every woman who ever mattered to him have to be so damn hard to get along with?

Chapter Nine

Glad that the nurse hadn't closed his blinds, Billy secretly watched the happenings in the hallway outside of his wall of windows. The pretty deputy who smelled like flowers, especially her hair—he'd noticed it when she'd bent over to kiss him—and a man who seemed strangely familiar had appeared, along with Doc Brown. Gathering in a group—no doubt discussing him—he waited to see what would happen. Soon the deputy and the doctor left, and only the unhappy man stayed behind. It was weird watching as the guy clenched his fists and then leaned his chin on them, almost like he was in prayer. He looked sad. *Poor guy!* Maybe he had a sick family member.

With misgivings, Billy's thoughts turned back to Deputy Shawna. She'd made him promises. Ones he knew better than to depend on. She'd never be able to keep them and he accepted that. Who cared anyway? Not him.

Shit, hadn't he always been unlovable, a bad boy? His own mother had taken great enjoyment in reminding him that it was because of him that his father had left. Billy figured she hated his father almost as much as she hated him.

And he didn't care. He'd never care again. The last time he'd put his faith into anyone had been his social worker, Gerda. She'd promised him a nice home, a loving family—people who wanted him—and look what had happened? He'd tried so hard to fit in, do everything they'd asked, even imagined at times that Mama Vole had cared for him a little. But that had turned out to be a pipedream, nothing but foolish hope. From now on, he'd be looking after Number One, and anybody who tried to get close could get stuffed.

And that stupid puppy that the deputy wanted him to like, he hated it more than anything. The nurse had told him it'd probably saved his life. He didn't know how that could be, but at the thought, sorrow flooded him. Why had the stupid animal been there? If he'da died, then he wouldn't ever have to be scared again. Never have to look in the mirror and hate what he saw... a bad boy!

Chapter Ten

Shawna knew John McCrae had taken the same route she had as she'd made her way home. Through the sheer white curtains of her living room, she saw him glance at her house before turning away. Then he cut across the snow-filled street and headed to the big blue-painted building across from hers, the one that had a Bed & Breakfast sign out front.

Quickly picking up the phone, she punched in Alice at the B&B's number, while she continued to spy. Her friend had already opened the front door to her visitor, smiling a welcome. The ringing phone was being ignored as she invited him inside.

Shawna hung up, quickly ran across the street and let herself in. "Hi, Neighbor." Shawna liked the other woman immensely and considered her a good friend. "Can I see you for a minute?" John McCrae's face darkened when he realized who was disturbing his discussion with Alice and his smile disappeared. But he said nothing.

Alice, not liking the interruption either but sensing the tension, nodded, excused herself and led the way into the kitchen. Before she could light into Shawna—the expression on Alice's face quite annoyed—Shawna cut her off.

"I know that man is requesting a room. And before you ask, I snooped from the window."

"And you're here because..."

"I don't want you to give him one."

"Any particular reason why not? He's a nice guy, says he's moving back to the Grove."

"You know him?"

"Sure, he's John McCrae. I've known his family for years. He and his wife used to live next door to my sister. And, boy, can she share some stories about them. His wife, Ada, was a real case, let me tell you—"

"Still, I don't think him living across the street from me right now is a good idea. I'll be bringing his son Billy home to stay with me for a while; the boy's foster family didn't work out and Social Services needed to place him. We just can't allow the father, who abandoned the family and has been out of the picture for years, living this close, Alice. In fact, Gerda Ward from Social Services has placed a restriction on him coming anywhere near the boy until she's done a study of the case. Do you understand?"

"Look, honey, you know I'd do anything for you, but times are tough. Number one, I need the money. And number two, that man got jerked around by a vicious bitch and there's no way I'll make his life more difficult now. He was a loving father and a good provider back in the day, and a wonderful neighbor: fixed my sister's porch after her husband fell through and broke his leg. Then he took care of the daily chores till Steve was back on his feet. Sorry, Shawna. Unless you can come up with a better reason for me to turn John away, I'll be welcoming him into my home and you'll just have to deal."

Totally shocked at having her request denied, Shawna wanted to argue but knew by Alice's demeanor she'd made up her mind. The loyal woman wouldn't be coerced into turning her back on a family friend and, in a way, Shawna couldn't blame her

The problem was that Shawna intended to do her best by Billy. There'd been a bond between them the instant they'd met, incomprehensible maybe, but nevertheless it existed. The boy had touched something in her and from that first moment she'd held him in her arms, her heart had melted and she'd known then that she'd protect him with her life.

Shadowing Alice back into the room where she began making arrangements for John to return that night, giving him the key to the basement suite, Shawna stood aside with arms crossed and waited. Smiling, happily sharing Alice's hug of acceptance, he left and she followed.

She'd wipe that grin off his face right now, the sneak. "Mr. McCrae, may I have a word, please?"

"I know what you're going to say, so save your breath. I've been kept away from my boy for half of his life, thinking it was best for him, believing that his mother with all her faults would take care of him properly. But it seems I was wrong." His voice became husky at this junction and he had to clear his throat before getting back to what he was saying. One knee bent slightly, his hands gripping the hip area of his jeans and his head lowered, he took some heavy breaths. When she tried to cut in, he held up his hand to stop her. "Look, I appreciate that you're stepping in to take care of him. I believe you will give him kindness and a safe place. But you can't possibly love him the way I do. So, please...." Again he choked up and had to look downwards and blink a number of times, "...Please, just let me watch over him from afar. I won't approach him until you say I can. I promise."

Shawna hesitated. Suddenly, a radiant sunset filtered through the snow-laden oak trees on the boulevard, peek-a-booing perfectly to cloak the man in a golden glow from behind. It was as eerie as it was beautiful, like an omen. A sound of pleasure escaped from her before she could stop it and it caught his attention.

Their eyes met and held. Slightly moist, his searched hers and he let her see into his very soul. All the love for his son he hadn't been allowed to reveal blazed there proudly. The truth in his heart couldn't be false or faked. And suddenly something else appeared. Interest in her he didn't hide quickly enough. It made her shiver with a strange excitement and a response that wasn't controllable.

Dazzled, she stepped back and wrapped her arms around her body, the cold suddenly seeping through her sweater. Hardness entered her words, and she added them on purpose: "If you hurt one hair on that child's head, John McCrae, I will shoot you with my own deputy's gun." She stuck her finger in his chest and pushed more than once. "That's not a threat, sir. It's a declaration of intent."

***

While running back to her house, she made up her mind. It looked like she needed to return to Alice's for a cup of tea and a chat. As a part of her job, gathering evidence often seemed a lot like gossip and over the years she'd gotten quite good at knowing whether it was pure fabrication or based on truth. In her personal life, she purposely stayed away from chitchatting with anyone.

But this was different. Shawna knew Alice's sister personally and trusted both women to only discuss the straight facts about the past. Plus, the information she'd collect on the McCrae family would help her decide in the future how to treat Billy's dad.

If this dude figured to get anywhere near Billy until she felt totally convinced he really was the person she was now beginning to believe he might be, then he'd better prove his innocence.

She went back to her small house, donned her jacket and picked up the phone once again. Then she hit redial. After a brief discussion, she replied. "Okay, Alice, you put on the coffee and I'll be right there with a plate of your favorite butter tarts."

By the time Shawna returned home with an empty platter and an earful of hearsay, she had made up her mind that she might just have to give McCrae some leeway. Billy deserved to have things go his way for a while. The kid needed a break, not rules and regulations. But, then again, he shouldn't be forced into relationships he didn't want either.

Therefore, when he finally met John McCrae, if he chose to have nothing to do with the man who was his father, so be it. No way in this crazy-assed world would she force the poor kid into doing anything he didn't want to do... no way!

Chapter Eleven

"What do you mean, you don't want the pup around?"

"I don't want it! Am I speaking French or somethin'? It follows me everywhere and cries when I ignore it. The darn thing is a pain in the ass." Billy glared at Shawna across the kitchen table while the pup in question sat like a plump ball, face turning to each speaker in turn as they had their say. In the silence that followed Billy's last statement, the pup twisted his face to the side and then added his sentiments. He barked so loudly that he comically toppled over sideways, and Shawna started to laugh.

"How can you not want a puppy around who's so darn precious?" She leaned over to pick up the silver-white fluff ball, cuddle him and scratch his tummy. When she looked at Billy to see his reaction, it startled her that the only expression he wore was fear.

"Billy, what's wrong?" She left her place at the end of the small table to go and kneel by his side, the puppy now on the floor running with her. His fat little body wriggled at her knees, whining, trying desperately to climb onto her lap.

Ignoring the pup, she imprisoned Billy in his chair by placing her hands on its arms, the wall behind effectively closing off his escape. She waited, forcing him to look at her. The pup, sensing an emotional moment, stopped his antics and stared at the boy also.

Accepting his confinement and not liking it whatsoever, Billy's scorn added validity to his words. "I don't like dogs, so there. My mom said they're dirty, smelly animals that only eat and shit. And she's right. They're so stupid; they get run over, don't look where they're going and then they die. I don't want a dumb dog."

"Aw, Billy! I'm sorry kid, but your mom was wrong. Sure they need to be trained and taken care of, but they love so hard that they've been known to give up their lives for their masters. It's a fact; look it up on the Internet."

But Billy wasn't budging. Her words had no effect, and he answered with the same stubborn point of view. "They're stupid."

Not wanting to admit defeat, Shawna pushed. "How can you say that if you've never had a dog before?"

"But I did." Anger fled, changing to introspection. "When I was a kid, I think my old man bought me a puppy before he left us. It was small and black. I liked it. Then, see – it got killed."

"What happened?"

"My mom ran over the stupid thing 'cause it wanted to go with her. It followed her to the car and got in her way. She drove over it, and the man next door came and tried to help, but it was dead."

"You saw it happen?"

"Yeah. She saw me in the window with the babysitter and she didn't even stop. Just drove away." Utter misery rang in his tone. His sickening words echoed in the dead silence that followed: *she just drove away.* "I'm tired. Where am I going to sleep?"

Shawna shook off her distress. After imagining the sorry scene the boy had just described, she knew she needed to lighten the tension.

"Well, my friend, since you swore three times, I'd say first you'll be clearing the table and helping me wash the dishes."

He interrupted, his young voice full of derision. "Give me a break! Don't you have a dishwasher in this dump?"

"Yes. But this dump, as you call it, also has a sink and two of us don't have a lot of dishes. Therefore, rather than waste a lot of water unnecessarily, we'll be going the old-fashioned route and taking care of them ourselves." *And hopefully, get some time for schmoozing...*

"Then can I go to bed?"

"Then you'll be going out with me for a short walk to take the little monster to the potty. You might not want the orphan mutt around, but we still need to take care of him until he leaves. Plus, it's time to see how well you can handle that ankle cast and crutch Dr. Brown gave you."

"Do I have to?" Billy's frustration rang clearly.

"Yes, Billy, you do. After that, you'll be getting at the homework I went and fetched for you from your teachers. Then we'll see about setting you up in your bedroom. And, Billy, if you're sure you don't want Fluffy around..." she pointed at the dog whose head was again twisted to the side in a comical questioning pose, "I'll try and find a home for him after the weekend. In the meantime, he'll have to stay with us until I do. Okay?"

"I'm not looking after him."

"No. that won't be necessary. As I explained earlier, a neighbor's daughter, Becky, will be staying with you after school and she'll look after the Fluff—"

Interrupting, his voice mocking her, he said, "He's a boy. You can't call him Fluffy. It's stupid."

Sighing, pretending to be annoyed, she replied, "Don't you know any other words besides stupid? For instance, I think it's kinda stupid that a guy with a very healthy IQ—yeah I saw it–needs to use such a stupid word all the time. Don't you know any other stupid adjectives?"

Grinning, his young boy's face alight for the first time since he'd entered the house that morning, he pointed at the now sleeping dog whose comical pose did look rather silly. Lying on his tummy, his paws splayed on the floor in the four directions, his tongue hanging from the side of his mouth, the puppy had decided that the humans weren't going to share their food or their laps and had given up begging.

"Right! Got it!" Grinning, Shawna added, "So what you do you think I should call him? How about Snow? After all, we found him lying over your body while buried in the stuff." She watched to see the boy's reaction and wasn't disappointed.

"Snow is a lot better than that stupi... ah, Fluffy. You found him on top of me?"

"Yes. At first, I believed him to be yours and so I didn't call the Humane Society. Then after interviewing Mrs. Vole and realizing she had no knowledge of Snow, I wondered if you hadn't befriended him without them being aware and he was important to you."

The boy collected his plate and utensils and stood up, purposely walking away from the dog. He answered with his back to her, his voice muffled. "I could care less about the mutt. I never saw him before in my life."

Chapter Twelve

For the next two days, over the weekend, she and Billy settled into a routine. He stayed in his room for longer periods than Shawna would have liked, but she'd made up her mind not to hassle him.

Not so for Snow. The little monster was determined to be in Billy's roommate, and though Billy would immediately remove him, the pup kept sneaking back, and many times when Shawna called he'd appear from his hiding place under Billy's bed.

Wavering, not totally understanding why, something in her insisted that the boy's door should stay open. Therefore, when she'd pass by on the way to the washroom, she'd peek in and see him either reading or sleeping and sometimes just lying in the darkened room and pouting.

Her frequent visits to the facilities meant she had the emptiest bladder and the cleanest hands of any woman in town, but she couldn't seem to stop checking.

Not wanting to intrude, she just kept coming up with chores or outings. Most times it worked fine and he'd join her quite happily. Then it dawned on her that he even needed to be summoned to watch television with her. In fact, he did nothing outside his room without an express invitation. That had to change. This wasn't the Voles' house, thank God, and her rules were different.

In the middle of Sunday afternoon, after standing at his darkened doorway for a few seconds, she stepped into his room and opened the blinds. Then she signaled him to move over so she could sit beside him on the bed. "Billy, are you tired?"

"No."

"Then why are you lying on your bed in the dark with your blinds closed?"

"I don't know what else to do."

"Did the Voles make the rule that you had to stay in your room?"

"Yeah. They didn't like me roaming around the house. And I had to keep my light off so I wouldn't use electricity. I try to sleep and if the room is dark, sometimes I can." His explanation sounded matter-of-fact and that alone sent shivers along Shawna's back and arms. Her stomach tightened with anger and she bit her tongue to stop the harangue that hovered so close, pushing to get loose.

The boy's previous existence sounded unimaginable to her. She'd grown up in a happy, busy house always filled with cheerful kids, noisy animals and with a mom and dad who sprinkled love around with the ease of two people who had so much to share.

"Well, now that you're living in my house, there'll be new rules. You will only be in your room if it's where you want to be; open or close the blinds, it's up to you. My electricity bill isn't a problem so turn on whatever lights you need, just turn them off when you're finished. The television is as much yours as mine; we share. If I'm not watching something specific, you get to choose, and vice versa."

"Seriously? You won't go spastic?"

"Seriously. And there're rules for the kitchen also. You eat what you want, when you want. I don't know when you get to feeling hungry, only you know that. Heck, my brothers were always eating; we used to tease them that they had hollow legs. So if there's something you want, help yourself. Since I don't buy a lot of junk food, you'll mostly find fruit, nature bars or homemade cookies and leftovers. Just don't pig out too close to suppertime so you'll eat your meals. And... clean up after yourself in there also."

"Sweet! You mean it?"

"Yes, Billy, I really mean it. While you're here, the house is yours as much as mine. Just remember, if you make a mess, fix it yourself and don't leave it for me."

His eyes bugged out of his head as he listened to every word. "Sure, I'll clean it up. I'm really good at cleaning."

Shawna got an uneasy feeling and added, "Honey, I like it spiffed up once a week or so, but in the meantime, if it gets a bit cluttered—no biggie. Okay?"

Within a few minutes, the happy boy had appeared in the kitchen, the puppy trailing him, fetched a glass of milk plus one of the oatmeal bars she kept in a glass jar on the counter and plonked himself on the recliner in front of the TV. She grabbed Snow to stop him joining Billy, though the puppy put up quite a fight.

Instead, she cuddled Snow on her knee and threw Billy the remote, then watched his eyes sparkle like those of a hungry wolf let loose in a henhouse.

Chapter Thirteen

On Monday morning, Shawna barricaded Snow on the veranda with lots of paper and the same litter box the smart little fellow had begun to use at night. She added a few treats: his food, a bowl of water and lots of toys she'd found for him to gnaw on. "I'll be back soon, sweetie, to take you for a walk. In the meantime, please don't chew my furniture. Okay?"

Snow barked and tried to lick her face yet again. She'd had it washed so many times this morning, it was a wonder she had any moisturizer left.

"Are you leaving him locked up in here all day?" Billy appeared at the door with his brace propped forward, stopping Snow from jumping up. He had his school books under one arm and his crutch in the other hand. "He's really stupid, you know. I keep pushing him away, but he doesn't stop."

Shawna had noticed that whenever Billy had prevented the dog from climbing up, it had been done in a gentle manner and so she hadn't intervened. "I guess the *stupid* dog likes you... can't figure out why myself. You refuse to have anything to do with him." She grinned to show she was teasing and Billy returned it cheekily.

Truly, she couldn't understand what drove the puppy. It was like he knew something they didn't—like he belonged with the boy, plain and simple. She looked at Snow now sitting in front of Billy, a questioning look on the pup's tilted face. Suddenly, his mouth opened into the famous Samoyed grin and she could have sworn he'd smiled at Billy on purpose.

Before Billy turned away, she saw the hunger on the boy's face and felt the yearning he couldn't hide fast enough. Whoa! The kid did secretly like the puppy. O-kay! Maybe if she kept them together long enough, Billy would get to openly accept Snow.

"You know Billy, even though I'll try and find Snow a good home, doesn't mean it'll happen overnight. After all, we want to be sure he gets with the right type of family."

"Yeah, whatever." Billy kept his face turned away and the moment was gone, but it left her with a lot to think about.

"Remember, I'll pick you up from school, and then Becky will be here to stay with you until I get home from work."

"I told you already, I don't need a babysitter. I'm not a baby." His tone turned snarky when he said the last word.

"It's the rules, bud. I can't leave you alone, you're a minor. Plus, you're on crutches. Becky's a good girl, you'll like her. Look, if you have any problems, you've got the cell phone I gave you so call me, all right?"

Billy leaned his crutch against the wall and pulled the treasured phone from his pocket. She saw that his eyes still lit up whenever he looked at it, which was often. Ever since the night before when she'd passed on her old phone and explained its uses, he'd listened totally engrossed and had worn a big grin.

"Sure. I got it. In fact, I actually got it the first time you said and the second—"

"Smartypants!" She shook her head and opened the door.

As they stepped outside to go to her Rav4 in the driveway, Shawna automatically looked over to Alice's house and noticed John McCrae also leaving. Only he was hurrying in the direction of the corner bus stop. He'd hesitated and waved, and without knowing it would, her hand rose. Quickly she pulled it down and checked to see if Billy had noticed.

The boy had already gotten into the front seat of the car and she hoped he hadn't been aware of McCrae. God, this was going to be awkward. Shawna didn't like to shut out a potential friend, it wasn't in her nature. Normally, she'd have offered the neighbor a lift. But the boy came first, had to.

No matter how drawn she felt to the handsome man, she had no business getting involved. If Gerda found out John McCrae was now staying across the street, no matter how close friends they were, the social worker would remove Billy from her house and that would be that.

"Shawna, see that guy across the street? I think I saw him at the hospital one day. I remember he looked kinda sad."

Oh no! "Do you know who he is?" She had to ask.

"Nope. Do you?"

"Yep. He's the new neighbour."

Chapter Fourteen

By Friday, Billy was glad that Shawna picked him up at the end of each day. His leg hurt from so much activity that it was getting more difficult to cover up the weakness. Some kids had offered to carry his books and so on, but he'd refused their help. Until one of the teachers had intervened and forced him to let the four-eyed kid, the one with the bottle-cap glasses, help him out.

"I'm Adam. We're in the same homeroom and math class."

"Yeah, I know."

"I've tried to talk to you before."

"Yeah. I'm not too talkative."

"No kidding. Even the girls can't get a word out of you." Adam appeared a bit envious that the girls bothered with Billy.

"Don't like girls." Billy hunched his shoulders and wished the nag would disappear.

"Are you gay?"

Billy swiveled and glared. "No! I'm not gay. It's just that they giggle too much and never stop talking... like someone else I know."

Grinning, Adam nodded. "I never stop. Talking, I mean. It's a good thing you're kinda quiet. I can make up for you, no problem."

The rest of the week, Adam reminded Billy of Snow. Each day, Adam appeared after their classes, snatched up Billy's books, whether he wanted to pass them over or not, and wouldn't be shut down. And, God knew, Billy tried. Even got downright rude, but it was like snow sliding off a slippery roof.

"How was school today?" Shawna asked him the same question every day when he got into the car.

"Okay." He always answered the same.

"Did you get a lot of homework?"

"A little bit; easy stuff."

He knew Shawna had checked in with his teachers, they'd snitched and warned him he'd better perform now that he had a cop on his case. They'd laughed, thinking it was funny. He'd thought it was stupid.

She noticed him rubbing his knee before he realized it totally gave him away. "Does your leg hurt?"

"Nope. I'm good." He turned to look out the window before she saw his cheeks heating up.

"You wouldn't tell me even if it did, would you?" She glanced over at him, then slowed down for the corner on their street.

"Nothing you can do. Doc says it'll just take time."

"That's true. But then there're ways to help with the pain. And one of them is for you to rest your foot up on a stool. Will you do that for me, please?"

"Whatever. I'm good."

She grabbed his books before he could and then came around to open his door, stopping herself from actually reaching for him. Instead, she passed him the crutch and stood back.

Once Shawna quit her fussing and left him in the kitchen with Becky, she headed out the back door to return to work. Rather than visit with his teenage babysitter, who was always full of questions too, Billy grabbed some cookies and decided to go to his room.

On the way past the front door, he noticed it sat open a few inches. *Oh heck, I didn't close it.* Though Shawna mostly used the rear entrance, it was easier for him to use the front because there were only a couple of steps. So, he'd been the last one to come through there earlier.

He remembered his crutch had gotten in the way and when he'd tried to swing around, a pain had caught him, almost putting him on his ass. After spending a few seconds to recuperate, he mustn't have closed the door firmly.

Moving quickly now to swing it shut, he had an unaccountable sense of needing to step out into the veranda and check on Snow.

When he'd come in earlier, though Billy had ignored his frantic attempts at begging for attention, Snow had been elated to see him. In fact, Billy had pushed him back with his crutch, not hurting the mutt but meaning business. Snow had given him such a pitiful look, Billy'd almost relented. Before he could, the dog had stuck his tail between his legs, let out a pitiful whine and circled back to his puffy pillow.

Nerves caught at Billy, making him feel sick. A thought struck with such an impact, it had his adrenalin surging. Why hadn't the stupid pest come inside the house? He knew Snow hadn't, or he'd now be tripping him up, hanging around his feet.

"Snow?" He moved awkwardly forward out onto the veranda again and his heart dropped. It was empty! No goofy white furry puppy in sight. Nothing! Instantly, his eyes flew to the outer door and saw it had been left open too.

Oh no! He'd really screwed up. Snow was loose.

Now totally scared, drawn to the open door, he stepped outside and saw Snow across the street. Everything happened at once, and weirdly, it appeared to be happening in slow motion. Seeing Billy, the Samoyed puppy began scrambling across the road to get to him, his earlier unhappiness forgotten. Bounding like a bunny, his ears perked and tail rotating like a flag, he headed straight for the one person who mattered.

A car, after turning the corner, sped up. Snow became invisible in the powered snow on the wind-blown street. And the driver wasn't slowing down, likely didn't see him. Instead, the vehicle was barreling straight for the furry creature.

Billy's cry ripped from his throat and the pain in his chest reminded him of another time, another pet.

The screech of the tires on the slushy road and the puppy's yelp could be heard by everyone on the street. Dropping his crutch, all his attention zeroed in on Snow's still body, Billy hobbled over, staying upright only through desperation and pure fear. A man, on his way to Alice's house, arrived at the accident the same time as Billy.

"Snow! Aw... dammit. *Snow!*" Billy slid awkwardly and dropped beside the animal who lay crumpled on his side, lifeless. Not knowing what to do, Billy automatically passed over control to the adult kneeling next to him. "Is he dead?"

The stranger checked to see if the dog was breathing. "No, son. He's breathing." The man's gentle ministration gave Billy hope.

The woman driver, who stopped the car and had gotten out to offer assistance, tried to touch Billy's shoulder, but he pulled away. "I'm so sorry, honey, I didn't see your puppy. It's so small and white, with the snow falling... but I don't think I actually hit it. I'm so sorry."

"Snow's a he not an it." Once he'd cleared up what rankled, he ignored her but looked hopefully at the man who had carefully turned the body and lifted it, looking for signs of injury. "Is Snow hurt bad?" *Please, no...*

"I don't see any wounds or signs of blood."

"I'm so sor – sorry he's hurt." A hitch sounded in the driver's voice.

The stranger calmed the traumatized woman. "It wasn't your fault, ma'am. He ran right in front of your car. I'll look after him. But thank you for stopping."

With one last touch on Billy's shoulder, she got back in the car and slowly pulled around them.

Billy reached over and very softly ran his hand over the soft fluff. "Aw, Snow Pup. I'm the sorry one." He searched the man's face, his own quivering. "I didn't mean to, but I left the front door open."

Suddenly, as if Billy's touch pierced his stupor, the puppy wriggled, sprung up and lurched right into his arms. The baby shivered, whimpering and crying, sharing a story that wrung out Billy's heart. In between his yips and whines, Snow tried to dig his way inside Billy's open jacket and right into his chest, burrowing, looking for tenderness, affection...acceptance.

Tears flooding, Billy very gently held Snow close and buried his face in the softness of the white fur. Embarrassed in front of the stranger, he tried to hide his eyes but was afraid to move too much in case his puppy really was injured.

With his voice shaking and body trembling, he asked, "Can we take him to the vet?" He fought the tears, trying to be strong even though he wanted to throw up. *Billy, you're so stupid.* The words echoed from memories he couldn't shake.

'I have a better idea, kid. My landlord, Alice, is a nurse. I'm sure she can tell us if we need to take him to the vet or not. Let's go and see what she says."

Becky, arriving just then, agreed. "Yes, Billy. Take Snow to Alice's house. She's Shawna's friend and will be glad to help. "I'll go and call Shawna and then come right over. You need to be there so your puppy has someone around him he knows."

***

Out on a call, Shawna couldn't respond to Becky's message right away. By the time she'd gotten free from the highway accident she'd been called to, and listened to Becky's voice, an hour or more had passed.

Squad car screeching to a halt in Alice's driveway, without ringing or knocking, she ran into the house and a sight awaited that brought instant relief. She swallowed the hovering hysterics, her mind much calmer for witnessing the scene in front of her.

Billy, smiling and relaxed sat with his foot up on a stool. John McCrae lit up like he'd won a million-dollar lottery, faced him at Alice's souvenir Peruvian chess table where they were deep into a game. Father and son, left elbows on the arms of their chairs and their cheeks resting on their hands, looked so much alike that Shawna stopped dead in her tracks.

Her attention wandered to Snow, who lay cuddled on Billy's lap while Billy's right hand stroked his fur. The pup glanced her way and his tail began circling in welcome.

Shawna swung to see the other two present, Alice and Becky, sharing tea at the low table across from the wide-screen TV, and discussing something that had both their faces wearing a smile. It was a happy, peaceful sight and one that Shawna could scarcely believe... or accept.

The boy laughed at something the man said, his voice ringing with a sound she'd never heard from him before – pure unadulterated pleasure.

Oh God! What the heck was she going to do now?

Chapter Fifteen

Refusing tea, grateful for the news that Snow seemed unhurt, Shawna greeted Billy with a touch on his shoulder that didn't get shrugged off as most of her touches did. Then she lifted the frantic puppy for hugs and pets.

Standing behind Billy, her glare at the innocent-looking John McCrae received a head twist to one side and a sheepish shrug. Brilliant blue, his eyes signaled his happiness and glowed with such joy that she noticed it immediately. In fact, they sparkled as brightly as the multi-colored twinkle lights on Alice's early Christmas tree. Glancing down under the table, she noticed his hand resting on his thigh. It was clenched so tightly that his whitened knuckles told their own story.

If ever a guy tried to look uncaring for his indiscretion, John McCrae was that man. *Could you blame him?* A headache started clamoring, needing medication, but instead she stretched her neck and made herself relax. For now...

Gathering her clan and getting them to go back home seemed rather rude and a downer, but she had no choice.

"Sir, can we play again?" Billy not using John McCrae's name seemed weird, but Shawna had the feeling that Billy still didn't know who John was and, therefore, didn't know of their relationship. No way was she going to be the one to spill the beans unless Gerda was on board.

John's sidelong glance told her how nervous he'd become since she'd arrived, but he smiled at Billy, held out his hand to shake the boy's and grinned his consent. "Anytime, champ. If Shawna approves, that is. You're a natural, Billy. Just like me when I was your age, only I didn't have anyone to play against."

"Me neither. A friend of my mom's taught me before she kicked him out. Then I played at school online. It's fun."

Before Billy and Becky left, Snow now clutched close in Billy's arms, the boy sidled over to Shawna and whispered, "His name is John Reid and he's a really good chess player. He says he'll teach me, Shawna. I like chess."

"Right! Good to know. It's time for you to go home with Becky now and get at your homework. We'll talk later. I just want to get Alice's diagnosis for Snow and see if we need to do anything special for him."

Once they left, Alice explained how they'd brought Snow to her and she could see that he'd been shaken, but after examining the puppy, she was pretty sure that he wasn't injured. Then Billy had spotted the chess table and one thing had led to another.

"Thanks for helping in the emergency, Alice. I appreciate it."

"It was John here who saw the accident and calmed the situation. You have him to thank." Alice looked from Shawna to John, who wouldn't meet her eyes and she took the hint. "I think I'll go and start dinner."

The minute they had the room to themselves, Shawna attacked. "What the hell did you think you were doing?"

"The dog got run over. I was there. This time, I was there."

That stopped her for a second. The emphasis on *this time* resonated clearly. But she had no choice. He must be made to see that. "Did you tell Alice that my ward was your son?"

"No, of course not."

Relieved about that, she added. "Do you want them to place Billy with another foster family, John? Is that it? You don't like me?"

Stiffening, he bristled and his tone hardened. "What the hell are you talking about? No, I don't want them to take Billy away from you... of course not. He seems happy. He has the puppy I always wanted to give him. And Alice says you have a huge heart and understand kids. Why in the world would you even consider asking me such a thing?"

His eyes now black with misery begged for understanding, but she had to freeze him out. "You need to realize that if Gerda knew you had moved in across the street, she'd most likely take Billy away just for that reason alone. But if she knew you'd made contact with him before she'd done her due diligence, he'd be removed *for sure*. She might be my friend, but that woman is all about the rules."

He slumped down on the flowered sofa and, without being aware of moving, Shawna knelt in front of him. "John, I know how much Billy means to you. Alice told me some of your history and how badly you were treated by your wife, but my hands are tied. There's a bond between Billy and me that I can't explain. Just the thought of them moving him somewhere else would break *my* heart. Look, he seems to be happy. We can't ruin it." Her voice had risen. Earnest, pleading, even a small sob escaped and added to her sincerity. *Please, please understand.*

John reached out and cradled her face between his hands. He slid his fingers over her cheekbones and brushed at the worry lines around her eyes.

Held spellbound, Shawna didn't move. Every cautious brain cell she possessed warned her to stand up and leave. But everything female inside her cried out for his mouth to descend, meet hers so she could taste him.

As if he heard her silent appeal, he lowered his lips ever so slowly, stopping at every inch forward to see if she was still willing. When their mouths finally met, he searched hers with such tenderness; moans broke loose and refused to be held in.

Gently, he pulled back. They gazed deeply, hunting to find answers, sharing, daring... Shawna allowed him to see her fascination; she couldn't have stopped it anyway. Never before had any man gotten such a response from her... ever.

Control in his tender hands, this time he turned their faces so he could delve deeper, get her response and give his own. It lasted forever and then another forever until they finally separated.

The shared bliss had to be acknowledged and respected. Their foreheads touched and she shut her eyes. His eyelids also hid the sparkling dark highlights that had bewitched her from the first moment. But he hadn't closed them in time, she'd seen the hunger. Drawing in a deep breath, she released it slowly, tremulously... *I'll remember this moment forever.*

Finally, he let her go and leaned back against the couch. His hands shook as he covered his face. They travelled behind his head, his fingers gripping together. He met her eyes; his flinched at first and then held firm.

"Fine. I won't contact him, I promise. But if he comes here on his own, my God, please don't ask me to turn him away."

Chapter Sixteen

"Why can't I go and play chess with John? He's my friend. He showed me all kinds of moves and he's smart, Shawna... really smart." Billy wasn't happy, and Shawna didn't blame him. Which made it harder than ever to shut him down and conceal a lie she wanted more than anything to share.

Lowering her pizza slice, she gave the boy her full attention. "*Because I said so* never cut it with me when my mom used it, so I won't even try it on you. But I do have my reasons, Billy. I don't want to lie, but I can't tell you the truth. So can you just please just go along with this for now. I promise we'll get everything settled soon and then you will be the first to know all the answers to your questions."

"Aw, Shawna. That's not fair."

"I know. Life sucks, kid, but that's the way it has to be. In the meantime, I'll get working on Gerda to try and expedite your case so I can be your actual foster mother. Then it'll be different. But right now I'm only a fill-in. So, let's not mess around, babe. Okay?"

Billy stomped to the kitchen doorway and leaned against the frame. He shoved his hands into his jeans pockets; his shoulders were slumped and he took his time.

Good Lord, she wanted to run over, kneel down and take him in her arms, promise him that he could have this way since it appeared so important. But she just couldn't. Instead, she waited and he didn't disappoint.

"Fine. I won't go over there. But if John comes here, I'm gonna let him in. So there." Billy disappeared up the hallway, Snow shadowing him, leaving Shawna with only one thought: *like Father like Son.*

As she cleaned off the table, wrapping Billy's unfinished pizza, knowing he'd want it later, she stared at the scene across the street. Through the uncovered window, she saw Alice and John eating together in Alice's dining room.

Snow that had collected on the roof and window grids gave the beautiful older home an appearance like one might have seen on a Christmas card or even in real life fifty years ago. The twinkle lights from Alice's tree glittered through a second window, the big bay one in the front room. And there were yet more lights decorating the outside of the house, from one roof peak to the other, with lit garlands around the front door that added to the cheerful scene.

Earlier, she'd seen John busy at Alice's house putting up the Christmas decorations and she couldn't help but admire his work.

Shaking off her wistful reflections, Shawna forced her mind to the problem at hand. How could she keep Billy occupied so he wouldn't feel resentful?

Aha! She pumped her fist and felt her heavy mood lighten. That's what she'd do to keep Billy's mind away from John... they'd get the house ready for the holidays. After all, Christmas was just weeks away and she decided right then: she'd make this the best Christmas Billy ever had.

But first things first. She needed to get the ball rolling with her plans to be Billy's foster mother, and to keep the boy with her until he could finally be reunited with his father.

Now why did that thought pierce her heart like an extremely sharp sting?

Chapter Seventeen

"What? You can't do that, Gerda. He's happy with me. You saw that for yourself last week. Remember when you stopped by and said he looked content. It's true. Now that he's made friends with Snow, he's more relaxed, cracks silly jokes and smiles all the time." Shawna lowered her voice to a dull roar. She'd seen her co-workers staring in her direction, their expressions confused.

Not being one to lose her cool, her behavior had them raising their eyebrows and looking worried. Nodding, her signal that all was fine, she closed the door to her office and returned to sit on the edge of her desk, facing the other woman.

"I'm sorry, Shawna. But you haven't been licensed as a foster home. And this opening just came along. I thought you'd be as ecstatic as I am over this opportunity. Billy will be placed with a really nice family; they have three boys they foster, two around his age. Don't get so upset. I promise he'll be treated well. Only one problem: he can't bring Snow. But you can keep the pup, and Billy can come and visit both you and the pooch."

"I don't want visits. I want him." Anger gathering, her throat reacted and Shawna all but spat out the words. "I thought everything was moving along fine. We started the paperwork, Gerda. I know what needs to be changed in the house. I'll get the other bathroom added on and his room made larger. I promised, didn't I?" Tears threatened and she heard the weepy echo in her shaky voice. She cleared her throat and blinked more than once.

"Honey," Gerda reached over and patted her hands. Shawna pulled them away and stood. "I'm sorry you're so upset. But face it; you're a single woman, a working one with long hours. Lois Phillips is a stay-at-home mom and she's a real sweetie. You know Lois. Billy'll be happy there."

Swiftly, Shawna paced to the end of the room and smashed the flat of her hand against the wall. Then she leaned her forehead against it. Closing her eyes, she gathered her thoughts.

Finally, shoving her fingers through her long hair to get it away from her face, she spoke. Her voice sounded conciliatory, pleading. "No, he won't, Gerda. Listen, you don't know him like I do. Billy's an introvert, a quiet kid who isn't happy in crowds. Hell, Gerda, he doesn't even like going to the mall. So far the only place with lots of people I can get him to go to is the movie theater, and even then I have to bribe him with popcorn and a hamburger. The kid's different... he's not into sports like other eleven-year-olds, even though he's good at it. He – he likes chess, for God's sake."

Gerda's expression hardened. She was no longer trying to get Shawna on board. Instead, she was telling her what was going to be. "Once he gets settled, that'll all change. He'll learn to enjoy being with a mom and a dad, part of a family. They have a huge house, lots of room and they're good people, Shawna. The best family I have on my list. I was ecstatic when they said they'd be willing to take Billy. You know his background as well as I do. He's always been a difficult kid, doesn't like rules, doesn't listen to the teachers at school. He has a problem with authority."

"And that's all changed since he moved in with me two weeks ago. He's been a lot better. I've worked with him. Remember I told you we got him a pair of glasses so he can now see the board. That was a big part of his struggles, not being able to read from the back of the room. He's even made a friend, Adam Small. He's trying, Gerda, and... *I love him.*" Hearing those words broke her completely. She'd never acknowledged before how much the snarky boy had come to mean to her. Now she understood so much better.

"I know you do, sweetie. You love all the kids at the center too. You've been good for him, I'm not arguing about that. But he needs more. The boy needs a family."

With her heart pumping so hard she wondered why she didn't pass out, Shawna, now down to begging, tried one last argument. "What about his father, John McCrae? He should have first dibs on Billy, right? After all, he's his flesh and blood. And he wants him. Doesn't that count for anything in your stupid rules and regulations? He's been in to deal with all your red tape, I know it."

Gerda sat forward, her voice sharp. "How do you know?"

Caught and not willing to tell the truth, Shawna hedged. "He said he would and I believed the man. He has, hasn't he?"

"Well, yes. But I don't like his background, Shawna.

Do you know how many incidents happened where Ada McCrae called 911 for the police to go to their house before he moved? Four times. What kind of a man is he? Letting his kid see him messing with his wife so they had to call in the police to split them apart?"

"I don't believe it." The words escaped before Shawna could tie off the loose end of her tongue.

Again Gerda's eyes narrowed and she snapped. "What don't you believe? That there are assholes out there who beat their wives? Or that they need the police to come and drag them away so women don't die from getting the shit kicked out of them. Or maybe that the kids don't get to see all this fun stuff happening? And in many cases, suffer from the animal's brutality themselves." She'd jumped up and screamed the last few words in rhythm with her fist pounding the desk. "Trust me, you innocent you. It happens all the time."

Silence settled over the two women, one looking pale and sick while the other was totally shocked. *So that's what drove the social worker.*

"I'm sorry, Gerda. I'm *so* sorry. That's why you're exceptionally protective of the children in your care. I get it now." Shawna moved to sit next to the woman who'd collapsed back in her chair, shaken and remorseful.

"I don't usually divulge my past, Shawna. It's painful and a horrible memory. But now you know why I'd do anything in my power to protect the youngsters under my care from suffering like I did. It's also how I know that a stable home can do wonders for a child on the brink. Having a family was all I dreamed about in those days, a loving environment to take away the fear I lived with every day. And, to my mind, John McCrae can't provide that and according to his previous history, doesn't deserve to get custody of Billy. I'm sorry, but until he can prove to me that he's gotten help for his alcoholism and anger management, I won't be letting Billy anywhere near him."

"He has a drinking problem?" Stunned, Shawna whispered the words.

"Maybe not now, but he did have at one time. And it created a lot of trouble in that house. Look, I'm still gathering evidence and I'd ask you to keep this under wraps, but I'll be appealing to the judge not to accept his application for custody."

Chapter
Eighteen

Shawna wandered from room to room, unstoppable tears pouring down her face. Gerda had come to take Billy away an hour earlier and she still wasn't able to control her crushing emotions.

When Gerda had called to say she'd be there that morning to pick up Billy, Shawna had once again begged her to change her mind, give them more time, even let her apply for a full adoption, but the other woman wouldn't budge.

Rethinking the moment when she'd tried to explain what was happening to Billy; Shawna couldn't get his shocked, incredulous look out of her mind. It played over and over, driving her half mad.

"You're letting them take me? You don't want me?" Shock evident, his big eyes had filled, their blueness disappearing behind a wall of tears.

"God, no, Billy. I'm not *letting* them do anything. I just have no rights to keep you against the decision of a government service. We're not related, and as far as they're concerned, I'm not even a qualified foster mother. Even my house doesn't fit their requirements. They only let you stay here because I pulled some strings and they didn't have anywhere else to place you. Now they do. The Phillips are a good family; they have three other fostered boys, a couple your age. You'll be treated well there."

"I don't want to go, Shawna. Me and Snow, we're good here. We like being with you." His pleading tone worked hard to win her over.

"Oh, Billy." She dropped to the couch in despair. "I love having you here. You know that. But I'm a deputy, an officer of the law. And the law says I have no rights. So as much as I hate the idea, you *have* to go with Gerda." She tried to harden her voice, state the case in a matter-of-fact manner, while at the same time as her heart ripped apart and bled inside her chest.

Her mind replayed how stunned he'd been when Gerda had arrived to fetch him and admitted that his new family had refused to accept Snow, said they had an older dog that wouldn't like being usurped by the little guy. He'd run back to Shawna then, grabbed her hand and begged again. "Let me stay, Shawna. I don't want to leave you, leave Snow. He's crying for me. Don't let the old witch take me."

She'd made promises then, unlikely ones, but she couldn't stop the words from flooding. "I'll do everything I can to get you back, Billy. I promise. Snow and I will be here and we'll fix the house to their damn codes and do whatever it takes. I'll apply to adopt you, I mean it. Whatever it takes."

Disapproval splashing across her expression, Gerda shook her head with impatience, took the boy's suitcase and handed him the box. "Come on, Billy. They're waiting to welcome you at your new home. Let's go."

After the door had closed behind them, Shawna had collapsed and cried until there were no tears left. She was still crying...

Suddenly the phone rang, but she ignored it. There wasn't anyone she wanted to talk to while she and the broken-hearted puppy both agonized for the boy they loved.

Eventually, it stopped. Within minutes, there was a pounding on the door that got so annoying, she finally gave in, picked up the pup and swiped at her face. Hesitating, swallowing, she moved forward and opened it.

John McCrae stood there, a worried look splashed across his features. As soon as he saw her misery, it turned into deep concern. Moving forward and closing the door behind him, he gently took Snow and lowered the pup to the floor, then folded her in his arms. His tenderness undid her and she broke down again.

Sobbing, she wailed, "Gerda took Billy away."

Chapter Nineteen

"I know. I saw them leaving out of the window. Honey, I need to know. Was it because Gerda found out that I've been teaching him chess? God, I'm sorry if that was the reason." John knew he had to come clean, tell her his secret and hope she didn't kick his sorry ass out in the snow. "We've only been together a couple of times."

"What?" Shock covering her features, Shawna leaned back to read his expression

Feeling sheepish, John added, "I know I said I wouldn't let him come to Alice's and I haven't. But I started working as a substitute math teacher at the school under the name John Reid, which is my real father's name. McCrae is my adopted family name. Billy waylaid me a few times in the hall and asked if we could play during lunch hour. I never wanted to go behind your back, Shawna, but he's my son and it's hell not being able to tell him. He likes being with me. How could I refuse such a small request, especially when I wanted it so badly?" His voice broke and he gath-

ered her back in close and squeezed her hard, his face lowering to her neck.

She held the trembling man in her arms and pity
stirred. "It's okay. I probably would have done the same."
She hugged him harder. "That wasn't why she took him.
She came by the office earlier and said she'd found a family
who wanted to take the boy, a good foster home, one of the
best. They have a huge house and other foster kids, two
boys near the same age as Billy. As much as I hate to admit
it, she only wants the best for him but she just doesn't
understand. Even if my house isn't up to their standards,
Billy was happy here with me and Snow."

Hearing his name and then Billy's, his furry companion ran to the door and scratched, crying and barking, his
small body squirming with desperation to find his master.

John released Shawna to scoop up the sad creature,
and they went forward into the family room where he set
Snow down on a chair with a pat and a soft command.
"Stay here, boy." They both watched as Snow ignored the
command and half leaped and half tumbled to the ground.
His chubby little legs ran as fast as they could back to the
front door where he circled around and finally laid down,
his head on his paws and his sad little button black eyes
begging.

Shawna collapsed on the sofa and John sat next to her.
He gathered her in his arms. "You mentioned the house
not being up to their requirements. What's wrong with
this house?"

Something in his voice caught her attention. "It's not
big enough. According to the regulations, Billy needs
access to his own bathroom. Plus, his bedroom was too
small. It's never been a problem before when they've
needed me to take in the strays. And as long as they had

no place else for Billy, Gerda was happy for him to be here. But it's not considered a suitable long-term foster establishment."

Wanting to keep her talking, he questioned, "I see. Is this your family home?"

"No. I grew up in the neighborhood, but Mom and Dad sold their big house and bought this one after us kids all moved out. Then they decided to retire to Florida five years ago. None of my brothers or sisters stayed here in Carlton Grove; they're scattered all over the States, so I was the only one who wanted it."

"It's small but perfect for a single woman. I know you've never been married—"

Shawna's questioning glare forced him to add, "Alice does like to... ah... visit. Trust me, everything she said was complimentary. For instance, I know you don't have a boyfriend, and haven't had anyone serious in your life since you moved in."

Shawna sniffed in disgust. "Just haven't met the right man. The nice ones are either hard to find, married or shell-shocked from a bad divorce. Since I'm only thirty-one, no matter what Alice says, I figure there's still plenty of time. I've done my share of dating, but it gets stale. Too often, I've spent an evening with someone else while wishing the whole time I'd stayed home wearing my PJs, watching TV and snacking on popcorn."

"I know what you mean. It's been the same for me—until I met you. I can't think of anything I'd rather do than join you for an evening. Hell, I'd happily provide the popcorn and, if it's mandatory, I'll even buy a pair of PJs." He hoped his teasing had taken her mind off Billy and, by her giggle, it had obviously worked. Now that she appeared more receptive, he shared his wonderful news.

"Alice is selling me her house."

"What?" She pushed away from where her head had rested against his chest, made him loosen his arms and she searched his eyes. "Alice loves this neighborhood."

"Yes, she wants to buy another place close by. But that big house is a lot of work for her these days. The bed & breakfast business is either too slow or when she does get visitors, it's too much work. Therefore, I've promised I'll pay her what the house is worth, and then I'll upgrade the kitchen and bathrooms, paint the interior and renovate wherever it needs to be done. I can do most of the work myself. She has a fantastic lot: her gardens are awesome and it's exactly the type of house I'd envisioned myself living in with Billy."

"You're buying it to give him a home, aren't you?"

"Of course, it's one of the conditions for getting custody. As a father, it's only right that I provide him with a decent place to live. After working all those years in South America and investing my money wisely, I can afford to pretty well buy whatever house I want." He wasn't bragging and hoped she didn't take his words in that way. It was simply a fact. He'd worked damn hard to be financially stable and he wouldn't apologize for it.

Bristling slightly, memories of Ada's so-called love returning to taunt and belittle, he waited to hear Shawna's comeback.

Something was wrong. She was going to hurt him; he knew the signs, only she didn't look happy about breaking his heart. Instead, she looked devastated. He swallowed and stiffened for the impact, stomach churning.

Reaching forward, she gently stroked his face. He searched her eyes and knew he'd hate the next words out of her mouth. Trying to stop her, he gently laid his hand over her lips but she shrugged away.

"You have to hear this, John. You need to understand what you're up against. Gerda told me she'll fight against you getting custody of Billy, she'll go to court and she'll win."

"What?"

What she said next shattered his dreams.

Chapter Twenty

Drunkenness, disturbances, cops called to the house? What the hell was Shawna talking about? The pounding in his head worked simultaneously: agitating his senses and encouraging his wild imagination. What atrocities had his little boy suffered at the hands of his crazy mother?

He slid away from the warm-hearted woman at his side and, leaning forward, hid his face in his hands until he could be assured that his reactions were calm, rational... controlled.

This ridiculous situation was like having to deal with Ada all over again. Only this time he wasn't a poor, defenseless man with no income, no job and a mother's tearful claims overriding the truth. This time, he could afford a lawyer. This time, he had right on his side–the right of a loving and stable father to bring up his mother-less son.

"She won't get away with it." He made sure his voice came out clear, no whining, no give, just a statement of fact. "I'll hire a lawyer and we'll take this to court."

"You won't have to. I've already dug into the matter

through official channels and I know the truth."

He spun to face her. "You didn't trust I'd tell you the truth? You had so little faith in my integrity?" Pain resonated in his voice. He heard it clearly. Before he could cover up his response, his eyes filled with hurt and distrust. Feeling colder as each second passed, he inched away.

She hadn't believed in him. That fact alone almost brought him to his knees. The woman he'd begun to worship, to allow space in his thoughts and, if he were being truthful, in his heart, had investigated his background like he was a common criminal. One who would have so little care for a wife and a son that the police would need to be called in to save them from his drunken behavior. She'd done a search on his background to find the *facts*.

"Stop being such a fool! As if you could behave that way. It was *because* I believed in you that I knew I had to find the proof to show Gerda that she was wrong. And I did find the truth."

He swung around, scooped her up and had her nestled in his lap before he even knew he would do so. *She believed in him!*

"You're the first woman who's ever seen me so clearly. That you would know I'd never act so underhanded is such a high for me, that I can't even begin to explain." Words left him. He wanted her to know how touched he was, but there was nothing he could say. He needed to show her.

At first, his kisses were full of the sweetness that poured straight from his overflowing heart and through his lips. Soft and gentle, he made his mouth touch hers with only love and tenderness.

She moaned her approval and so he continued until

passion ignited and changed the dynamics. Now she was spurring him on, her tongue foraging for his, ramping up pleasant affection to a whole new level. Her movements against him, her hips and her breasts, rubbing, tantalizing, were signs she was getting carried away, and he wanted it to happen more than anything.

He dragged his lips from hers. "Sweetheart, if your intentions are to stop this from going all the way, tell me now. It's been a long time for me. I want it to be right."

"Hell, from the way I feel after a few kisses, I'd say it's perfect. Please, don't stop. If you do, I'm afraid I'll have to shoot you."

He laughed, stood up with her in his arms and headed for the hallway that he hoped led to her bedroom. With her arms wrapped around his neck, she just continued to lay one kiss on him after the other, quick kisses of approval that provoked and teased. "Through here."

Holding her protectively, he lowered them onto the end of the thick white comforter, and this time when she kissed him he got involved and took it much further. His mouth gently sucked at hers until they were both breathing hard and shaking with barely-restrained desire.

Somehow, they'd fallen back and were half on and half off the end of the bed. He lifted her further up and followed so that they were lying with their heads on the pillows, both facing each other, her eyes blazing with a lustful softness that made every molecule in his body stand at attention.

This gorgeous woman wanted him, John Reid McCrae, and he would do everything in his power to satisfy her cravings.

Chapter
Twenty-one

Shawna had never felt this way with any other man before. Like there was no need for shyness or worries about whether her performance would pass muster, or if he'd find her naked body attractive.

Getting her clothes off became the ultimate goal, and with his help, it happened faster than she'd ever thought possible.

During those precious moments, his lips searched out erogenous zones she didn't even know existed. Turned out she had a lot of areas on her neck that were linked to a lustful appetite and by the time he'd covered most of them, she was a pitiful bundle of cravings.

Now his golden hands were doing amazing things to her body, his fingers warm and gentle as they squeezed and caressed her breasts and stomach, intensifying her hunger beyond what she could bear. "John, hurry. I'm dying here."

His chuckles against her breast made her arch her body, inviting him to enter, to plunge and feed her appetite.

"Hold on, beautiful. If I come near you now, it'll be over with before we've had time to learn each other's preferences."

"Preferences? I love it all, and I'd *prefer* that we hold your survey for next time." Giggling, she added, "John Reid McCrae–don't you make me beg."

Running her fingers through his thick hair, loving the male scent of his shampoo, she nipped at his earlobe gently to let him know she meant business. Not too slow on the uptake, he must have understood because, within a very short time, he'd filled her body with his and her heart with sweet love.

***

Later, while waiting for him to return to the bed, Shawna thought about their earlier conversation. She knew that her confidence in John's honor had made a huge difference to him, and there was no way she'd ever admit to the hit she'd taken when Gerda had first told her about his past.

Reasoning her way through everything she'd recently learned about the man had spurred on the realization that the guy she knew, albeit not for long and mostly by instinct, couldn't be the same man showing up in Gerda's files. Certainly, training had also kicked in. Once she'd calmed down and pieced the facts together, there was no doubt they'd need proof of his innocence to help Gerda see the light.

Spending the morning on the computer, calling in IOUs and getting others on board, remembering the remark Billy had made about his mother having a boyfriend living with them, she'd amassed a strong case in John's favor. The first two times when the police had been to his home, John had been overseas attending his job interview. On the last two incidents, he'd been away working. Obviously, Ada's boyfriend had used John's name, and since no charges had been pressed, the police had separated the adults, written up a report and left. Therefore, John couldn't be the vicious monster Gerda imagined.

Shawna had also paid a visit to Alice's sister, Claire. And in a very short time, she'd gained a clear picture of John's lifestyle while he'd lived with Ada and Billy. Turned out the man had seldom taken a drink because his wife had needed to be looked after when she'd become intoxicated... and that was often the case.

Also, Ada had never been any sort of housekeeper but had relied on John to clean keep things tidy. So, before he'd left, John had arranged for a woman to go in and clean every week. From what Shawna could tell, the man had done everything he could to leave his family in good shape while he worked abroad for their future

Since the maid and Claire had struck up a friendship, between the two of them, they had tried to do right by Billy. Too bad Ada had rejected any overtures and soon locked them both out. Then she'd moved and Claire had lost track.

But explanations didn't seem to matter to John right at the moment. This night belonged to them. He appeared from the kitchen, wearing just his jeans unbuttoned and low on his hips. There was a tattoo on his chest with the name *Billy* hiding in swirls of filigree. If one didn't know his son's name, they'd miss it altogether.

Coming close to serve Shawna, he balanced two cups of hot coffee, and between his teeth hung a bag of home-made cookies he must have found on the counter. They were the ones she and Billy had baked together.

Seeing them, her heart dropped and she had to swallow back the threatening tears. Quickly he put down his offerings and slid back in beside her, cuddling, stroking and whispering, "Don't be sad, honey. We'll get him back. I promise. It might take a bit of time, but it will happen. In the meantime, at least he's safe."

"You aren't worried?"

"Nope. I have the truth on my side, and as soon as the court learns Gerda's mistaken, it will come out all right."

"Okay, I know that's true. It's just that Christmas is only a week away and we had such big plans. We were going to watch some specials on TV and open a few presents on Christmas Eve. I'd promised the kid he could eat whatever he wanted that night and he chose – get this – thick-crust pizza. And it had to have loads of cheese and pepperoni... but no mushrooms."

"And you'd let him get away with that?" John chuckled as if he knew the answer.

"Of course not. I made him a deal that if he'd eat a few mushrooms, I'd let him help me make it. That part he liked. He also wanted us to invite you and Alice for turkey dinner on Christmas day, and I had to say no because I worried that if Gerda found out, she'd take him away." The last word came out in a pitiful moan. A sob escaped and the dam broke. Soon her whole body shook from the emotions raging inside her.

Scooping her close, rocking her, John's gentle voice trembled noticeably. "Darling, I almost forgot Christmas is so close. We'll get him back... we will. I promise. I'll do whatever it takes. Remember, we have right on our side."

Wailing her reply, she answered, "Yes, but we don't have much time."

Chapter
Twenty-two

"What do you mean you're going to run away? You can't do that, Billy. You're already in loads of trouble. I overheard the math teacher talking to Harry Hockey-stick, saying that you'd slipped back to being a hindrance, worse than you ever were."

"Mr. Harry? What does he know?"

"He might be skinny, but he's the Principal."

Billy hid his eyes, not wanting his buddy to see the lie. "I don't give a darn."

"Yeah, you do. Geez, man, you gotta stop making so many waves. What's your problem anyway?"

"What do you care?"

"We're friends, right? Friends care."

"Nah! We aren't friends. You just latched onto me 'cause no one else likes you." The minute the words, formed by bitterness and anger, escaped, Billy knew he'd gone too far. Adam's face turned bright pink and his eyes held a distinct glimmer of shame, hurt and tears.

Billy stepped back, thinking to make himself scarce, but Adam didn't let go. "So this is what you do when you're feeling shitty. You make everyone else suffer. No wonder... " Adam stopped. He fought with himself, obviously holding in the insults that were struggling to get out. Instead, he stood and stared at Billy, his hands fisted at his side.

He'd been a jackass. He had to leave soon or he'd cry too. Only Adam had stuck by him, the one friend who'd put up with his bad attitude. Billy reached out. His hand grabbed the front of Adam's hoodie. He shook it and words burst out that he knew should have been said in a nicer way, but the mad was riding him and he figured he was lucky enough to get them out at all.

"Why do you care about me, you dork? I'm a shit! Just like my mom used to say. Like everyone believes. So why do you even give a damn about me?"

"'Cause you're the only one who listens when I talk." Adam's voice wobbled, but he forced out what he wanted to say. "I didn't think you did, but you proved me wrong. You listen."

"Well, yeah, man. You're smart. The things you know about are interesting. Course I listen."

"See, that's why I care." Adam grinned in a way that had Billy returning the smile. "So, what are you gonna do? Do you want that I should go with you?"

"Hell, no, your dad would kill you if you took off. No one really gives a damn about what I do. Except maybe that Gerda and she's the cow that took me away from Shawna."

Adam, standing straight now, nodded. "Yeah, Shawna's cool and you know she really likes you a lot. They shoulda left you with her and Snow."

"I'm going to take Snow with me."

"How can you do that?"

"You know Shawna leaves him out on the front veranda when she's at work. I'll just stop by and pick him up. He'll be happy to see me. Shawna said that he was crying in my room and she had to close the door so he couldn't get back in, silly mutt. Then she said that because he's been sleeping by the front door, she's put his cushion there."

"Dumb dog likes you too."

Billy grinned and nodded. "We can catch a ride, maybe to Seattle and find someplace to live there. I saw on TV that they have homes for kids with no family. As long as I don't tell them my name, they won't know where I come from, right?"

"I don't think it's that easy, Billy. They'll put out an amber alert, and anyone who sees you will contact the authorities here in Carlton Grove and they'll bring you back."

"Maybe, but then they'll know I'm serious about not wanting to live with the Phillips family. Maybe then, they'll let me go back to Shawna."

Chapter
Twenty-three

Late the next day, Shawna opened the front door to a very disturbed Gerda. "Lois Phillips just called and said that Billy never came home from school." Gerda stepped into the lit foyer of Shawna's house, agitation riding her hard. "I'm not fooling around here, Shawna. Tell him he needs to go back."

Shawna stared at the woman and couldn't seem to digest the words. She glanced behind Gerda to the outside and saw all the Christmas lights radiating from the opposite side of the street. But there wasn't anyone there. Confusion made her ask, "He's missing?"

"You haven't seen him?"

John appeared from around the corner and joined the two women at the front door. "My son isn't at the Phillips' home? Where is he?"

When she saw Billy's father, Gerda's face dropped. She watched as he stepped closer to Shawna in a protective way. "What are you doing here?" Not at all polite, she fired her question.

"I live across the street, and we've been keeping company since you took Billy away." He said the words with pride and a hint of warning that Shawna recognized as protection for her. She cut in to stop the looming argument.

"Gerda, did you read the files I emailed to you at your office yesterday? We've been waiting to hear from you."

Gerda backed up a step. "No, I didn't read them. I've been too busy looking after kids from dysfunctional families who are having their Christmas ruined by screwed up folks like John here."

Shawna recognized the fury in her friend's eyes and gave John the look that said, *back off.* Then she took Gerda's hand and led her to the living room where they could sit. "Would you like something to drink, Gerda? John just made us some hot chocolate so it wouldn't be any problem. We needed to warm up because we've been hunting for Snow all over the neighborhood. When I got home from work, he was nowhere to be found. I have no idea how he could have escaped; the door was closed. We were thinking maybe some kids let him out and he's roaming around, lost. We've searched for a few hours, but we're freezing so we came in for a hot drink."

Not sure what was happening between the two adults facing her, Gerda's expression clearly showed her confusion. "No thanks, there's no time now that I know Billy's not with you. I'm sorry about the puppy. Billy talks about him a lot." Seeing John's expression, she added, "I'll have a glass of water if you don't mind."

John vanished to the kitchen and the minute he stepped from the room, Gerda was onto her. "What the hell are you playing at here, Shawna? You tell me you want

Billy, and then you go behind my back and hang out with that loser? Are you kidding me?"

Shawna cared about her friend, but no one was going to get away with calling her man names, especially since they were so untrue. John worked as many hours as he could at the school as a substitute teacher to help out his old buddy, the Principal, who couldn't find anyone else to take on the math classes so close to the Christmas holidays.

He'd also shouldered the bulk of Alice's chores and was helping her find a new home, driving her to see potential properties.

Plus, he'd started working at Shawna's to take down a wall between a small den and Billy's bedroom to increase the size of his space. Since Shawna still hadn't given up hope that she might get Billy back, even if only temporarily, she was glad to see this renovation moving along. The man was a dynamo and Gerda needed to know what a good heart he had.

Unable to stop her rant, she let Gerda have it all, and the poor woman sat there shell-shocked. Finally, she got a word in edgeways.

"A snake doesn't change its way of slithering. They're born that way. I saw it happen too many times."

"Gerda, you have to quit comparing your experiences with other people. I've just told you the man is a hard worker and you can verify that with Alice across the street, and Harry the Principal at the school, and—"

"You're saying you think he's reformed?"

"What I'm saying is you need to read your emails. I've amassed a huge folder of files on John McCrae. Just got the final papers from the army yesterday verifying that he won a medal in Iraq when he was just twenty-one. He's since qualified as a mining engineer and has glowing references. He's also a carpenter; used the skill to help put himself through college after he left the military. Most important to your case, the man is not a drinker and never has been. The times that the police were called to his house, John was already out of the country. Ada's drunken boyfriend was the perp, and those files hold the proof."

John came in carrying a glass of ice water and set it down in front of Gerda. "What's this about Billy being missing? Did you check with his buddy, Adam, from school?"

Gerda's discomfort was palpable. "Lois is doing that now. I took for granted that he'd snuck here and you were letting him hang out, so I came right over. "

John stiffened. Shawna's disquiet soared and the worry hit her like a ton of bricks. "You mean he's actually missing and you don't know where he is? He's run away again?"

Hunched over, Gerda hid her face in her hands. "Yes. He must have run away. The boy's been so unhappy and I didn't pay attention. He liked it here with you and I made him leave. I'm so sorry."

Within a few moments, Shawna was on the phone to the precinct, giving orders to her co-workers. When she came back to where John and Gerda were talking quietly, she said, "We've set up an amber alert and I e-mailed them his most recent photograph. It will be on television in the next few minutes. I'm heading over to the Phillips' house to get the details and see what he might have taken."

John spoke in a no-nonsense tone. "I'll go and talk to Adam again and see if he's hiding anything."

Gerda piped up. "We talked to him and he says he doesn't know."

John looked crestfallen for a few seconds and then he

brightened up. "Yeah, well, that was before he knew that Billy would be living with his father from now on and, if my luck holds out, with Shawna as his mom."

What? Heart tripping, pulse already out of whack, Shawna allowed the answer to blaze from her eyes as she nodded her acceptance of the strangest proposal any woman was likely to get. "Right, tell Adam that Billy will be living with his own family when we find him. Now I need to move. An eleven-year-old out there on his own is a frightening thought. If I didn't know just how smart he was, I'd be terrified."

John added. "You mean a boy and his dog."

Ah... Shawna understood what he meant. "Yeah, a boy and his dog. Look, the last time I came home was at lunchtime and Snow was here, so they must have left sometime after that. I already have the crew checking the bus depot and every place where he could have paid for a ride. My fear is that he might have hitchhiked."

"Oh God, that's dangerous." John's face lost all its color. "We have to find him."

Chapter
Twenty-four

Billy was nobody's fool. When he lifted his thumb and a car stopped, he checked out the driver. He saw a woman with a small child in the back seat and felt pretty secure that she wouldn't hurt him. The window slid down and the blonde-haired lady was even prettier close-up.

"Hi, there. Can I give you a lift?" She even had a nice voice.

"Okay. Where are you going?"

"I live just on the outskirts of town, on the north end. Where were you headed?"

"I kinda thought Seattle."

"That's pretty far to go for a youngster alone like you. Come in out of the cold." She smiled and waved him into the front seat next to her. Once he was settled, she put the car in gear and started to drive. "What's your pup's name?"

"He's Snow. What's your kid's name?"

"She's Laura, and I'm Andrea Mollet."

"I'm John." He lied and decided it was good he'd

thought to.

"My turn," she chuckled. "How old are you?" A smile accompanied her question, but Billy knew he needed to be careful.

"I'm fifteen. How old is your baby?"

"Twenty." She raised her eyebrow, and Billy knew she'd lied because he had.

He turned away and hoped she'd keep driving. It had been cold out there. Even Snow had begun to shake. Besides, dusk had settled in and he knew darkness would soon follow.

"Are you hungry?" Andrea reached over and petted Snow's head, and the puppy wriggled to get closer to her. Billy had to restrain him and didn't see her dial her phone through the entertainment system on the dash. All of a sudden, a male voice answered her call.

"Hi, honey. Where are you?"

"I'm almost home. I'll be bringing a guest with me. He's hungry and so is his pup, Snow. Hitchhiking makes a guy tuckered out and I'm hoping he'll stay with us for a while."

"Roger that. I'll be waiting. Cooked spaghetti and meatballs tonight, so I hope he likes Italian."

Andrea turned to him and asked, "Do you like Italian?"

Billy nodded and then settled back against the seat, happy to be letting an adult take over, if only for a few hours. If he could stay with Andrea and the man who sounded so nice for the night, he'd be off in the morning before they even knew he was missing.

Chapter
Twenty-five

"Are you sure this is the address they gave you?" John's nerves were on edge and the only thing that would settle them down was to see his boy and hold him in his arms.

"Yes. This is it on the corner—Andrea and Hank Mollet. He's a cop with the north division, and his wife is a kindergarten teacher."

Shawna opened the door of the SUV and John quickly circled the vehicle to meet her and take her in his arms. Holding her face gently, he kissed her hard. "Did you mean it? About maybe getting married and being a family? We can be together, you and me and Billy?"

"Yes. I meant it, and the sooner, the better. After my first marriage disaster, I never thought I'd trust another female enough to ask her to be my wife and a mother to my son. But you've given me back my faith in the gentle sex, baby. I've never met a woman like you. I know I couldn't be happy without being close to you every day for the rest of my life."

She kissed him, his eyes, his cheeks and then his lips, feeling the flow of emotion that happened every time their lips met. Nestling herself into his arms, her face nuzzling his neck, she said, "I was closed to love for the longest time, John. When I was a girl, my brother was killed in a car accident and I escaped with just a few scars. It broke something in me. The unbearable pain drove me into a kind of shell. Oh, I could deal with everyday life, the center, my police job, even the occasional date. But anytime I felt someone closing in, something inside me, the scared little girl who didn't want to take a chance, well she shut the door. Until your son came into my life. The minute I held him in my arms, my heart opened and swung wider when you showed up. So now I figure once you're both safely inside with me where you belong, I'll lock it tight."

"And open it again when our first baby comes along, right?"

Laughing gaily, she nodded. "Right." An image of a blond-haired baby with sparkling blue-gray eyes appeared and made her heart sing. "I hope Alice finds a place to live soon. Then we can be together in our new home as a family."

"I've found her a place."

"You have? That's wonderful." Shawna laughed happily and swung around so she could see his eyes.

He winked at her and made her wait for his answer. Finally, he added, "Yep. She can buy your house."

Of course! A sledgehammer of yes's bashed in the side of her head. "How dumb am I for not thinking of that myself. It's the perfect solution."

Looking a bit smug, John smiled. "I kinda like the ole girl, and she'll make a great babysitter for Billy and his brothers and sisters."

Catching his meaning, she giggled. "Good idea! Let's go and get our boy." Walking toward the house, that had decorations in every window, a big white blow-up Santa waving in the wind and multi-colored lights strung on the all trees on the front lawn, Shawna stopped and added. "I love Christmas."

Chapter
Twenty-six

Shawna rang the bell and smiled at the blonde woman who answered with a baby in her arms and a white puppy bouncing by her ankles. A creature who began howling and skipping with joy as soon as he saw who was at the door.

"I'm Deputy Shawna Mallory, and this is my friend, John McCrae. We've come to fetch Billy."

"Ah! His name is Billy. We only know him as John. I'm Andrea Mollet. Please come in."

Snow, now wild, jumped up at Shawna until she bent over and gathered the excited canine close. She welcomed getting her face washed and her hugs let the little fellow know she shared in his happiness. With his soft coat all fluffed around him, adoring black eyes alight, he was a sight for sore eyes.

Andrea spoke low. "Please come in and make your-selves at home. Hank has your Billy downstairs in his man-cave. They're playing video games. He's a sweet kid. Don't know why he ran away, but I wouldn't want to see him get into any trouble." Her gaze didn't waver as she scrutinized both Shawna and John before relaxing her stance.

"No trouble at all." Both Shawna and John assured their hostess. Then Shawna decided the woman deserved more of an explanation.

"Billy was forced into a foster home he didn't want to be in and he ran away. What he wanted to do was stay with me, but his social worker wouldn't let him. But that's all settled now and he'll be coming back with me where he belongs."

Andrea smiled, looking relieved. "Okay then, just go down those stairs and my husband will leave you with him so you can get it all straightened out. Then maybe you could join us for a spaghetti dinner. It'll be ready whenever you are."

"How sweet. Thank you." Shawna was so over-whelmed that a hug seemed in order and the other woman was more than happy to oblige, baby and all.

When they stepped into the room with the wide-screen TV, brown leather couch and boy toys everywhere, it was the obvious place where Hank most likely hung out.

John hesitated at the entrance and Shawna saw his shyness. She knew he was worried about Billy's reception once he learned that John was his dad. The kid was smart and would want to know where his father had been when he'd needed him the most.

Hank saw them while Billy was deep in his moves and he stood, ruffled Billy's hair, and then headed for the stairs. He slowed down and gave them the once over, then seemed satisfied. With a nod, he continued on his way.

"Billy?" Shawna moved to sit on one side of him and watched his expression change from overjoyed to worried and then to confused. She took the controls from his hand and laid them on the table. "Hank is a cop and saw the amber alert we set up for you. As soon as his wife mentioned you had a pup called Snow, he knew you were the boy being looked for and he called it in. I'm just glad it was Mrs. Mollet who picked you up."

"I screened the cars, Shawna. I knew I had to find people to ride with that would be safe. I'm not an idiot."

Shawna nodded and smiled. No way would she argue right now but one day they were destined to have a serious talk.

Billy stared at her nervously. When he swung his head and saw John, he grinned and his whole face lit up. "Hi, John. You came to get me too?"

"Yeah. I was scared for you until the call came in that you were safe. Man, you mustn't ever do this again. My old heart can't take the beating."

Billy laughed and, at the same time, looked kinda curious. "Why would you be so worried? I'm a pretty smart kid; you said so yourself."

John glanced at Shawna and she saw the sweat on his forehead and the nerve twitching under his left eye. The man looked frantic and she felt her heart soften at his predicament. Smiling, she nodded.

John took hold of Billy's left hand and unconsciously began to play with his fingers. "Billy, I was worried because I'm your dad, and dads can't help themselves when it comes to their kids."

A silence followed and Billy's face broke into a happy grin. Finally, he answered. "So you do want me to know."

John looked mystified. "Know what?"

"That you're my father."

"Hold it. *You knew?*"

"Kinda. I wasn't sure, but I have a picture of you holding me as a baby, the only one Mom didn't destroy. I found it in an old textbook. My dad sorta looked like you and I pretended it was true. But then when you never said anything, I decided it couldn't be. Either that or you didn't want me."

"God, kid. That's so far from the truth that I don't know how to tell you." John's voice wobbled and he looked to Shawna for help.

Not in much better shape, tears close, she took Billy's other hand and held it between both of hers. "Your dad wasn't allowed to say anything, Billy. Gerda wanted to make sure all the paperwork was complete before we broke the news. Mainly, she didn't want you to be disappointed that it took so long."

No way did Shawna want to explain how the system that should have protected this boy screwed up again. "But it's fine now, Billy. You're coming home with me tonight, and you'll be staying with me just until your dad can get his new home fixed up."

Billy threw himself into her arms and clung. "I knew *you'd* want me, Shawna. I knew it."

Shawna threw a look at John that spoke volumes. *He needs you now. You have to tell him.* She eased away from Billy and picked up Snow.

Billy turned to John shyly. But John wasn't having any more nonsense. He picked the boy up, held him on his lap and wrapped his large arms around him. He nestled his son's head into his shoulder and began to talk. He told him about how heartbroken he'd been when Ada had refused to join him in Chile. About the lonely nights when he yearned to be with his boy, but he knew that they needed a place to live and, being the man of the family, he had to be a provider. But how it had backfired and how Billy's mother had turned against him.

He didn't spare himself or Ada in the telling. Admitted they were both at fault for how they'd handled their son. Finally, his voice broken, he said, "Billy, can you ever forgive me? For leaving you? For having you believe that no one cared? For letting the broken system dictate to me how to be a father? I love you, son. If you don't believe in anything else, please, please believe that."

Billy pulled away and wiped his face though the tears kept spilling over. "I love you too, Dad. I'm glad we can be together now, you, me and Snow."

Shawna felt her heart drop and her eyes flew to John's face. He looked like a deer caught in the headlights, floundering, unsure.

Not being too stupid, the boy looked first at his dad and then grinned at her. "And maybe one day, Shawna."

Find Me a Home

Holiday Heartwarmers Trilogy
Book #3
Wheelchair bound, Amelia Lloyd is embarrassed when the neighbor calls the police to deal with her out-of-control brother. Her old dog tries to protect her but it takes the combined efforts of a handsome police Sergeant

and a crabby puppy to put a stop to her sibling's shenanigans. At first, she hates to be caught in such a situation. But then she accepts an important truth. The big-hearted man, her savior, wouldn't have come into her life otherwise.

Sergeant Harley Carlton is exhausted from dealing with a car accident where everyone is killed except for the darling cherub who mistakes him for her daddy. How can a man with a heart as big as his, correct the precious little blind orphan? Within a few hours, he gets a call to save a blonde-haired beauty from her crazy brother. The thing is – how can a man fall in love twice in one night?

Dedication

I want to dedicate this third novella to Melody Williams, the lovely lady who suggested the title **Find Me a Home**. Once I had that, the rest of the story came easy.

Have a wonderful Christmas Season, my friend. May you be blessed with family, friends and lots of fun.

XO

Mimi

Prologue

Dark and frightening, the night sounds of busy birds, buzzing insects and muted traffic from the faraway streets created a racket that disturbed the terrified puppies. Rustling of the tree branches added to the discord, as did the wind sweeping up dry leaves and forcing them against solid objects where they splattered and crumbled.

The overwhelming, surrounding scents were tantalizing, yet not familiar and, therefore, not comforting. Only the smell from the teats and the warmth of their mother's body was yearned for by the pups and missed.

Inside the cardboard box, the one female puppy communicated with her two brothers; he's gone!

Scampering to the corner of their flimsy prison, she thought back to the fight that had ensued between the man and her mistress before she and her brothers had been thrown here.

"Amelia, you kept those mutts? Before I left last week, I told you to get rid of them."

"But, Jimmy, they were too little to be weaned from Bella. I was waiting until this weekend to try and sell them." Her mistress's lovely voice had sounded placating and miserable all at the same time.

"Who's going to buy these three? Their mom is a fat, ugly, overly-friendly lab with no guard skills; don't know why I let you talk me into keeping her. And that vicious Samoyed brute across the way, who's no doubt their father, is meaner than the devil who owns him."

"Jim, they're cute pups. I bet I can get a few dollars for them."

"Sure, and until then we have to listen to them kai-yiying all the time, clean up their messes and feed them. No more! I want them gone. It's bad enough we have to trip over that bag of bones without having to deal with her stupid offspring too. Never mind! Since you're as useless as a garden hose in a forest fire, I'll take care of this myself."

He yanked the three pups out from under the tummy of the keening dam where they'd burrowed in fear. Grabbing a nearby box, he hurled them inside. After a short drive in a car, he carried the carton for a few minutes and threw it down.

"Good riddance!" Those were the last words the puppies heard from him. The fading sounds as the man crunched away were terrifying.

Whimpering at the memory, after multiple tries, the female puppy bounced until her front paws gained purchase on the box's edge. Straining her neck, she peered out.

The moon, riding high in the starlit sky, provided illumination for the snoopy pup. *I think it's a park,* she told the other two, whining, sharing her thoughts.

Chubbs, her roly-poly brother, subsided lazily into his corner, his furry body falling over and staying there. *What are we going to do?* Little beady black eyes watered as he howled pitifully.

Stop that caterwauling! It hurts my ears. His brother's normal cranky manner was evident in his insensitive attitude. *We'll sleep now, and in the morning, Sis can go and find us some help.*

Okay! That's a good idea, right, Sister? Chubbs yawned and curled up next to his brother. Both were asleep in seconds. Only their sister snoozed with one eye open, guarding their new dwelling.

In the morning, sounds of human voices woke the three. Again, the female bounced in the corner until she had her front paws clinging to the side of the carton. In the distance, she saw a lot of water. There were people running along its edge. To her left, there was a grassy field where humans were playing a game with a big brown ball.

Cranky wanted to see the world she was describing. When he got close, she used his butt as a ladder and worked her way up and over his head, landing ungraciously in a heap on the grass outside of their container.

Go, Sis. Find us help! Chubbs and Cranky whined together.

***

Early the next morning, cold and hunger driving him, Chubbs escaped over the edge of the box and disappeared. Cranky never saw him again. Left alone, as the hours passed, the remaining pup became crabbier than usual.

He spent most of the day by himself and the loneliness ate at him almost as much as the hunger roiling in his belly. Falling snow collecting in the box didn't help the situation whatsoever, other than giving him something to stop his thirst. Without his sister and brother there to share his woes, the time had come for him to fend for himself and do something about his situation.

Pushing against the side of his prison got him nowhere. The pitiful cries he'd been forcing out periodically hadn't worked either. He had to make a plan.

First he leaped at the corner of the box and felt it tilt just a little. Putting more oomph behind his thrust, he backed up and threw his whole furry ball of fat puppy against that same corner, this time at a higher level, and over it went.

Only the box played a trick on him and it flipped, landing on top of him. Growling, turning circles, darkness surrounding him, he began to lunge at the walls and attack them with his sharp teeth. Suddenly, the box began moving. As it slid over a low spot, he felt a breeze. Seeing an opening, he scratched at the ground.

Snarling, growing fierce in his need to escape, he lunged once more, and with a Herculean effort, he found himself half outside the wall. One last thrust, and freedom became reality.

Still angry, he shook himself, tripped over his chubby legs and fell to the side, where more snow clung to his cold little body. He looked around and saw the same white icy stuff completely covered his surroundings.

Sniffing the air, he ran to a tree and did his business. A memory appeared about how pleased his mistress had been when he'd learned that the yard outside was his bathroom. She'd cuddled him, petting and praising. *"What a smart boy! You're the best puppy in the world."*

Warmth spilled into his small being and brought with it an overwhelming urge. He needed to find his home, his mother and the lady he liked more than anyone else. Sniffing the air once again, he turned north.

This way...

Chapter One

Normally, Harley Carlton liked his position as a police sergeant for the Carlton Grove Police Department, but he didn't today. The bodies strewn around two crushed vehicles had to be dealt with, and since he'd come upon the accident while on his way home, after working his butt off all day, it fell on him to take charge. Being alone at the scene meant that the total responsibility hung on his shoulders.

Two dead male drivers were bad enough, but the lone woman's bruised and torn body added to the horrific scene, making it heart-wrenching. Her eerie screams of pain and cries for her baby made his skin crawl.

Feverishly searching everywhere, looking frantically for the baby she called for, Harley's gut tightened when he found nothing.

"Lady, I'm here to help. Please be calm. If you can, tell me where she is."

"Katrina." Again, her words tore through him, leaving shivers in their wake. "Oh, God! Help my baby!" He pulled at the crumpled metal, trying desperately to get to her, question her.

There was no baby.

Continuous screams ripped through the darkness and made the hair on his head feel as if the end of each strand had nerves and they all tingled. It was totally disconcerting. Though what was even worse was when quiet erupted like an agonizing scream itself.

Sliding his hand through the narrow opening, and with an intense effort, he ripped the door wide enough so he could reach in and search the woman's neck for a pulse.

One that wasn't there...

Dammit!

Refusing to allow his intense grief to influence the necessary actions his job demanded, he quickly set up a road block so others wouldn't plow into the carnage that was taking up a good portion of the road. Still searching in vain for signs of an infant, he'd called in for assistance and ambulances.

Frustration grabbed at him and made him cuss loud and hard. *Nothing.* His investigation of the mangled vehicles only made him madder. Still no sign of any baby.

In his hunt, he noticed that the left side passenger door had been ripped off, probably while the car had rolled, and there were torn harnesses. Could they have held a child's seat?

Suddenly, a faint wail caught his attention. He followed the sound to where he found an infant seat had been thrown clear across the road and had landed in the bushes on its side. Gently as possible, he righted it and found a little girl, a toddler of about three years old, still strapped in.

Overpowering fear erupted. Scared to touch, he forced himself to gently pick her up, still in the car seat, and hovered over her like a dithering idiot. Her large eyes were filled with terror, and silly bastard that he was, he couldn't remember a blasted thing from the first aid classes he'd been forced to take in training.

All he could do was hold her tiny hand, scatter kisses on her forehead, her cheek, and whisper silly phrases like what a beautiful angel she was and how she'd be fine. Her mama was fine. Everything was freakin' fine... *except for him*

He was breaking up inside and that wasn't part of his role. As the officer at the scene, he had a duty to take over, handle the details and deal with the accident, the roadblock.

Except that wasn't possible. How could he leave the precious darling who held on to his hand and looked at him with more love in her glazed eyes than he'd ever experienced in his life.

Hearing the sirens in the distance gave him his first breath of relief. "Stay with me, sugar. The doctors are coming to look after you, and take you to the hospital. They're almost here."

"Can Mommy come too?" Her voice was weak but more powerful than any sound he'd ever heard. Thank God, she was coherent.

"Sure she can. Except she'll probably go in a different car, but you don't need to worry. The doctors will be with you, sweetheart. They'll make everything better."

"Stay, Daddy."

"Daddy?"

Before he could answer, the paramedics rushed over and shifted him to one side in order to make a preliminary examination. They saw what Harvey had already noted: the infant's head wound had bled a lot, and it appeared she couldn't see.

"Daddy? I 'ant my Daddy." Her shriek made everyone jump into action.

"Where's her daddy?" They looked at Harley. He shook his head.

Another heart-wrenching scream ramped up everyone's nerves. Harley moved in and spoke. "Shush baby, don't cry."

"Daddy?"

"Yes, sweetheart. Daddy's here."

It took a harsh order and an *I'm-not-leaving-her* stare before they allowed him to go along with her in the ambulance. But once he knew the parents weren't going to be any help ever again, what else could *a new daddy* do?

Chapter Two

Using his voice to keep the terrified youngster calm until the sedation kicked in and the loudness of the MRI machine didn't scare her anymore, Harley spent the next few hours at the child's bedside.

He tried to understand the medical jargon about a swollen brain needing pressure released, possibly having to put a shunt in... on and on until the frightening words drove so much dread into his heart that he broke into the doctor's litany and begged, "Just tell me she'll live, Doc. That's what I need to hear."

"Sure, Harley. Thanks to the fact she was strapped into a proper seat, she's perfectly fine, except for the head trauma, which most likely happened from debris hitting her before she was flung clear. We'll need to do more tests, but for now, she's slipped into a coma and we'll keep her there to let the swelling recede naturally."

"Great! Thanks, Doc. You can't know how much better that makes me feel."

"Take it from me; it's beneficial that she's under. We'll monitor her constantly, but she'll heal better if she isn't able to move. It's all good. Stop fretting."

Harley nodded. "The poor little orphan needs some decent karma. I just found out that they haven't been able to locate any family members who can come in and stay with her. There's one great-grandmother on her mother's side, but she's in a home. No aunts or uncles so far; seems like she's all alone in the world."

"Poor little mite. She's a real cutie is Miss Katrina Simpson." Doc Brown read her name from the file he held, shook his head and sighed, disgust plain to see on his tired features. "Terrible accident—terrible. I saw the bodies of the other victims arrive."

"Yeah, I was there. Couldn't do anything for them; it was too late." Harley stuck his hands into the pockets of his dark blue officer's jacket and looked down at his feet. No way did he want the doc to see a grown man, a sergeant no less, having trouble keeping it together. The memory of the mother's screams wouldn't be erased anytime soon.

Doc Brown's expression mirrored his own disgust. "We're running out of space here; the beds are all full. We'll be moving the patients into the hallways soon. I hate to grumble but gosh darn, Harley, this isn't the time of year we want to see the hospital full."

"I know what you mean. Just wished these crazy idiots would learn to drive according to the weather conditions. With the freak snowstorms that can hit at any time, those roads are so hazardous."

Doc Brown grunted. "I know what you mean. We're run ragged here in Emergency with all the crashes today. Why the hell people don't stay home, or at least slow down when they're behind the wheel is beyond me. They should spend a day in the ER and they'd get the picture soon enough."

"If only, Doc." Harley rubbed the back of his head before he let the older man see his expression. "Is it okay if I stay with Katrina?"

Doc Brown searched Harley's face. "If I say no, go home and get some sleep, will you listen?" Doc grinned without any humor. "No, of course you won't. She'll not even know you're there."

Harley gazed at Katrina, so tiny, surrounded by scary equipment and with nurses coming to and fro but no one staying to comfort her. This wouldn't work. He turned back and glared at Doc Brown.

"Look here, Harley, I've known you all your life, delivered you for crumbs' sake, and you're as stubborn a man as I've ever met. At least go home and have a shower and change out of the uniform so you'll be more comfortable. I'll arrange for them to bring in a cot for you. And, until you return, I'll get one of the nurses to stay with her." He patted Harley's arm, smiled and left, his head slowly shaking from side to side.

Chapter Three

Glad that one of his officers had remembered to drop off his squad car at the hospital for him, Harley started for home totally exhausted. Intending on showering and returning to Katrina, he couldn't believe his rotten luck when the dispatcher's voice cut through the silence. *Idiot!* He'd forgotten to turn down the sound on the car radio, and there was an emergency call coming over the line.

Sharyn, one of the older employees in the department, had never learned the proper call etiquette. She tried hard to give the necessary information but did it in her own unique style, and he hadn't had the heart to give her too hard a time about sticking with procedure.

"Home disturbance at 310 Durban Road. Neighbor called: assistance needed for a woman in wheelchair. Some male bastard assailant is drunk and disorderly and kicking the crap out of her. Is there anyone in the vicinity?"

Harvey hesitated. *Man, you don't need this now. You've done your duty today.*

He would have kept driving, he should have, but his unwavering sense of duty kicked in and he couldn't. The house was only a block away, and if that woman died because he'd ignored the call, he'd never be able to forgive himself.

He radioed back, "On it!" and punched the pedal, wheeling around the corner faster than he should have. The car swerved but he had the skills to control it and soon arrived at the address.

A woman, bundled in a heavy coat and waiting outside by a fence, looked frantic, and the dog, barking from across the street sounded ferocious.

"Ma'am, you called for the police?"

"Yes, I did. Amelia is in there all alone with that crazy young step-brother of hers and he's tearin' up the place. He's a lunatic. She shoulda kicked his ass outta there a long time ago but she's too damn nice. If'n it was me, he'da been long gone by now." A scream and then a male's roar could be heard. "Good Lord, he's a killin' her this time."

Harley moved. He sprinted up the steps of the older-fashioned house and stopped at the entrance. First he pounded and then he yelled, "All right, break it up in there. It's the Carlton Grove Police Department. Open this door. Now!"

He leaned over to peer through the curtained window and saw a woman on the floor beside the body of an animal. She was crying, and a large man was heading for her, holding a chair in one hand, and the other one was fisted.

Harley backed up and lifted his leg. One hard kick and he was inside.

Chapter Four

With darkness closing in, the cranky pup's legs were tired from lumbering through so much snow. He fell over in a heap on the edge of the sidewalk and gave up for a while. Something had driven him in this direction; he didn't know how he knew he was going the right way, he just did. Only he hadn't realized the distance.

Panting, his tongue lolling, he cried out his vexation. Just then, an older boy smoking a cigarette stopped next to him and reached to touch. A disgusting smell hit his nostrils and put the crabby animal in an even worse mood. He growled, and when the kid's fingers touched his fur he snapped at them.

Backing away, the boy, not liking this treatment, cussed, kicked the pup and left.

That hurt! The mutt wriggled around, checking the damage. *Good riddance!* The miserable pup didn't like strangers and he especially didn't like male ones. In fact, he didn't like any males. He'd watched the way his mistress's man had treated her, and if he would have been bigger he'd have chewed him up real good. A growl ripped through his throat at the memory and gave him some satisfaction.

Suddenly, he heard a barking in the distance. He knew that sound, had heard it many times. *Home!* He was close. Struggling to his feet, shaking the snow from his fur, he started off at a rolling gait.

Chapter Five

Amelia couldn't believe Jim's lack of restraint. Just because Belle had accidently tripped him, he'd pushed the dog out the door so hard that she'd slid and fallen down the stairs. It had taken Amelia an hour to coax her pet back into the house. Though usually good-natured and easy-going, Belle's growing hatred for her brother had become more obvious, and Amelia couldn't blame her.

Smart as a whip, Belle must have connected him to her pups being taken away and not returning. And ever since they'd disappeared, the momma dog had lost her old zest. She'd aged overnight from being a relatively healthy animal to one who refused food, turned away from taking the walks she used to love and stayed on her mat under the table most of the day.

Bathroom breaks became the only time she'd move, and Amelia had begun to think a broken heart wasn't Belle's only ailment. "Leave her alone, Jim. I don't think she's well. I'm going to call the vet for an appointment."

"You will like hell."

"It's my money. I'll do what I want. She's suffering, and

you throwing her down the stairs made her worse."

"Are you blaming me for that dog being a useless piece of shit? Go ahead. It's just like you to put it on me. I can take it."

"Don't be silly. She's isn't useless, and I never said any such thing."

Jim flew into a rage, picked up a dining room chair and heaved it at the wall. "You've always hated me, don't think I didn't know. Mom and Dad left you the house, gave you everything—"

"Stop it! My father bought and paid for this house before he died. And when Mom married your father, you both lived here for free. I own the house because my dad willed it to me, and your father was in full agreement."

Snorting with fury, Jim came at her. She never realized his intentions because Belle suddenly rose and moved faster than either one of them expected. With a snarling roar, she attacked.

"Belle, no!"

Jim, taken by surprise, kicked at the enraged canine, but she wouldn't release the grip she had on his leg. The valiant dog shook his limb like she had a plush toy in her teeth, all the time growling, her fangs dripping; she meant business.

He went down and tried to grab at her, but she pivoted from side to side, gnawing with her teeth, not giving him a chance to touch her. Swearing his frustration, he finally used his other foot to let her have it in the head. She squealed and dropped, panting with exhaustion.

Distressed, Amelia slid out of her wheelchair to the floor and crawled over to her beloved pet. Tears poured down her face and landed on Belle, who licked her hand and whined before her head dropped down to the side.

Jim, using the counter to pull himself upright, surveyed his ripped pant leg, saw the blood pooling and
glared Amelia's way. "Now see what you made me go and
do? She's crazy. She attacked me. You saw it."

Amelia had always cared for Jim; after all, he was her
step-brother. But this time, he'd gone too far. Taking away
Belle's puppies had started the hostility, but having him
treat her beloved pet like this was the final straw.

"Get out!" She screamed the words, anger and disbe-
lief ringing in her voice. "You're a mean jerk who's never
satisfied with anything I've tried to do for you. I supported
you when you refused to work—"

"Hey, you don't mean that. I can't work with my
asthma. You know that."

"Yes, you can. Many people do. You need to leave. I
don't want to see your sneering face ever again."

"Just 'cause you're a nurse an' all, you think you're so
special. Well you ain't. You're pathetic. There's no man in
your life. You need me to look after you." His tone took
on the familiar wheedling sound he usually used to get his
way.

This time she was having none of it. This time he'd
gone too far. Scorn coloring her features and in a tear-
filled voice, she dismissed him by flinging her hand in his
direction. "I need nothing from you. Pack your things and
get out."

Reacting to her angry dismissal, Jim picked up another
chair and headed her way. Before he could use it, a crash
sounded, and a furious police officer tackled him, pinning
him down.

Chapter Six

Amelia shifted to the other side of Belle and tugged the animal out of the way of the grappling men. The cop had an advantage because he was taller than Jim, bigger around the shoulders, and was trained to handle men in a fight.

Jim, on the other hand, had the chair in his hand ready to use when tackled and he brought it down over the head of his assailant. The policeman dropped and Jim, fast as weasel, shot to his feet. Straddling the dazed man on the floor, he lifted his leg to aim a kick. But before he could follow through, a growling white fluff-ball shot through the door and latched on to his sloppy sweatpants at his groin.

Grumps? What in the world? Amelia would know that puppy anywhere just by the sound of his growls.

From the scream Jim let out, Amelia had no doubt those sharp little puppy teeth had found their target and Grumps had no intention of letting go. Jim tried to bat him away, but since the pup had latched on from behind, her brother was having a terrible time. Circling, legs kicking up, screeching his pain, he swung around, while the puppy flew through the air still attached.

Amelia giggled. Hysterically maybe, but it loosened the ball of pain gathering in her stomach and that smidgen of fear she always experienced whenever her brother lost his cool. A happening, she noticed, that had occurred more often since she'd been home and off work. It was like her being there, watching him laze around made him ashamed, which in turn caused him to act out.

Groggily, the cop, shaking off his disorientation, stumbled to his feet and took in the hilarious scene. Seeing his attacker's situation brought a grin to his face. He pulled out the handcuffs from his belt and grabbed the frenzied man. Before he threw him to the ground, knowing the full weight of the man landing on the puppy could do damage, he tried to pull the mutt loose, only to have the manic pup turn on him. "Jesus! Calm down, little guy. I'm on your side."

Amelia seeing the puppy was just in the way now, called out, scooted over and grabbed him in her arms. Then she rolled back to Belle and safety. As soon as he saw who had him, Grumps became a baby again, whining, licking her face, wriggling with joy at being with her once more.

Belle, having heard her baby's cries, lifted her head. Grunting, making an effort to reach her puppy, she fell back. Amelia released Grumps and had to swallow the buildup of emotion that had gathered at her throat. Grumpy began investigating the side of his mother's face, licking her and patting her with his paws.

Amelia watched the two greet each other and knew her cranky pup, Grumpy, was home for good. If Belle's happiness depended on having one of her babies near her, then so be it. Grumpy would be staying home and no one would take him away again.

Weepy now, sobs broke through Amelia's restraint. From a mind still reacting to what just happened, she didn't know what to think or where to turn next.

All she knew was that the man in his officer's uniform taking charge made her feel safer than she'd felt in a long, long time.

Chapter Seven

For the second time that night, Harley called in for backup. He needed his officers to take the attacker away so the poor victim on the floor could feel safe again.

He threw his prisoner onto a chair near the door, "Shut up your whining and stay there or, so help me God, I'll shoot you. I've had a hell of a day and I'm that close to losing it completely." Harley held up his hand, thumb and finger within an inch of each other, and shoved them in the guy's face. Gritting his teeth, he glared, not wanting the prisoner to have any doubts as to his intention.

"I need an ambulance." Ignoring Harley, Jim bent over and let his tears gather. He began to cough, but to Harley it sounded fake and so he ignored the fool.

Instead, he turned to the real sufferer, the lady on the floor next to her turned-over wheelchair. It shocked him to discover that she wasn't a senior as he'd assumed when he'd looked through the window. Her hair wasn't white but spun gold, so blonde that a rainbow of sunshine might describe it perfectly. Streaming over her shoulders now, having broken loose from the clip she'd been wearing earlier, the glowing mass made him want to touch.

She stopped fussing with her dog and instead she looked right at him, her eyes clouded with tears. Their gazes caught and the floor under him rocked. The world spun crazily and he wondered for a second if the chair he'd been clobbered with had done more damage than he'd thought.

This female wasn't pretty, nor was she sexy. There had to be a word that would describe her: *lovely* slipped into his head and wouldn't let go. He'd never seen a lovelier female with such telling blue eyes. Her distress was so palpable; it was all he could do to stop himself from running over, sweeping her up in his arms and keeping her for his very own.

"Amelia. Please. You've got to tell this lunatic that I'd never hurt you. You're my sister. It was the dog's fault. Tell him... " Jim pleaded and drew her attention. He coughed and then did so again harder, making a rasping sound that wasn't quite convincing.

Sister? Okay, a small amount of the tightening in Harley's gut loosened, as did some of his mad. He checked to see what her reaction was to her brother's words.

For a few seconds, he saw her weaken, but just then the crazy puppy ran out from where he'd been nuzzling with the other dog and started to bark. He was giving the man the what-for in puppy talk and Harley had no doubt that if the canine could speak English, they'd be mostly cuss words he was using.

Jim, not liking this at all, kicked out at the little fellow, and even though he never touched him, the cantankerous little devil let out a squeal as if he'd had a foot planted up his backside. It did the trick, though, and if Harley didn't know any better, he'd almost wonder if the animal hadn't planned it that way.

Amelia opened her arms to give the pitifully whining pup shelter and her expression hardened. "I don't want you here anymore, Jimmy. You have to leave. Tonight." Once the words were spoken, she looked at Harley as if for confirmation that this could be worked out somehow.

"Oh, he'll be resting in the Jailhouse Hotel tonight, ma'am. And, we'll have you press charges so he won't get out anytime soon. Once I tell the judge that I witnessed him attacking you with a chair, he'll be looking at doing a fair bit of time."

Jim bellowed and tried to rise. "I didn't do no such thing, you liar. I'd *never* hurt my sister."

The truth, ringing in his voice, made Harley hesitate for just a second, before he added, "Hey, bud, I saw you." He switched his attention to Amelia. "Your sweet brother also resisted arrest and assaulted an officer in his line of duty. I'm afraid Jimmy here is in a lot of trouble."

Amelia had heard the horror in Jim's voice when he'd been accused of abusing her. Though he frightened her terribly, much more lately, he'd never struck her... yet. But he'd hit the dog she loved and that couldn't be tolerated anymore.

On the other hand, she'd promised Jim's father, a man who'd treated her like a beloved daughter all of the time he'd lived with her and her mother, that she'd look out for his son, and she'd tried her best. Obviously, her best wasn't good enough. The mean-tempered, foul-mouthed slacker had scared and manipulated her for the last time. She should have cut him loose long ago but she hadn't, and now she could see that she'd aided and abetted his nonsense and it had to stop.

Straightening her back and stiffening her resolve, she

admitted, "It's true he's never hurt me, but his behavior is spiraling and it's probably just a matter of time. I th-think he should leave. But I don't necessarily want him to go to jail."

Chapter Eight

Harley heard the hesitation in her voice and knew from experience that if he didn't step in, she'd reconsider and probably not follow through with charging her brother. That scenario happened all the time. Women getting beaten by their men seldom pressed charges. Most times, they knew they'd have to pay for it later and so they refused.

Where the hell was his posse? He needed the victim separated from her attacker, but he didn't want to leave her and no way did he trust leaving Jimmy unattended in the squad car.

Slowly, he moved closer and reached out his right hand. "Let me help you into your chair, Amelia."

She looked startled and he added, "Jim used that name, and so did the neighbor lady who called 911."

Amelia's head lowered while her hands covered her cheeks. Then she straightened her shoulders, allowing him to see her concern. She spoke in a gentle tone. "Yes. You're right, I'm Amelia Lloyd. He's my half-brother, Jim Rogers."

"I'm Sergeant Harley Carlton." He knelt beside her, his hand still out until she noticed and waved him away.

"No, it's okay. I can stand by myself. If you don't mind, can you bring my chair closer so I can sit down right away?"

She's not crippled! Why that mattered so much to Harley, he didn't take time to consider. It just did. "Sure, here." He picked up the chair, set it real close and put on the brakes. Then he hovered, watching as sweat broke out on her forehead. She bit her bottom lip to keep from making any sound and, clutching the side of her chair, she strained to rise.

He couldn't stand seeing her in pain. Before she tumbled over, he swung her up in his arms and rested her back into the chair. Then he backed away with his hands up defensively. "Sorry, just didn't want you to fall on the dog."

"So you were only worried about Belle, is that it?" A smile lit up her face and dazzled him. His tongue lost the ability to function and his brain shut down leaving him with only one thought. *Wow! What a beauty.*

For the second time in a stressful evening, he heard the sounds of sirens approaching his location. *Finally!*

"I just didn't want you to injure yourself again." Suddenly, an idea took hold and wouldn't be shook loose. Pointing at the sorry loser, who now sat with his knees up under his chin, rocking from side to side, Harley demanded. "Did he put you in that chair?" Surprised by his fierce tone, he tried to lighten it so his accusation didn't reflect on her in any way. "Did he hurt you before?"

Chapter Nine

Amelia noticed the hardness in his eyes before she heard it in his voice. This police officer wasn't anyone she'd want to mess with. Good thing, because he made her feel stronger than she had in a long time. Strange, because she'd always carried the majority of the load while at work in the ER, but at home a garden snake had more grit than she did lately.

After Amelia's mother had passed away, her step-father lost interest in his surroundings, his son—in fact, in everything that had once been important to him. Within a year, he'd succumbed to lung cancer and left the responsibility of the house, the finances and Jim on the shoulders of Amelia, whose heart was much bigger than her backbone.

Skimming the next five years, she'd reached her late twenties, attended nursing school and had become a skilled ER technician, while Jim had finished high school and become accomplished at starting new jobs and quitting them all in a very short time. He had a myriad of excuses, but the upshot was, the reasons why he left were never his fault.

Not having the will to argue, trying to be a good person and a good sister, she'd made so many allowances for his behavior that even she'd run out of excuses as well. The twenty-one-year-old toddler had to grow up, leave the nest and learn to fly.

She realized the officer was still waiting for her answer, but lost in the past, she'd forgotten the question. "I'm sorry. What?"

"Has he attacked you at other times? Was he responsible for you being in that wheelchair?"

"Good heavens, no. He's not an animal. He's just a young fool who won't grow up." She tried to let the Sergeant see her conviction, but her voice broke and gave lie to the words. "I don't want to be the one responsible for putting him in jail."

"Okay. Tell me before the others arrive. Amelia, I need to know how far to go with this. Are you afraid of him?"

His question made her understand one thing. He'd seen the fear she thought she'd hidden. "I don't want him living here anymore. He needs to find his own place. I'll help him financially to get a room or even a bachelor suite, but then it's up to him." Twisting to see around the broad shoulders of the policeman kneeling beside her, she added, "It's time, Jim."

Jim stared at her and his sneer fell short of the one he'd perfected lately.

Taking the handles of her chair in both his hands, the officer made her face him. "Sleep on it. But don't make a stupid decision to let things stay the way they are. Maybe he doesn't need a record, but he does need a good slap on the wrist so he'll know what to expect if I ever catch his ass in trouble again. "

Amelia appreciated that Officer Carlton had spoken loud enough that Jim would hear his promise. She nodded. Tired, heart-sick, she reached down and picked up the pup whining by her chair. Placing him close to her chest, she whispered. "Grumps you were marvellous."

Sergeant Carlton, obviously in agreement, reached out to add his petting, only to have the wicked, crabby beast snarl a warning.

"Guess he doesn't realize I'm here to help you."

"Oh, that wouldn't matter to Grumpy. He just hates all men."

Chapter Ten

By the time Harley had dealt with the ruckus between Amelia and Jim, had the younger man taken into custody and made sure she'd be able to handle being alone for the night, exhaustion had all but put him under. Only the hot shower and quick coffee he grabbed before returning to the hospital kept him from ending up as a victim in his own car crash on the treacherous, snow-packed streets.

Once he got back to the hospital, the situation there appeared daunting. Seems that after he'd left, none of the medical personal had been able to calm the restless child. Reluctant to use more drugs because of her head injury, they'd tried soothing her every way they could, but with negative results. Her coma hadn't taken her completely under, she'd fought it, and everyone knew that complete rest was imperative for the healing process.

Thank goodness when she heard Harley's voice, Katrina curled against him, sighed one of the few words she'd spoken so far, "Daddy" and relaxed.

While Harley watched the beautiful child now peacefully slumbering, he realized he'd gone way past the sleep stage himself. He'd hit the space where the mind recharges and refuses to settle down.

Automatically, his hand caressed the little girl's shoulder and her arms. In the dim lighting of the hospital room, now lounging beside her, he noticed a smear on her cheek and gently wiped it away. Also, her dark blonde hair, which was grubby with sweat, some leaves and mussed with tangles, became a focal point for his attention. Gently, he worked out the twigs and foliage.

Bandages had been placed over the deeper lacerations on her face and head, and though most of the blood had been washed away, there were still traces of it on the edge of her little ear.

He wondered what color eyes she had. Since the darkness at the accident had made it all but impossible to see them clearly, and because by the time they'd arrived at the hospital she'd been in a light coma, that secret hadn't yet been revealed.

True, she'd looked right at him at the scene and it'd seemed like she was searching his features, but she hadn't really been able to see. Though she'd called him 'Daddy', the male victim in the accident hadn't looked anything like him whatsoever.

Maybe his voice had reminded her of her father's. He didn't know. All he knew for sure—this little girl had wormed her way into his tightly guarded heart and from now on, she'd be his to protect. No matter what it took!

A small grunt escaped and pulled him up. *What are you thinking, man? You have no idea how to take care of a kid. Good Lord, you're a bachelor, and damn happy to stay that way.*

Little Katrina snuggled closer as if she'd heard his inner struggle. His arms tightened and he whispered, "I'm here, baby. I won't leave you, kitten. Shush now and sleep." Like a miracle, she smiled, snuffled and settled back into the healing slumber.

Harley leaned his head back and let his mind ramble at will. *Hell, you've been busy tonight, dude.* The golden-haired female he'd held earlier in his arms stirred in his memory and wouldn't be shaken loose. Funny thing, he'd had the same reluctance at letting her go as he was experiencing with the precious bundle he held at the moment.

Amelia Lloyd's haunting blue eyes had mesmerized. If he didn't know better, he'd almost think he'd fallen under a spell. He zeroed back to earlier when they'd hauled her brother away and the nonsense that the man-boy had spouted: "Sis, it's you and me. Dad said so. You gotta help me. I can't go to jail. You can't let them take me. Please!" And then his ultimate plea, "I'll be better" had sounded so earnest that the arresting officers had stopped and looked her way.

Those final words had made her hesitate, until Harley had lowered himself to his knees, taken her hands into his and made her return his look. He'd spoken with his eyes, brown to blue, no nonsense at all. Then he'd added. "My dad told me this once and I've always believed it. Right is right and wrong isn't acceptable. Your brother did wrong tonight. And it isn't acceptable."

She'd nodded, sighed and, as if her strength had completely vanished, she'd leaned toward him until her forehead had rested against his chest. The odd gesture had had him wishing he could take her in his arms and shelter her from the painful indecision he'd seen clearly stamped over her delicate features.

Of course, they'd taken Jim away, and Harley'd promised to stop by the next day at the same time as her brother returned to get his belongings, just to lend moral support.

Her words came back to him. "I'm truly grateful that you arrived tonight when you did. I'm positive he wouldn't have used that chair on *me* but..."

"But what? You wouldn't lay money on it?"

"No. I wouldn't lay money on Belle surviving the night."

As if her name had a magic effect, the dog had turned her head away from licking her pup and looked straight at Amelia.

Harley had seen the stiff way the dog moved. "Did you want me to take her to the vets? I have a friend here at the Grove who has a clinic and would open for an emergency."

Amelia had looked uncertain and called to Belle. The older dog had gained her feet with little difficulty and approached, her back end swaying in a relaxed manner, her tail circling. The puppy had come along with his mother, and the two had greeted their mistress with affection. After licking her hand, the older animal had laid her head on Amelia's lap and gazed at her with love blatantly expressed for everyone to see.

It'd caught at Harley. Messed with his macho and made him swallow. This woman was loved dearly by her pets.

"She seems to be moving much easier than after Jim first kicked her. I don't think anything's broken." While she said the words, Amelia's hands had travelled gently over the dog's body, manipulating, feeling her way for painful areas. Other than letting out one small cry, the dog hadn't seemed to be suffering from serious injuries, but then Harley wasn't a veterinarian. "Just say the word and we can get her into the squad car and have her checked out."

"She's walking fine, no limping, and the puppy's arrival

has cheered her immensely. I don't believe even a short separation will be good for either of them right now. So, thank you, but I'm thinking we're fine."

"Did this one have a sister in the litter?" He pointed to the puppy. "If so my brother found her yesterday by the lake. In fact, he rescued the little one after it fell into the water and has adopted her. If the pup's yours, hope it's okay. Reed's a doctor and will take good care of your pet. He's a bachelor and needs some company."

"Oh, I'm so glad you told me. There were three pups in the litter. Jim put them in a box and drove off with them the day before yesterday and I've been frantic about it ever since. Was it at the park where you found his sister?" She pointed at Grumps.

"Yep. Didn't see any others though. I'll put the word out at the office. Sometimes we get people phoning in about lost animals."

"I'd appreciate that, Sergeant. Thank you."

"Right. Then I'll be on my way. I'll have to drop off a report and leave them instructions at the department that your brother's not to be let out until I come for him. Then I'll accompany him here, wait while he gets his gear and take him to a shelter."

"I can't thank you enough, Officer Carlton. You have no idea how much having you here lessens my anxiety to face him again."

Harley had driven away with her words ringing in his head. He remembered his unconscious reaction and smiled. *Lady, you have no idea how much it'll lessen my anxiety too.*

Chapter Eleven

"Doc Brown, Katrina is still out of it. You don't think that's a problem?"

"It's best for her right now, Harley. Put her down, man. She'll be more comfortable on the bed, and you need to get to work. The nurses told me that you've held her for most of the night."

"When I arrived, she was restless. Having me hold her and talk to her seemed to soothe."

"Well, I believe she's slipped deeper into the coma now and you can safely let her go. She doesn't know you're even here." Seeing Harley's negative response to his orders, the doc added. "Let the nurses do their morning rounds, wash her and make her comfortable. You can return later if you must to check on her. Though, I'm not sure it's good if she gets too reliant on you. It seems she's an orphan now and will be a ward of the court."

"No one's come forward yet?" Harley had been so busy the night before that he hadn't given much thought to the child's imminent plight.

"Not yet. Human resources, with the help of the Feds,

are still digging. This is what they've uncovered so far. Her father was brought up in the system, never did stay in one foster situation long enough for it to be considered family. And the mother came from a broken home with members scattered far and wide. They're still searching. In the meantime, we'll give her our best care and let God look after the rest."

"I guess you're right. Let's just hope that God's in a better mood for the little angel because, so far, he hasn't done such a good job with her parents."

"Oh, she'll heal just fine. Only thing I can't know just yet is if her sight will return. We've tried to trace any medical records that might exist for the child, but either she's been incredibly healthy or her parents have been incredibly lax."

"Or incredibly poor! The old vehicle they were driving had seen better days. And from the gear they'd packed in the back, I wondered if they'd been moving. Looked to me like the belongings scattered over the highway were pitiful and just maybe everything they'd owned." Harley remembered the car seat that had protected the child, the rips on its side, its grubby appearance. The boxes and suitcases piled in the back of the old van hadn't registered at the time, but they did now.

"Whatever she needs, Doc. If the system won't fork it over, let me know and I'll take care of the bill."

Old Doc Brown smiled and nodded. "You're a good man, Harley Carlton, a good, decent one. We'll take care of your little angel, have no fear." With a final pat on Harley's arm, the doc moved on to his next patient. While the older nurse who just arrived looked on expectantly, Harley self-consciously laid his precious bundle on the bed. "We'll look after your little girl, sir. Don't you worry yourself."

Harley couldn't correct the kind-hearted soul. Instead he nodded and watched as the older woman leaned over, and very carefully began disrobing the tiny body, using a washcloth on disfiguring marks that didn't actually wash away.

Chapter Twelve

Jim's hands were sore but he couldn't seem to stop torturing them, cracking his knuckles and twisting his fingers. Now in a holding room, he awaited his future. After a night of pure hell in a cell full of weird losers, he had no idea what to expect.

Yesterday, after he'd picked up the chair and headed toward his sister, he'd recognized fear on her face, the way she'd cringed. She'd been terrified... of him. A howling noise had sounded inside his heart and wouldn't be silenced. His best friend, the one person in the world who he trusted, had cowered from him and he couldn't stand the thought that she'd been right to do so.

He still had no idea what his intention had been. One minute he'd snapped and the next, he'd needed to hit something. So far, he'd managed to take out his frustrations on the dog, but that wasn't right either. He'd never cared for Belle the way that Amelia did, but he'd never thought he'd be capable of hurting her either. Sure, the mutt was Amelia's pet, and sometimes he felt she loved the stupid thing more than she did him. And when the puppies had come along, she'd hovered over them all the time and ignored him even more. But that didn't mean he was the kind of guy who'd stoop so low as to injure dumb animals. Except that he had, and it made him sick.

If only he'd had someone to talk to about these things. He rubbed his hands through his greasy hair and swallowed the building sob.

Feeling sorry for himself had to stop. True, he'd tried to open up to Amelia. But when she did make time for him nowadays, she'd yell or call him on his stupid behavior like she had every right to do. Stupid didn't begin to describe his latest choices.

The walls of the small interrogation room began closing in, suffocating him. He stood and paced. Suddenly, the door slowly opened and the officer from the night before entered. His expression scared the hell out of Jim. Then the other man did something totally unexpected. He smiled and held out his hand to shake like Jim deserved the compliment. His trembling hand enclosed by a warm palm was all it took: tears gushed uncontrollably.

Chapter Thirteen

Amelia appreciated the phone call she'd received from Officer Carlton warning of his and Jimmy's arrival within the hour. The long night had passed slowly with a lot of self-recrimination and hard talks to convince herself of the necessity of this step. Making her brother move, get a life of his own and learn to be independent, had to be done. She understood that, but it didn't make it any easier. After all, she loved the silly idiot and, up till now, had done everything she could to help him make the right decisions.

But lately, looking after him had become a chore, a noose tightening around her neck which now choked. She couldn't trust him. He'd steal cash from her purse, act as if he had the right to anything in the house, no matter who had bought it, and he'd even sold some of her mother's expensive knick-knacks when Amelia'd refused to lend him any more money.

She knew that having her home to herself would make her happier. Hadn't she loved the time he'd recently spent on a camping trip with his friends? The truth is, she'd dreaded him returning and that wasn't healthy, not for either of them.

Aware that young men who had no goals, mentors or role models to look up to could get lost, she'd cut him a lot of slack. But enough was enough. Lately, he'd taken his temper and frustrations out on Belle and the pups, and Amelia knew she had to draw the line.

If he could be saved from getting into real trouble, he had to be stopped now. Forced to face choices ahead, she only prayed he wouldn't take the easy road with any of the thugs in the neighborhood.

The one she'd seen him hanging with lately was bad news, and that had started their argument the night before. She knew she'd been right to ride him, but he'd hated being in the wrong.

"Jim, Tommy Wicks is nothing but trouble. He was in the juvenile system most of his youth and has now escalated to more serious crimes. Mrs. Moore next door has witnessed him selling drugs, and it's a well-known fact that the police are at his house all the time. Is that how you want to live?"

He'd been furious with her for calling him on his activities. "I can take care of myself, Amelia. I don't need you harping on me."

"You do when you're bringing those people into our home, Jim. I don't want that guy here, he scares me. And he should scare you too. He's gone bad and you need to stay away from him."

At first, Amelia had seen the indecision on Jim's immature face. Then he'd gotten angry, worse than ever before, and he'd started screaming. Things had escalated quickly and fear had ridden her hard. Maybe if she hadn't been tied to the wheelchair, she wouldn't have felt so powerless, but he'd scared her and she didn't like it.

No more... He had to go. But then why did she feel so damn sorry, like just maybe, she was giving up too soon?

When Officer Carlton rang the bell, his image reflected through the sheer curtains at the window. Amelia couldn't wait to get started, let Jim get packed and have it over with. Carefully maneuvering her walker, she hobbled to the door and let him in.

The officer seemed shocked to see her up and around. With worry etched on his features, he greeted her. "Hello, Miss Lloyd." He surveyed the room. "Where's your chair?"

Opening the door wide, she backed away. "I try to get up every morning for the first few hours, do my exercises and get practice. It's only the latter part of the day that I'm forced to use the chair. My goal is to get back to work soon and I need to keep up with my therapy. Please come in."

"May I ask what happened to you?" He stepped past her which made her feel absolutely tiny next to him. She stood at five and a half feet, so he must be well over six. Shivers of reaction thrilled her body and were as shocking as they were pleasant. His soft brown stare snared hers and she couldn't look away. Her breath caught in her throat. Finally, it broke loose and made a loud sighing sound that had him narrowing his gaze. "What?"

"Nothing. I mean, I'm fine. What did you want to know?"

"Did your brother put you in that chair?" His question transformed his features from kindly to deadly.

Without intending to, Amelia reached out and touched his chest. "No! Oh God, no. Jimmy wouldn't hurt me. Or at least he hasn't yet. I was attacked by a patient at the hospital where I work in the ER. Some crazy guy, high on crack cocaine, didn't like us trying to help him. He shoved me and there was equipment in the way. I fell and broke my hip. It's healing well but I have to make sure it doesn't stiffen up too much."

Sargent Carlton's whole attitude underwent a change. He smiled. "Well, then, I guess I can make the suggestion I had in mind."

Amelia swivelled to look out of the window. "Where's Jim?"

"I didn't bring him in with me. I wanted to broach this subject first with you before offering him a chance to decide. They have a new program starting here in Carlton Grove for young people in trouble. Jim's a bit older than our usual candidates but he fits the bill otherwise. It's a way to keep juvies out of the system, and we could use someone like him to work with the younger ones."

Hope flared, but she had reservations when he added the last part. "How could Jim teach youngsters when he's so mixed up himself? He's started to run with one of the gangs around here. That's what we fought about last night."

"No. Actually, they're blackmailing him to deliver packages for them. He did deliver once, but I guess you'd gotten through to him and he'd refused to do it again. Problem was, they'd taken a video of him making the drop and threatened to send it to the police. Even worse, they threatened to show you. So, they've been forcing him to do things until it's spiralled out of control and he had begun to feel helpless."

"Oh, no. My goodness, why didn't he tell me? I wouldn't have been so hard on him."

"He knew you'd force him to do the right thing, come to us and make a confession... or at least that's what he told me after we had a long talk this morning. I guess a night spent in the cell with some of the more hardened criminals around town turned into a real eye-opener for your brother."

Amelia noticed the twinkle in Officer Carlton's eye and something fell into place. "You orchestrated that to happen, didn't you?"

"I might have arranged for him to be in the cell with some pretty wild dudes. But he needed a wake-up call. Those men have been through the mill a few times and are hardened criminals. No reason to shield Jim from a bird's-eye view of where he'll most likely end up in a few years. Turns out that my plotting has paid off. It doesn't every time, trust me. Your brother's one of the lucky ones."

"Lucky ones?"

"Yeah, he has someone who loves him, and even more important, wants to believe in him. Trust me! That goes a long way when it comes time for these youngsters to make choices that they can't undo."

Chapter Fourteen

Now satisfied that Jim had told the truth, that he hadn't hurt his sister, Sergeant Carlton called him in to talk with her, a shamed-faced, sorry-looking guy who took one look at Amelia and fell to his knees in front of her chair. He lowered his head onto her lap, wrapped his arms around her knees and sobbed out his sorrow. "I'm sorry, sis. I never wanted to hurt you. You have to believe me."

Leaning over him, kissing his cheek, Amelia's voice wobbled and then broke. "Oh, Jim, you've been so lost and I didn't know how to find you. I've worried myself sick that you needed more from me and I just didn't know what to do."

"It's my fault, Amie. I got caught up in something I couldn't get out of. I'm so stupid. They played me like a fiddle and I fell for their bullshit. I knew better but I wasn't strong enough to turn away."

"From now on I'll help you, Jimmy. I promise. We'll start again. Sergeant Carlton explained to me about the program he wants you to join. Are you willing to do whatever he says?"

Jim's tear-stained face looked up at her and she saw enthusiasm in his green eyes for the first time in the last few years. "Yeah. I want to try, Amie. It's kinda like the Army: they make everyone learn skills and take on a lot of responsibilities. But it's only a six-week course, and then Harley said he'd help sponsor me into criminology at the college, or whatever course I want to take." She noticed his words came out fast. It was like eagerness powered his brain and his mouth couldn't keep up.

"Harley?"

"Sergeant Carlton. He went outside to wait, said he'd give us some time alone. He wanted me to explain things to you before we headed to the camp." Jim didn't tell her that the actual words the Officer had used were... *I'll kick your ass from here to Jericho, bro, if you don't make things right with your sister. It's your starting line, Jim.*

"Can I see you while you're there, Jimmy? At least for Christmas?"

"I don't know. I promise I'll ask, though. Amie, I have to go. First, I'll grab a quick shower, and then pack my gear. I don't want to keep Harley waiting too long."

She kissed him one last time and then nodded. "Yes, go. Get ready. You need to know how proud I am of you. And your dad would be thrilled right now."

Jim stopped and turned back to her, a glint of tears still noticeable. From the swelling around his eyes, she figured they hadn't been the first he'd shed today, but it had been a long time since he'd walked with his head up and pride covering his features.

He took a few steps and then turned to her pet who'd been lying next to her, watchful the whole time. The bad-tempered puppy hadn't left her side either. When Jim had first entered, he'd growled his dislike but then had been surprisingly quiet.

Jim knelt down in front of Belle and held out his hand. "I'm sorry, Beauty, for the way I've been treating you. I'm afraid you suffered from my dislike of myself. I hate that I treated you this way."

Beauty! Amelia remembered that Jim's father had often called Belle by that nickname. The dog must have sensed Jim's sincerity. She licked his fingers and whined her acceptance. Grumpy, on the other hand, growled, stood up and turned the other way. His refusal was so blatant that Jim grinned, and Amelia answered with her own smile. "I guess it'll take more time to get Grumps to forgive. But he will, Jim."

"Yeah. I can wait. I'll just go and signal to Harley that we've talked so he can come in and wait for me in here. It's damn cold outside."

***

Jim hadn't felt so light in a long time and he liked the feeling. Opening the door to his room, he stepped inside only to have two arms swing him around and a finger held close to his mouth, the warning clear.

"What the hell?"

"You didn't think I'd find out, did you? I know all about the cell you stayed in last night." Tommy Wick's eyes dug a hole into his before Jim yanked out of his grasp.

"How did you get in here?"

"Through the window, of course. Just like I did the last time I dropped off your package for delivery."

"Yeah, well, about that. I'm not going to be making any more deliveries. The cops aren't going to charge me, but only if I agreed to go to into a program for six weeks. I had to sign up, man. So I'm finished now." Saying the words gave him so much satisfaction that cockiness sounded in his relieved tone.

"Ahhh... not so fast, my friend. So they didn't charge you with anything, right?"

Not sure what to say, Jim looked at the door, trying to think if he should tell the truth or lie. He hid his hands in his pockets and struck a stance he'd recently perfected. The *you-can't-push-me-around* one. His mind fluttered, like a bee caught in a tightly-closed jar. *I'm so close. Can I bullshit my way out of this situation?*

"If they haven't charged you, then there's no way you have to do anything they tell you to do. Trust me."

Still not sure where this lawyer-crap was leading to, he decided to try honesty. "Tommy, I promised. Look, my sister won't let me stay here anymore. She's fed up with me. But the cop is giving me a chance, man. And I don't want to mess it up."

Tommy's thin face, sallow from using too many of the gang's products, was intimidating. "Nah! He's playing you, is all. Hey, Jimmy, you can stay at my place. They won't find you there. Look, our business is growing with more customers all the time. We need dependable guys like you to make those drops, and you know Jordan won't like it if you turn on us. And when Jordan doesn't like something, someone gets hurt."

"Can't you just tell him I flew the coop? That you couldn't find me."

"Not gonna happen. Look, bro, the last guy who tried to cut loose had his family's home broken into and his sister got hurt... bad. See what I'm getting at? I'd hate for anything like that happen to you."

Nerves at breaking point, Jim wanted to sit and howl.

He'd been so close. "Maybe you could tell them I already left?"

"Nope. This drop-off is too freakin' important. Look, if you promise to make this last delivery, I'll pretend afterwards that I didn't catch you in time. But this has to be done, Jimmy. Make no mistake. And I can't do it myself. They're expecting you." Tommy handed him the brown package and headed to the window. "Remember, your sister lives here alone." He waited to see Jim's nod and then he left.

Chapter Fifteen

Amelia heard the knock at the door and knew by the shape of her visitor that Sergeant Carlton had seen Jim's signal. "Come in. It's open."

Nervously, she sifted her fingers through her hair, wishing she'd thought to get her purse and the lipstick inside it. "Jimmy's having a quick shower and packing his gear. He shouldn't be much longer. Come and sit in here with me, Sergeant." She motioned for the man to sit in the easy chair across from hers.

He walked over and stopped at her side. "Call me Harley from now on, Amelia. Sergeant Carlton gets a bit wearing." His smile wasn't one that strangers shared. It held warmth and, if she didn't know better, she'd say he cared about her. It felt wonderful!

"I wanted to tell you how proud I am of Jim, and to thank you sincerely for what you're doing for him. The drastic change in him blew me over. He's like the boy he used to be, determined and with a goal. You can't know how much this transformation has meant to me, to us. He's promised to do his best at this program you're setting him up with and I know he'll try hard."

Harley shrugged self-consciously. "I gathered from his behavior last night that he's going through a rough patch. Not a bad kid, just a bit lost. I've run into his type before. They need guidance to make it easier for them to do what they know they should have been doing all along. I'm good at being the heavy. And this program is kinda like a boot camp, with a lot of discussion on his future possibilities mixed in with physical exercise and counselling. He'll be better for the discipline and the hard work."

"I think he knows that. You need to understand how much this means to me. Having Jim away from the gang he's begun running with makes me breathe a whole lot easier."

Harley checked his watch. The hospital had called. Katrina was showing signs of coming out of her coma and he needed to be there. "Is he packing everything he owns? I told him to bring a few changes and that he won't need a lot."

"I'll go and see what's keeping him." Amelia stood and painstakingly moved over to her wheelchair. She manoeuvered it up the hallway and headed to the last room. "Jim, Harley is here waiting for you." She opened the door to emptiness and a burning started low in her gut. *Something's wrong!*

Officer Carlton followed. "He's gone."

"I know." Tears close, she bowed her head and knew the tone of her voice revealed her despair. "I know." A warm hand squeezed her shoulder and made her feel that she wasn't alone in her heartbreak. "Harley, I'm so sorry."

Chapter Sixteen

Later at the hospital, Harley thought back over his conversations with young Jim. He could have sworn that the kid had been totally on board. Well versed in reading signs, he knew when someone was lying to him and Jim had been sincere, he'd swear on it. Something had happened between the time he'd let the boy leave the car and visit with his sister, to when he'd gone in to fetch him.

He'd questioned Amelia, they'd gone over her version, her excitement at the change she'd found in her brother and his remorse for what had happened the night before. She'd believed him too.

Then what the hell had happened between the time she'd spent with him and when they'd gone to his room? Harley felt like he'd been played for a fool and he didn't like that one bit. After all the years he'd spent on the job, he prided himself on having a second sense when it came to the young people he'd helped. And he'd never been wrong.

Until now...

A shuffling came from the small bed he sat beside.

Springing up from the visitor's chair, he leaned over the tiny form of the child who struggled to break through the fog of her coma. Sweat beaded on her forehead and he reached over to wipe it away, to lift her straggly hair back from her face. A nurse entered the room and checked her vitals and the digital screens surrounding her bed.

"It shouldn't be too long now." She read the chart and made ready her injection that would be fed in intravenously.

Harley barely moved. His heartbeat sped up and made talking difficult if he wasn't to give away his nervous foreboding. What if she still couldn't see? What if she had brain damage and they had to put the poor little doll into care? So many things could have gone wrong. Doc Brown had explained earlier, warning Harley, preparing him for the worst. *Please God! She's already lost so much!*

Another hour passed while he prayed and waited. Then suddenly she called out. "Daddy..."

Like a shot, he had her hand in his and he leaned over her protectively, his hand gently rubbing her arm. "I'm here, kitten. I'm here."

Tears started to gush through her still closed eyes, and the baby girl held out her arms, waving them in front of her. He turned to see Doc Brown who'd just entered the room, his expression begging for permission.

As soon as the Doc nodded, he carefully scooped up Katrina, blankets and all, into his arms and rested beside her on the small bed so the tubes attached to her wouldn't be in jeopardy. "Don't cry, sweetheart. I'm here with you."

Whispered words, barely heard. "Mommy? I 'ant my mommy."

Harley had to swallow the boulder stuck in his windpipe before he could answer. Wildly he looked at the professionals for help but they had no answers, only shrugs. "Mommy isn't here now, baby. She loves you, though, so much, and so do I. You must get better, okay?"

As if she had no strength, the whimpering slowed, then stopped. All the while, Harley gently rocked and patted, loving the sweet smells that wafted from her clothes, praying for the child to open her eyes. Except that didn't happen. Instead, she nestled closer and fell asleep.

"Best thing for her now, Harley." Doc Brown lowered the bed so he could stretch out while still holding her. "If you can stay with her until she wakes again, she'll settle better. She's restless without you. Guess she senses safety in your arms, and since her body is fine and we're only concerned about the head trauma, make sure not to jar her in any way. The nurse will call me as soon as she wakes again."

"Thanks, Doc, I'll stay. No problem."

"By the way, they've found a distant relative on the mother's side. Like I told you, she came from a broken family, and it turns out that Katrina has an uncle who lives here in the Grove. They're trying to contact him now."

Suddenly a mewing noise caught their attention and they turned to the child. Her long hair streamed over Harley's blue shirt, her tiny fingers clung to his thumb, while her gorgeous blue eyes, vacant yet lovely, stared into his face. "Daddy?"

Chapter Seventeen

"Harley, I'm sorry to bother you, but would you be free this afternoon, say at one o'clock? I'm expecting a visitor and I'd feel a lot better if I wasn't alone. It's to do with Jimmy." Amelia's hand shook as she held her phone. Harley'd given her his number and had made her promise to call if she needed anything. Well, today she needed a friend. Only she wasn't in the habit of calling men and asking for favors, so she'd had to pump up her nerve and, at the last minute, force herself to carry through.

"I'll be there. Anything you want me to bring?" Amelia pictured Harley smiling on the other end of the phone and her spirits lifted.

"Can you stop at the bakery for some cookies? I guess I need to serve something with coffee. Thank you. You can't know how much this means to me. I have a feeling it's going to be a very upsetting meeting, and I know I'll handle it better with someone else there for support."

Amelia couldn't believe how her world had been so

bright one week, and so horribly sad the next. After Harley had left the day of Jimmy's disappearance, she'd tried calling everyone they knew, hoping to find her brother and talk some sense into him. But she'd come up empty. Just like how she'd felt after they'd realized he'd fled.

Days had passed and she was still praying that Jimmy would come to his senses, return and try again. But, so far, he hadn't shown up and she had no idea where he'd gone.

To make matters even more complicated, others were looking for him too. Amelia knew he had a half-sister from his mother's second marriage, whose family, it seemed, was now in dire need of help. Amelia wasn't sure what it was all about, but Gerda Ward was coming this afternoon and, though Amelia probably should have admitted he'd disappeared, she hadn't. Instead, when the secretary from Gerda's office had called a few days earlier, she'd put the social worker off until today, praying Jimmy might return in time. But since Gerda was arriving shortly, realistically, that wasn't going to happen.

Working hard at her exercises had paid off and she could walk quite well now. A cane, used periodically when tiredness claimed her, came in handy, but otherwise she'd given up the wheelchair except for extreme emergencies—mostly at night when she'd overdone things during the day.

Proud of her accomplishments, she had to admit that Harley had been a great help. He'd stopped by most evenings for a short while, helping her set up the equipment and working with her on her exercises. He'd even loaned her a stationary bike that had gone a long way towards strengthening her leg and hip muscles.

The gentle massages to keep her from stiffening had been her favorite part of their regime and she hoped he never picked up on just how much she loved having his hands on her body. The man's aftershave, a scent she'd recognize anywhere, started the awakening of her senses, and then when his sure strokes on her back and side followed, they usually put her in sensual heaven.

Suddenly, she heard that strange noise coming from the back of the house, sounds she'd been hearing a lot lately. Though Belle didn't react, Grumpy started barking. Amelia never knew if it was in reaction to her edginess, or if he actually heard something, but he always ran to Jimmy's bedroom door and she'd follow.

Each time she checked, everything seemed in place, but it gave her the willies. Also, she could have sworn money had gone missing from her purse. Only who could have taken it? With Jimmy gone, her imagination was constantly spiralling out of control and she didn't like it at all.

But just to be sure, she slowly inspected each room at the back of the house and found nothing amiss... like all the other times.

Chapter Eighteen

Harley smoothed the hair back from Kat's forehead. "Honey, I have to go to work now. I'll be back soon. You know that—right? And Nurse Kim will be here to look after you."

Sniffles followed his announcement, but Katrina nodded and released his hand. The little one seemed to sense when she could cling and when she needed to let go. Since he'd always kept his promise to return, the words – *I need to go to work* – usually made the difference; as if she understood he didn't want to leave her but had no choice. Usually, she'd pull her hands back, wipe her eyes and turn her face to the side. But she didn't scream anymore, thank God. That had broken his heart.

Stopping at the bakery, Harley made sure to select a Christmas decorated cupcake for Katrina, and then chose the cookies he'd promised to bring for Amelia. For a bachelor who, just a short time ago, had been as free as most men wished they could be, his life had certainly become complicated nowadays. Not that he minded. And that surprised the hell out of him.

Driving up to Amelia's house, his heart sped up in the same way it did every time he'd visited lately. Acknowledging that the blonde witch had cast a love spell and it was the best thing that had happened to him in a long while, he sat for a few minutes surveying her property. He'd always known there was a young lady out there in the world just for him and he had no doubt that that Amelia Lloyd was that special person.

Shaking off his romantic notions, he inspected Amelia's snow-covered street and especially her house. The stuccoed front of the older home with its stairs and front porch reminded him of his brother Reed, and how Harley'd recently helped move Reed's girlfriend, Belinda, her daughter and Grumpy's sister, Cloud, into a new place with an old lady-friend of Belinda's. When he'd told Amelia about Reed finding the Samoyed pup, she'd realized that this had to be the Crank's sister, and had been delighted to learn that the other pup had found a good home.

What was that?

Something or someone had moved the bushes at the back of the house. Immediately, Harley bolted from the car and began running in that direction, his heart pumping faster than his legs. When he arrived, nothing appeared to be out of place. The gate was closed and when he approached, an old tom cat meowed, hissed and jumped the fence. By the time Harley had made up his mind he'd been wrong, the back door opened and Grumpy flew down the stairs, yapping and heading right for his pant leg.

Having had this same experience every time he'd visited, Harley waited until the puppy came closer and then pointed and yelled, "No, Grumpy. No. It's just me." Normally it worked, and it did so this time too. The puppy skidded to a stop and growled at his finger. Then he turned to the closest bush, lifted his hind leg and let the stream loose; his way, no doubt, of letting Harley know what he thought of him.

Laughing at the pup's antics, Harley replied to Amelia's question of who was there, and rubbed Belle's head after she approached with a swagger of her back end and a wag of her long tail. Once the puppy had finished his business, he glared at Harley, ran over to the gate and jumped at it, his barking now annoying.

"Hey, little buddy, stop that noise." Harley made a move towards him and Grumpy ran to hide on the other side of his mother. But the growls didn't stop—his warning that this battle might be over but the war hadn't ended!

"How come you're in the backyard?" Amelia stepped gingerly onto the deck and waited for Harley to approach.

"Thought I saw something moving out here, but I guess the old cat from down the street prefers your yard."

She laughed. "It's true. He likes to tease the puppy. Belle and Blackie declared peace a long time ago, but I think the old tom gets a kick out of annoying Grumps. Are you coming in?"

"I'll just fetch the stuff from my car and be right there." Harley watched as Amelia made her way back inside. His eyes glued to her swaying hips started a reaction in his lower body as well as his imagination. And her lovely hair blowing in the breeze made his heart swell with macho pride. Hell, the woman turned him to mush, and he wished he had the right to scoop her into his arms and show her how important she'd become to his happiness.

Chapter Nineteen

In the kitchen, Amelia let Harley make the coffee while she set up a tray for her guest. She loved having him help her in the small room, maybe because they constantly brushed against each other and it felt kind of homey and sexy at the same time. Being aware every time his big body loomed behind hers, she played games with herself that, one day, he'd wrap his arms around her and they'd kiss.

Harley broke into her daydream. "Can you tell me what this meeting is all about?"

Clearing her tight throat, she replied. "Not really. Gerda didn't say much on the phone."

"Gerda?"

"Yes, Gerda Ward from Government Child's Services. She's coming for a visit and says she'll explain everything once she gets here. We've become quite good friends through our jobs. She often calls in at the hospital and we've worked on a few cases together. But it's Jimmy she's looking for, and I didn't have the heart to tell her that he wasn't around. I guess I hoped he'd return in time."

The doorbell rang and cut off further discussion. "I'll get it, if you don't mind carrying the tray into the living room."

Harley heard the two women greet each other with hugs and friendliness, and he stood when Miss Ward entered. As soon as he saw her, he recognized the woman. He'd dealt with her before and had always found her to be fair and caring about the youngsters that were her responsibility. He stepped forward to welcome her. "Hi there, Miss Ward. Nice to see you again."

"It's Gerda. Hi, Harley. Nice to see you also. "She shook his hand and shivered slightly. "Goodness it's cold out there. Looks like we'll be having more snow for the holidays." He helped her with her coat and went to hang it in the hall closet. Returning, he saw that Amelia had poured coffees all around and he took a seat, anxious to learn what this woman had to do with Amelia and her brother

Gerda Ward started the discussion. "I guess you're wondering why I'm here, Amelia. I'm trying to reach your step-brother, Jimmy Rogers."

Amelia gestured to Harley, leaving the explanation about her brother's absence to him. She didn't exactly know what his status was with the law, but when it came to their home life, as far as she was concerned, he had disappeared and she had no idea where he'd gone.

Harley looked a bit uncomfortable. Whether an outsider picked that up, she didn't know, but to her, it showed quite clearly.

"Jim's away right now. We're still hoping to get him involved in the Youth program, Gerda. Then have him counselled about his future career choices. He's a twenty-one-year-old toddler right now, but we'll straighten him out given time." Hearing Harley's words, Amelia wanted to rush over and kiss the wonderful guy for not yet giving up on her idiot brother.

Gerda grinned. "Aren't they all big babies at that age nowadays? Well, I've been able to ascertain that he had a sister, Tamyrn Simpson. Is that right?"

Harley jumped at the surname, his inner antennae spiking to attention.

Amelia, attuned to his moods, glanced first at him and then she turned back to Gerda. "I don't understand. Yes. Jimmy does have a sister but they lost touch with each other. After Jim's mother and father were divorced, his mother remarried and she had a daughter. Therefore I believe Tamryn is Jimmy's half-sister. They only met a few times."

"I see. Well, there was a car accident recently and, unfortunately, Tamryn and her husband were killed. But their three-year-old daughter, Katrina, survived and we're looking for any relatives who might be in a position to step forward and offer the child a home. When our search found that, possibly, an uncle lived here in Carlton Grove, I thought I'd visit and see what his circumstances were, and whether he might be able to help us locate other relatives, or even offer her a place himself."

***

Harley had to contain his rage, stop from bellowing his response at the idea of his Katrina being shuffled off to the likes of Jimmy. Having existed in a dream state ever since he'd rescued Kat, he hadn't given any thought at all as to what would happen to her eventually. Well, it was past time to get his head out of his ass and start being more proactive about her fate. Before he could form a response though, Amelia spoke up.

"Oh, the poor darling. Of course she can come and live here with me and Jimmy, Gerda. He might be away right now, but he'd say the same thing. He's shown me the photos that his half-sister e-mailed him the Christmas after Katrina was born. She's a lovely child. You know we'd take good care of her."

Gerda sighed loudly and clasped her hands like in prayer. "Thank goodness. You can't know how much this means to me, Amie. I've got a huge caseload right now, and this sad story breaks my old heart. She's a delightful child, except for one thing. The car crash has left her with temporary blindness, or at least we hope that's the case. Doc Brown thinks so. We know from speaking to neighbors in the family's old apartment building that Katrina could see before this all happened. Now we're hoping that the swelling she suffered to the brain is the cause and, once that lessens, her sight will return."

Harley held back the response he had and waited, wanting to learn as much as he could about this legal search the agency had conducted. Why hadn't he thought to follow these lines of research himself? Heaven knew, he had the resources. Sick inside, realizing he'd been wallowing in a bubble, he determined then and there to find out everything he could about Katrina Simpson and her circumstances. After all, if she'd decided he was her daddy, then it was way past time he began acting the part.

Zeroing back in on their discussion, he heard Amelia say, "I'll be off work for the next few weeks. It's a perfect time for Katrina to settle in here with me and see how things go. Jimmy should have returned by then and we'll be able to give the little one a nice Christmas at least. After that, we'll make some solid arrangements for day care, etc.

How's that, Gerda?"

"You've lifted a huge weight off me, Amie. With the 'flu season upon us and these treacherous road conditions, the hospital desperately needs the bed. As you can imagine, they're chockablock full of patients right now, with more arriving every day. I was desperate about finding a placement for Katrina. So thank you for relieving me of that worry. As far as your brother is concerned, we'll look into his involvement in the beginning of the New Year. If his circumstances are such that he can be responsible for the child, and of course he's over twenty-one, I see no problem with him eventually becoming her legal guardian."

"Him or me. After all, I am legally her step-auntie also, right? And you certainly couldn't complain about my references."

Gerda grinned. "A step-auntie! Well... Let's just wait and see how everything works out. In the meantime, I'll get started on the paperwork, and if you could come and see Katrina at the hospital, let her get to know you and catch up with Doc Brown on his instructions for her care, then I don't see why you couldn't bring her home in the next day or so."

Chapter Twenty

By the time Gerda left, Amelia had wrapped herself around the idea of giving a home to the desperate child in need. The poor little girl had no one else and the thought of her entering the foster care system made Amelia cringe. She knew that some of those places were wonderful, but many weren't, and the thought of Jimmy's niece, that beautiful toddler, having to go to a loveless home couldn't be tolerated.

Returning to the living room, she realized that Harley had said almost nothing during their exchange and she looked at him questioningly. "What do you think?"

He stepped into her space and let loose. "I think your heart is bigger than your head, Amie Lloyd. Are you seriously considering taking this stranger, even though she's just a child, into your home, loving her and becoming her mother? She's three years old. You realize that, right? If she turns out to be blind, what then? She'll need constant care, a truckload of compassion and a whole hell of a lot of support. Are you telling me that you'd be up for all that commitment?"

Bristles appeared after his first words, and by the time he'd run out of steam, she'd had enough. "Don't you bully me, Harley Carlton. That child needs family and if Jimmy and I are her only relatives, then you're damn right I'll be up for taking her into my home... and my heart."

When he lifted her into his arms and began swirling her around the room, she didn't know whether to laugh or be frightened that the man she'd begun to fantasize about had lost all his marbles. "Harley? What in the world is wrong with you?"

He lowered her in front of him, letting her body slide down his in a romantic way like he'd never acted before. He framed her face with his large, visibly shaking hands. "You're my dream woman, Amelia Lloyd. I'm nuts about you and your gigantic heart. Remember me telling you about the child from an accident that happened the same night I got the call to come and rescue your from Jimmy? Well, I was talking about Katrina Simpson. She's the second love of my life and there's nothing I'd like better than to be involved with you in helping give that little angel a home."

Amelia's heart-rate sped up and she hoped the glow she felt inside her body wasn't blinding the man smiling down at her so adoringly. She saw his eyes search her face and they stopped on her lips. Shyly, she wet them and noticed the loving look in his eyes change to that of a man hungry to taste.

Unaware of her own intentions, she stepped closer until her chest touched his and her arms lifted around his neck. Without disengaging from his seductive gaze, she fingered the short hair on each side of his head, sifting her fingers gently through the strands.

She felt him stiffen, letting her take her time, giving

himself over for her to toy with, to enchant and she loved the power. Finally she lifted her face and pressed her lips to his chin. And that was all it took for him to lose control.

Once again, he swept her into his arms but this time his lips weren't talking. They were too busy making her melt. At first, sweet and soft, he searched her mouth, his tongue gently encountering hers... licking, engaging.

His hands travelled her form, starting at her back, moving to her hips and then cradling her bottom. He devoured her and her body heat rose in waves of passion so quickly, she felt faint.

As if he knew her problem, Harley lifted her like one would a child and then lowered them both onto the nearest sofa. On his lap, she cuddled into him and their kisses became more inflamed until he'd stolen the very breath she needed to continue. Dragging her mouth from his hungry lips, she kissed his neck instead and almost passed out when his wandering, busy hands began searching for her breasts.

"Oh, Lordy! It feels wonderful. Yes, Harley. Please!"

"It is wonderful, darlin'. You're wonderful."

Heavens, she'd spoken those words aloud, not just in her mind as she'd imagined. "Oh, Harley, I love what you're doing to me." Though whispered, she knew he'd heard every word because he moaned and his movements become more feverish, as if he couldn't contain himself.

His hands began seriously searching, sliding under her blouse, stroking her skin, moving upward until he found her brassiere. Working his way around the back, he undid the hook and sighed loudly. His lips on her neck, he scooped her breast into his warm hand and began to squeeze, rubbing his thumb over the nipple until she all but screamed her joy.

Not wanting to be left out, Amelia began undoing the buttons on his denim shirt, then slid her hands inside so the warmth of his skin could satisfy her hunger a little.

Soon his lips followed his hands and he licked and kissed her chest, both sides, until she couldn't stand the torture any longer. Wet, hot, ready for him to come to her, she began to wriggle and noticed the powerful reaction his body had to her movements.

"Baby, your hip. Be careful."

"It's fine. I'm fine. Don't stop." She kissed him again, drawing it out.

He grunted his pleasure, letting her have her fun. Finally, he lifted her up and away. "We have to stop, baby. I'll be too heavy. Stop, Amelia."

Sliding to the rug on the floor, Amelia reached to him and smiled. "We have more room here and I'll be fine, love. Come"

Without another word, Harley slid into her arms and began helping her strip. In no time, he'd taken her clothes off and had himself naked as well. With the room now darkened at the day's end, the fireplace he'd lit earlier brandished waves of warmth and a romantic glow. He again searched out the vulnerable places on her body, first with his hands and then his lips.

Following his example, skimming her fingers along the muscled ridges on his back, down his hips and stopping at his buttocks, Amelia marvelled again at the shape of the man in her arms. He obviously worked out and she loved his lean strength.

All of a sudden, his searching had taken him to the ravenous part of her body, the inflamed erotic area where wet heat burned its way into her core. Consciousness clouded, and then totally disappeared while she gave herself over to the pleasure that his hands were creating. His fingers, which had slid over every inch of her body, were now entering her wetness, delving, plundering, taking her to new heights of pleasure.

Her sighs were impossible to control. Nor did she want to do so. They were her way of telling Harley she loved what he was doing to her. And, in fact, she never wanted him to stop... ever. Opening wide, giving him total access, she arched her back and moved with him, pushing against the pressure his palm inflicted on the nub where joy lay in waiting.

Spiralling quickly, her orgasm hovering, panting, breathing harshly with sweat breaking, she soared until she heard him say. "Come, baby. For me."

Moaning her release, she heard him groan his reply. Once she settled down, her racing heart easing its pressure and the pulsating quivers fading, she slid her body over his and began her attack.

Chapter
Twenty-one

Harley loved the sounds of the woman under him. Her squeals of delight, moans and heavy breathing meshed with his own and drove him on so he could hardly think straight, only smoulder and throb.

Hot, wet and tight, every man's fantasy of a woman in his arms, Amelia delighted him completely. Though not prepared when she turned the tables on him and took over, he succumbed, giving her control.

Having her straddle him, impale him, ride him, she took them both to heights unimaginable. Words broke loose and couldn't be contained. "Yes, baby. Do this. I love it. Yes."

Holding her hips, careful to balance and support the newly-healed side, he watched as she pleasured him. Her eyes were slits, glittering in the half-light. Her hair, wild now around her shoulders, curtained his face when she bent to tease him with kisses so enticing they made his blood boil hotter.

Close, knowing he couldn't last much longer, he growled his excitement, telling her she'd accomplished her goal. That's when her body shuddered with surrender, tightening around him, seducing him to heave one last time.

After their shared orgasm subsided, she lay over his chest, her arms lax, her breasts heaving, harsh breaths emitting little sighs and moans of pleasure.

As he hugged her to him, their sweating bodies began to cool. Not wanting to ever disengage or let her leave, he held on gently. If he could stay like this forever, it still wouldn't be enough time together.

Finally his heart's rhythm slowed. They hugged. They kissed. Then they began to chuckle softly, until another kiss stopped that foolishness and they hugged again.

***

Later, in bed, Harley lay with a smile on his face that echoed the one in his heart. He'd had never had a woman so responsive to him before. One who seemed to fit so perfectly, and who knew what to say, how to act. One who looked at him like he held all the secrets in her world.

That he was in trouble didn't take a genius to figure out. That he liked being in such a spot? Oh, yeah. He'd been searching for this woman forever and now that he'd found her, nothing and no one would be allowed to come between them.

Admitting now that he'd been a fool—a man not wanting to face the potential problems of finding a home for Katrina—he'd ignored the issues for far too long. Hell, what had he been thinking about? That child could have been anyone's niece and how the hell could he have let her go to strangers? Just the thought of that possibility, plus the tightening in his gut, let him know he'd have fought it happening.

Thankful for the ideal way things had fallen into place, he should have known Amelia' sweet soul couldn't stand the thought of a homeless child. That if they had any chance at all for a future, it would have to include his little angel. He could no more have walked away from his crazy role as her daddy as he could have given up Amelia. Now, thanks to the mysterious ways of all things good, he didn't need to worry about either of his girls anymore.

One last time, he softly kissed the sexy bare shoulder near his lips, cuddled her closer and drifted off.

Until Grumpy began to bark.

Chapter
Twenty-two

Thudding noises came from the back of the house, sounds that weren't normal. Harley fought with his pants in the dark, righted the knocked-over chair and ran to the end of the hall where the vigilant pup scratched madly at a closed door.

Growling, flinging his small body at the wooden barrier, incensed, the little beast shared his warning with Harley, as if he knew the man was there to help. By this time, Belle had become involved and she added her snarling until Amelia, now in her housecoat, called her back.

Harley opened the door and switched on the light, all in one quick movement. The curtains, blowing in the breeze, gave truth to the fact that someone had been in the room and had escaped through the open window.

Before Harley could stop him, Grumps jumped up on a chair and flew through the window in hot pursuit.

Suddenly, Harley heard Bruno, the vicious Samoyed

from across the street, and the huge canine didn't sound very happy. Growls filled with rage overlapped bloodcurdling screams, an unmistakable tip-off that the prowler was now under attack.

Amelia appeared suddenly with Harley's boots and his jacket. In no time at all, he ran through the front door and saw the fight going on, under a lamppost, in the middle of the icy road.

His first thought, that Jimmy had come home, disappeared. This guy didn't look at all like Amelia's brother. He was skinnier. His voice sounded higher, at least when it was screaming in pain. And he had a mouth on him that needed more than one bar of soap to clean it out.

Grumps, not liking being left out, added insult to injury by biting the fellow's pant-leg while Bruno had a grip on his flailing arm. The pup's snarls were less terrifying but just as keen.

Once Harley got close, a command rang out from the front steps of the house across from Amelia's, and though the bigger dog whined in frustration, he did let go of his victim and backed off, watchful, letting Harley have control.

"Thank you. I'll take it from here." Harley raised his voice so the neighbor could hear.

"Bruno, come."

Moving in to take the dog's place, Harley twisted the trespasser's arm up behind his back and held on grimly. Speaking loudly, he added. "Give your dog a pat for me. Because of him, I can arrest this creep for breaking into Miss Lloyd's."

"Good! Me and Bruno are at your disposal, anytime. Think you'll need his services anymore tonight?"

"Not unless he knows how to use a phone."

Laughing, the voice answered. "He can't, but I've got a knack."

"Could you call the department and tell them to send a car to this address?"

"On it."

Harley twisted the younger man's arm behind his back, and frog-marched him forward to sit on Amelia's stairs and wait for the squad car to show up. Thoughtful as always, she'd turned on the porch lights and he saw her peeking through the window.

He didn't want to frighten her more than necessary and so he'd decided to keep the snivelling lawbreaker outside and question him there. After all, Jimmy's disappearance still rankled, and though he'd followed up as best he could, there had been no answers to that mystery.

Along with his fellow officers, he'd searched high and low for Jimmy Rogers, pulled in favors, paid snitches and basically torn up the town, all to no avail. It was as if the guy had disappeared off the face of the earth. Now, having this shithead break into Amelia's place infuriated him, yet it made no sense and only created more questions.

Throwing the foul-mouthed whiner onto the top step, Harley stood over him threateningly. "So Tommy Wicks, you've got about three minutes to tell me what the hell you were doing in Miss Lloyd's house earlier, or I'll get the neighbor to let his dog loose again."

A voice rang out. "I can arrange that."

"See what I mean. That Bruno hated you, man. One command and he'd be all over you again." Harley watched the coward cringe and swipe at the blood dripping from the wounds on his arm. Grumpy, still in the picture, growled his agreement, and suddenly the door opened and Belle appeared to add her snarling two cents.

Threats surrounding him, the sorry-assed dude broke down. "I came to get what's mine, is all. Jimmy promised me he'd take care of it and then he upped and disappeared."

"What's yours?"

"A package. And I'm not saying anything more. You got nothing on me."

"Have you lost all sense, you idiot? I've got you breaking and entering, disturbing the peace and unlawful possession."

"Hey! I didn't take nothing."

"I saw you with my own eyes making off with Miss Lloyd's valuable pet."

Are you crazy, man? Both those mutts attacked me. You can't prove I was making off with the little shit."

"I'm a witness too, saw it plain as day." The voice echoed through the dark, a mocking smile obvious.

"See. Two against one. And I'm an officer of the law. Who do you think they'll believe? You'll be behind bars for quite some time, unless you tell me what I want to know."

Wiping his shaking hand across his nose, tears choking him, Harley's prisoner queried with a look. "If you're asking what was in the package, I haven't a clue."

"Right. I can believe that. What I want to know, Tommy, is what made Jimmy take off? Him and me, we had a deal, and the last time I saw him he was cool. Next thing I knew, he'd disappeared. Why?"

"Officer? When you're free with scumbag over there, can you come and see me for a minute?" Again the voice from across the road cut into the conversation.

"Sure can, neighbor, soon as I get this situation settled. Now, where were we?" Harley got into Tommy's face in a menacing way. "Tell me now, what happened to Jimmy?"

Greasy strands of dark hair surrounded Tommy's colorless cheeks. His reddened pupils were ultra-large and his wide-eyed look of innocence not at all convincing. Harley had seen these signs many times and knew the pot-smoker for what he was. "You're in with your brother, aren't you? Gotta tell you, man, that sorry-assed dude is heading for a permanent jail cell very soon. Are you sure you want to be his cell-mate?"

Fear blanketed the other's features. His lips began trembling and he bit them to stop the tell-tale signs of agitation. Harley had seen this many times. When these younger fellows were in with their gangs, they had balls of steel. But if you got them alone, hung something on them that would stick in a court of law, they turned into little girls, crying for their mommies.

"See, it's like this. I want Jimmy. And you want to get out of jail with a misdemeanor, like a slap on the wrist. I can make that happen. But it's up to you man. I gotta tell you, you'd be a fool to pass up this chance."

A whining sob broke through and then another. Kicking out at the annoying Grumps still trying hard to take another chomp or two out of the leg so enticingly before him, the prisoner wailed his exasperation. "That's what I bin trying to tell you, cop. I came here to find Jimmy. I've been looking for him for the last week. If I knew where he was, do you think I'd be breaking into his house?"

As soon as the squad car stopped in front of the gate, the siren's wail ended. The sudden silence held a menacing quality in the snow-filled street. The same quality that Harley felt toward the sorry sucker he forced down the stairs in front of him. "Wrong answer, asshole. You're time's up."

Chapter
Twenty-three

"You wanted to see me?" Harley had dealt with the arresting officers quickly, making arrangements to sign their reports at the department the next morning. The he'd remembered the neighbor's request.

Forgetting Amelia's dogs were still with him, he laughed at their antics when greeting the vicious Bruno. Like three silly clowns, the dogs wiggled and whined their joy at being together. Belle especially acted familiar, while even Grumpy seemed to sense Bruno was an ally. Harley saw the resemblance immediately and knew that there were three sides to the big guard dog now leaping like a puppy in the snow: killer, father and lover.

"Yes, I did. Thanks for taking the time. Come in out of the cold. I put some coffee on; thought you could use a quick cup to warm you. It's brutal out there tonight."

"Thanks. I'd appreciate one." Harley joined the other man in the warm kitchen and saw that his helper was middle-aged, a good-looker wrapped in a navy robe and wearing pajama bottoms similar to a pair that Harley often wore himself. Holding the mug in his hands and leaning back against the counter, Harley added. "I'm glad Bruno was around tonight. Thanks to him, the trespasser didn't get away."

"Yeah, well, about that. I wanted to tell you that I overheard you talking to the idiot, and there's something you need to know. First, you must understand, I wasn't aware that Jimmy was considered missing."

"He took off about a week ago, and Amelia's terribly worried. I've had the department searching high and low but there's been no sign of him anywhere."

"That's just it. I know where he is. I just had no idea that no one else did."

Harley watched the other man's features as they expressed total perplexity. "This is going to be good, isn't it?"

Grinning, the neighbor nodded. "He's at Amelia's like always, only I've seen him lately coming and going from the door in her basement. Of course, I never thought anything of him being there because, as far as I'm concerned, he lives there. It seemed a mite strange that he'd started using that entrance, but I just put it down to the fact that he'd finally gotten off his lazy ass and decided to do some work down in that black hole."

"Seriously? You've seen him?"

"Almost every day. I'll admit it's usually at night when I'm walking Bruno. And he's not very friendly. But then Jimmy and Bruno have never been buddies and so I just put his strange behavior down to him wanting to stay away from the dog. Now that I think back, he kind of skulked around, his hoodie pulled low not wanting anyone to recognize him."

Harley put down his cup and held out his hand. "Thank you, sir."

"Name's Justin Raldon. I'm glad I could help."

"Well, thank you, Justin, I'm Harley Carlton, Sergeant with the CGPD. You've helped more than you can know. I think I'll just go now and pay a visit to Amelia's basement lodger and find out what the hell is going on. Good night."

Harley moved to the door and whistled softly for Belle, who appeared instantly. Grumps came up beside her, covered in snow and looking like a portable snowball. He sneezed and fell over from the inner force. Justin laughed and winked at Harley. "He's a cute bugger, maybe Bruno's best work yet."

"No maybe about it. I'd say he's inherited his father's personality too."

Justin laughed and added. "Bruno's a marshmallow to those he loves, and the best guard dog in the neighborhood."

Grumps, obviously feeling silly over his latest antics, growled and turned his back, his expression distinctly cranky. "Well, at least his offspring has taken on one of his attributes."

Chapter
Twenty-four

Amelia knew that Harley had gone to talk with Justin across the street and so she waited patiently. She'd overhead most of what he'd said to the boy he'd held on the stairs and none of it made any sense.

What in the world had Jimmy taken that belonged to the loser who'd broken into her house tonight? And why had Jimmy disappeared? Her brain felt overworked from all the whys and what ifs, and the rioting going on in her stomach made her feel ill with worry.

Not being able to stand the anxiety a second longer, she started to cry, apprehension overcoming her normal stiff-upper-lip way of dealing with crises. Her optimism had faded, replaced with depression after Jimmy's disappearance, and now she let lose all the frustrations that had built over the last week.

"Damn you, Jimmy Rogers. Where could you be?" Speaking out loud loosened the ball of pain that made swallowing difficult. As she leaned back against the sofa, she pounded on the cushion held against her knees.

"I'm right here, sis. Please don't cry." Abject misery surrounded her pale brother as he stood at the entrance to the basement stairs.

"Jimmy! My God!" Her hands clutched her heart and then swiped at the waterfalls dripping from her eyes. "Jimmy. You're here." Without any conscious thought, she raised her arms in his direction.

He moved forward, sank into her hug and brother and sister rocked back and forth. "I don't care what you've done, Jimmy. Nothing matters except that you're safe and all in one piece." She kissed his cheek and squeezed him harder. "You can't begin to imagine what I've been thinking these last few days. How I've pictured you lying injured in some dark alley, alone, scared."

His voice broke. "You watch too many cop shows, Amie. I've been here, hiding in the basement all along. Tonight, I snuck out to get some groceries, and when I got back I saw Harley on the porch with Tommy. I hid and listened. I know Tommy's looking for me, but I never thought he'd break into the house."

"I think he must've come more than once. I've heard noises in your room at other times since you've been gone." She felt his body stiffen and leaned back to see his shamefaced expression. "It was *you* those other times?"

"Yeah. Mostly I waited until you were at your physiotherapy appointments to come in, but a few times I thought you'd left and you hadn't. I needed to get cleaned up; there's nothing to use in the basement."

"I can't believe that you've been downstairs, right under me and I never realized."

"Hey, with your bad hip, I knew you wouldn't be tempted to use those rickety old stairs. You never went down there much anyway."

"Yes, well, I'd have found you tomorrow because I had plans to go down there and get the Christmas decorations. With you gone, I'd been putting off decorating, but now I have a good reason for wanting to celebrate."

He looked at her strangely. "I don't understand."

"Well, now that I know you're safe and that whatever nonsense you've gotten yourself into can be dealt with, we can move on. Plus, I have another surprise for you. There's a sad part to this story so brace yourself." She took both his hands and let him see her emotion, sharing her compassion with him so he'd know he wasn't alone. "It seems that your half-sister, Tamryn, and her husband were in a car accident just recently and they were both killed."

"God, no! Where... wha..."

"Here in Carlton Grove. Maybe they were coming to see you."

"She never wrote or nothing. I know they were trying to find a new place to settle down. Last I heard, her husband had lost another job because his company was downsizing and they needed to make some changes. I'd written back and said that Carlton Grove had work. So maybe they decided to come and check it out." He covered his face, his hands shaking. "That's terrible." Suddenly, he looked up, horror now showing through tear-filled eyes. "What about Katrina, their little girl? Was she killed too?"

"That's the good news." Amelia rubbed his cheek, encouraging him to be strong. "Katrina survived. But there's a small problem with her sight. According to the social worker they brought in on the case, Gerda Ward, she told me that they think her vision will return slowly, and that the head trauma she suffered created swelling in her brain. In fact, Gerda was here earlier, asking to talk with you. Looks like you're the only relative between both parents and she came seeking answers as to whether or not we could provide the little girl with a home."

His eyes widened. He looked stunned. Then a smile broke through and gathered force until it filled his face. "Of course you said yes."

"Of course."

"Sis, have I told you lately how much I really do love you?"

"It's reciprocated, bud. Believe me. You're my only family." They shared another hug. "We have to stick together."

"Not for long..." Harley's stern voice broke into their conversation.

Chapter
Twenty-five

Amelia saw her lover leaning against the doorway that led into the living room, his arms crossed and a frown covering his face. Belle and Grumps swarmed into the room just then too and all conversation came to a sudden stop.

Grumps headed for Amelia's lap, and other than sniffing disdainfully in Jimmy's direction he pretty much ignored him. Belle, on the other hand, greeted him with a lick on his hands, allowing his pats, even going as far as laying her muzzle against his knee to show her affection.

Cuddling her cold puppy, Amelia took the proffered towel Harley handed her and began wiping his snow-covered fur. Amazement written on her features, she stared at Belle and Jimmy and couldn't help the questioning stare.

Jimmy caught it and flushed. "We made friends. She was the only one I had to talk to. Cranky-face over there tried to bite me a few times and she actually nipped him to protect me, craziest thing I ever saw. He stopped growling and barking after that."

"It's too bad. If she hadn't muzzled him, we'd have known what the hell was going on a lot earlier." Harley looked to be in a very bad mood. Tonight was the first time Amelia had ever seen him in cop mode and it made frissions of pleasure start up along her spine. She liked knowing that this strong character wanted to be with *her*, cared about their relationship and intended for them to be together. There was a lot of feminine pride singing in her veins that whispered, *this magnificent man is yours.*

Jimmy flushed. "I can explain." Let me fetch something and then I'll tell you everything.

Harley trailed him to the door of the basement and even down the first few steps, as if he needed to be sure that Jimmy wouldn't try disappearing again.

Amelia understood his concern and smiled her agreement when his questioning gaze caught hers before he followed Jimmy. No way did she want to go through hell again, worrying about her oddball brother.

Soon, Jimmy reappeared carrying a package, which he handed to Harley. After passing it over, he sighed. "I didn't know what to do with that stupid thing. Now it's your problem." So saying, he wiped his hands together as if cleaning dirt from his palms. Then he sat down again, close to Amelia.

Harley tore open the brown envelope and saw the plastic bag full of multi-colored ecstasy tablets. Instantly, he recognized them and knew them for what they were. "Where did you get these pills?"

"I can't tell you. What I can say is that I was supposed to take them to a drop-off place and I couldn't do it. The day we set up the deal for me to go to into the program, I made a promise to myself that I was done with Tommy's gang. No more being involved. I knew they were luring me in deeper and deeper and I'd soon be past the point of no return. Then later, when I came to pack my stuff, Tommy was waiting for me in my room with this delivery."

Amelia broke in "Why didn't you tell me?" She rubbed his arm. "I would have helped you, Jimmy. We could have dealt with this together."

"I couldn't tell you because they threatened to hurt you if I didn't follow through. Even though the creep promised it would be the last time they'd ask, I knew he was lying. I couldn't do it. I tried to tell him but he just got more threatening."

"So you did nothing?" Harley seemed incredulous.

"Man, you don't understand. I felt like I was being tested somehow. I was dammed if I did and dammed if I didn't. I thought of coming to you, Harley, but then I got scared they would get to Amelia." Jimmy lowered his face into his shaking hands and his voice got husky. "I couldn't stand the thought of anyone hurting her. I had to stay and protect her. So I hid in the basement. I only intended to stay there until I decided what to do, but one day turned into the next and..."

"And you didn't know where to turn." Harley words finished off Jimmy's sentence, and the younger man reared up, hope blazing, obvious for Amelia to see. It turned out that Harley did understand.

"Yeah! Until I heard you talking to Tommy tonight. Seeing you arrest him made everything fall into place for me. I knew he couldn't hurt Amelia now, so I could give myself up. I don't care what happens to me, man. Just promise me that'll you'll make sure she's safe—her and Katrina."

Amelia saw Harley's expression and it mainly showed

shock. Jimmy must have seen it too because he added an explanation.

"Amelia told me that she's going to bring my niece home to live here with us. I'm glad."

Amelia experienced a strange sensation after hearing Jimmy's words. Relief, love and a lot of pride, feelings she wouldn't normally equate with her brother. Happiness flared and she beamed at Harley. Taking Jimmy's hand in hers, she said, "What happens now?"

Chapter Twenty-six

Harley saw two pairs of brown eyes watching him hopefully and his mind spun in circles until it settled on the only answer he could give them—the one that would work for him.

"Now... Jimmy is going to see the Captain and he needs to confess everything. I'll go with him, but he also needs to face up to his part in the unlawful trafficking of narcotics. Because this is his first offence, and with him turning over evidence that will convict Tommy and his brother, they'll probably be lenient. But it's up to the courts. The other program is still on the table though. And I'll put my ass on the line to lend support. The thing is, he needs to pay the piper."

Harley watched to see what reaction his words had on the two who had bonded together, showing unconsciously that they felt it was them against the system he stood for.

Amelia turned to Jimmy, and Harley saw she was holding her breath, waiting, praying he'd man up.

"I'll do whatever you say, Harley. If you want to take me into custody, I'll go with no arguments. Now that I know Tommy's out of the picture."

"No. Tomorrow morning we'll go see the Captain with the goods, you can explain your part in the crime and he'll make the final decision. Tonight, enjoy your time with Amelia." Harley picked up the package and stuck it inside his jacket. Then he winked at Amelia.

She looked back at him, a question in her eyes and he nodded and added, "By the way, Jimmy, your sister and I are a couple now. I'll be here to take care of her and your niece while you're away. You got any problems with that?"

Jimmy laughed, a happy sound not often heard. "I kinda hoped you were spending so much time here lately because you'd figured out what a great catch she is. Even if she is my sister, she's a good-looking chick, and man, can she cook." Jimmy's expression turned grave and he added. "You okay with taking on someone else's kid? From what I remember, Katrina's still a toddler, maybe two years old."

"Katrina's actually three and we've met. I was the officer who came across the accident that night. And to answer your question, yeah... I'm fine with having your niece in the picture. In fact, I'm delighted. She's a sad little angel who needs a family, and we'll give her a good one. If you want, we can stop off at the hospital in the morning for you to have a short visit before we pay our respects to my boss. Okay?"

"Okay, man. And thanks."

Amelia followed Harley to the front door to say goodnight. The minute they were alone, her arms wrapped around him and she hugged him real hard. He got the impression that she'd like nothing better than to climb into his clothes and meld inside his body. He treasured the emotion this created, making him feel loved like never before. "Sweetheart, I don't want to leave but I think it's best."

"I know why you're going and I adore you for being so sensitive to what has happened. For understanding how important it is for me and Jimmy to settle everything tonight. I've never seen him so vulnerable, and I know I can get through to him more than I've ever been able to before. We'll talk and we'll both be stronger for having spent this time."

"I know you will and I'm happy for you. Enjoy this night and I'll be here to pick you both up in the morning. We'll go and see our little girl together. You up for that?"

"You know I am." She kissed him then, sweet tenderness flowing from her lips. Her hands caressed his face and she gazed into his eyes, sharing her sentiments with him, showing him just how much he was cherished.

As he walked to his car, he felt taller than the snow-covered spruce tree blocking out the full moon.

Chapter
Twenty-seven

Amelia fell in love at first sight. The tiny girl lying in her hospital bed had dark blonde hair almost to her waist, a slender body that was a mite too thin and her small hands clutched a new-looking stuffed toy, a fluffy white puppy. Katrina shied away from her visitors until she heard Harley's voice and then her arms raised and she called out, "Daddy."

The roomful of people stilled. All noise stopped. Amelia and Jimmy looked behind them, wondering, confused. Then Harley stepped to the bed and lifted the clinging little girl into his arms. "Hi, kitten. I've brought some people for you to meet: Uncle Jimmy and Auntie Amelia. Your mommy and Uncle Jim were brother and sister."

Katrina hid her face his shoulder, her arms wrapped tightly around his neck and her long curls splayed over his big hands. He looked rather red-faced and Amelia saw him swallow. Then he shook his head as if to clear away a fog and he spoke low. "She mistook my voice at the scene and we haven't corrected her misconception. I'm so used to it that I'd forgotten to warn you."

Amelia thought she couldn't be any crazier about the man standing in front of her, cuddling the tiny girl and trying not to look inflexible but feeling exactly that way about what had just happened. "Of course you mustn't say anything." She moved forward and spoke soothingly in her nurse's voice she knew charmed most patients. "Hello, sweetheart, I'm Auntie Amie. Can I come and visit with you for a while? I like reading storybooks. Do you have any I can read to you?" Since she'd seen a stack near the bed, she felt pretty confident the little girl would agree.

"Yes. I like puppy stowies." Katrina's voice was delightful, and Amelia was immediately charmed.

Aha! She stroked the little girls arm gently and whispered, "Do you like real live puppies?"

"Yeth. I like fluffy ones."

Amelia caught Harley's flush and she just knew he'd laid this trail.

"Your Uncle Jimmy and I have a fluffy white puppy called Grumpy."

When she heard the name, Katrina giggled. "Gwumpy?"

"Uh, huh! He's a cranky little guy who only likes girls. He likes me and I bet he'll love you. Would you like to come to stay at my place and meet him?" Everyone held their breath. The petite girl hid her face against Harley once again and didn't answer. It was as if she had to think before making any commitment.

Jimmy moved forward and gently took her hand in his. "I'm your Uncle Jimmy and your mommy was my half-sister. She was beautiful. Now all I have to remember her by is you, Katrina. You look just like her."

His charming words shocked Amelia. She didn't know her brother had it in him to be so sweet, but then memories started flooding of the thoughtful younger boy who her step-father had first introduced her to years back. This man had reverted to that younger version.

Katrina didn't pull her hand away. But she didn't speak until Harley kissed her cheek and nuzzled her neck. She giggled, delighted with his teasing. "Then she rubbed her cheek against his and said, "Daddy, my auntie has a puppy. A fluffy white puppy called Gwumpy. Can we go see him?"

A sigh of relief broke out from everyone in the room. Step one had been successful. She was willing to come and visit the crabby little mutt. Now they just had pray Grumpy would take to the little girl and fix things so that she'd never want to leave.

Chapter
Twenty-eight

Amelia stayed at the hospital with Katrina while Harley took Jim to see his captain. She read stories to the toddler then, while Katrina had a nap, Amelia visited with Katrina's physician, her old friend.

"Hello, Harry. How're you holding out with all these patients I see crowded in everywhere?"

"Well, if it isn't Amelia Lloyd, my favorite ER nurse. Aren't you tired of lazing around yet? We'll gladly put you to work anytime you want." He grinned, the teasing note in his voice obvious.

"Sorry, my doctor says I have to stay off my feet for long hours until after the holidays."

"Damn idiot! Who could he possibly be?"

"His name's Doc Brown. You might have heard of him. Handsome as sin and very knowledgeable; all the nurses are crazy about him."

"Ha! Silly old fool, you mean. But he's right about you taking the time to heal properly. What are you doing here then?"

"I understand Katrina Simpson is your patient. Did Gerda Ward explain what she's arranged for the little one?"

"She did mention something about Katina having an uncle here in town, a Mr. Jim Rogers, and that she'd made arrangements for Katrina to go and live with his family for the foreseeable future. I was happy to hear the good news. That poor little girl needs a break."

"Just so you know, Jimmy Rogers is my half-brother and I'm the family Katrina will be coming to stay with. I was hoping you could tell me something about her case."

"Well, now. She's got a guardian angel taking care of her after all. Sure, I'll pass on her files so you can go over them. Just come to my office before you leave and I'll give my secretary instructions. But for now, I can tell you she's a healthy child suffering from temporary blindness. We know for sure it's just a matter of time before her eyesight returns because we've seen small signs of it coming back already. When she doesn't know she's being watched, the nurses have witnessed her reaching out for things with no searching involved. I'm beginning to think she might be afraid if she lets on that she can see, that her world will change too much." He shrugged and spread his hands." Who knows what's going on in that gorgeous little head? Two things I'm positive about though; she needs Harley to be in her new world, at least for a while. And, I'm pretty sure that when she's in a happy environment, surrounded by people she trusts, you'll begin to see a huge improvement."

"I'm so glad, Doctor. We'll be taking very good care of the little minx, don't you worry about that."

"Hell, Amelia. Now that I know she'll be in your care,

all I can say is, she's a very lucky little girl."

Chapter Twenty-nine

The next day, while Amelia and Harley were feverishly decorating the Christmas tree, he grabbed her for a kiss. "Lady, you sure have a lot of stuff for Christmas. I thought I'd never get all those lights up around the house."

She pulled out of his arms and slapped her hands on her hips. "Don't tell me you're a Scrooge for the holidays, Harley Carlton, because if so, it could be a deal breaker."

Though she'd spoken teasingly, her heart dropped at the idea that she loved a man who might not share her excitement for this season. It was her favorite time of the year. If it hadn't been for having had her life turned upside down first with her injury, and then all the worry about Jimmy, she would have had all her beautiful decorations in place weeks ago.

"Calm down, sugar. I'm a sucker for Christmas. In fact, I'm usually the one who helps Mom get the house ready. Only this year, things have been a bit crazy and poor old Dad had to step up. The old complainer called to let me know he was only a temporary employee."

"He sounds like a real joker. You don't talk much about your family, Harley. Are you close, you and your brothers?"

"Reed and I hang out quite a bit, or we did until recently. My second oldest brother, Terry, is working out of town right now. He's a helicopter pilot in Alaska so we don't get to see a lot of him, but he's a cool guy. Yeah, I think we're a close family. Our biggest problem has always been that we have no sisters, no-one to boss us around except for my mom and she's like an Army major, tough as nails on us poor boys."

Amelia laughed along with Harley and then got sucked into another long kiss. "Stop! Harley." She batted away his wandering hands. "We need to get this done. Katrina is coming for her first visit tomorrow and I wanted to have the house ready. I told you Doc Brown thinks she can see a lot more than she'd letting on, right? So I want the place to look special."

Harley let her go and crossed his arms; making her think he had to contain them in some way or he'd be reaching for her again. Warmth flooded her and she kissed him for being so sweet. Then she pulled away. Thinking to get his mind off the longing she saw clearly written on his face, shining from his eyes, she spoke. "I meant to ask. You seemed shocked when I told you about my conversation with the doctor. Didn't you *know* Katrina could see a little?"

"I guess I'm just a fool wanting to make everything right. It never dawned on me the little monkey might be hiding anything. Now that I know, I'm thinking it means she must know I'm not her daddy."

"That makes sense. But I heard her call to you as soon

as she heard your voice."

"At the scene of the accident, when I found her on the side of the road in the dark, she called me that and I never corrected her. It didn't seem to matter at the time whether she thought I was her daddy. All I cared about was keeping her calm until the ambulance came. Then something strange happened and it was as if by her calling me daddy, I felt like I had to be. I was all she had. The rest you know."

"Well, as far as I'm concerned, she shouldn't be corrected. If you don't mind, then you'll be her daddy until she decides differently."

"Let's pray that never happens."

"Amen to that!" Not able to help herself, Amelia flew into his arms and the next hour passed in shared ecstasy. After they'd dressed, she started dinner preparations and let Harley finish tying up the last of the garlands around the fireplace. She carried their full plates of lasagna and salad into the living room, went back and fetched the wine and glasses and was sorry the smell of the tomato sauce from their dinner had engulfed the cedar scents from the many lit candles.

Once they were seated on the floor together, Grumpy on her lap eyeballing Harley nastily, she couldn't help herself. "You promised to tell in detail what happened this morning at the police station, between Jimmy and your captain."

"Yeah, well, things couldn't have gone any better. As I mentioned earlier, Captain Johnson took the fact into consideration that Jimmy had not only come forward of his own accord, but that he also hadn't delivered the package like they'd wanted him to. As it turns out, when I arrested Tommy last night, his brother, Jordan, turned himself in and took the rap. He's the one behind the gang activities and according to him, Tommy had always gotten off with probation and light sentences before because he'd been a minor. This time, now that he no longer fit the bill, Jordan knew the law would come down on him hard. Says he couldn't let it happen."

"I guess Tommy is lucky it was his brother who was in charge."

Harley nodded. "Baby, you can't believe how many young fellows get caught up in this kind of a racket. Once in, they can't get out. The gangs suck them dry, blackmail them and get them hooked, so they feel as if there's no hope anyway—might as well go along."

"I'm so glad Jimmy pulled back in time. Just the thought of him living that life terrifies me."

"Yeah, well, Jimmy had someone who loved him, someone he cared about more than himself. You're the reason he couldn't go through with that delivery; he worries too much about your safety and your opinion of him. It matters. A lot! Look, he's very lucky. After he told us everything he could about the operation, the Captain agreed he needed to start on the program, the sooner the better. I have a sneaky feeling he wanted to get Jimmy out of town as much as I did so there wouldn't be any backlash. He got him a ride with one of the other young men we hope to save." His thumb swiped at her tears. "He'll call you on Christmas Day, okay? They are allowed that one time—it's more about their families who miss them."

"Okay." She sighed and gave him one last hug.

Amelia felt tears welling and she hid her head against his chest, feeling a puppy's tiny tongue on her chin, trying to soothe.

"Tell me again about the drugs."

"Right. They raided the drug lab and it turns out that the ones in the parcel were the same batch of tainted drugs that had been poisoning a lot of people over the last week. Some takers are hovering on the brink, sick, minds broken. It's a good thing that Tommy's brother, Jordan, came forward and turned State's Evidence. He's in a lot less trouble now, having helped with the case against the distributers. The district attorney will be a bit more lenient, especially for Tommy."

"I'm just so thankful it's over now, and Jimmy got out before it was too late."

"Says he wants to study the law, maybe be a police officer in the future."

She shared her grin with him, loving the pride she'd heard in his voice. "I wonder who could have influenced him in that direction."

Chapter Thirty

All the way to the house, while Amelia drove, Katrina sat quietly in her car seat. Harley stayed next to her in case memories of another dark snowy night might return and haunt the little tyke.

Relaxed, a diminutive angel staring out the window, her new white hat and fluffy coat to match gave her the appearance of her favorite stuffed animal that was clutched in her arms.

When they arrived at the house, she said only one word. "Gwumpy?"

Amelia and Harley had discussed this moment and what they would do if the cranky puppy refused to be nice and ignored the little girl. But now that the time had come, both were nervous as hell. She glanced at him and saw him swallow, his Adam's apple moving up and down in his throat, a sign that he must be worrying too.

"Grumpy's in the back yard, Sweetheart. Let Har... daddy help you off with your coat and I'll go fetch him." Amelia hung her jacket in the closet and stood for a moment watching as Harley carried his precious bundle to the living room sofa and gently lowered her to sit. Then he carefully undid the coat he'd bought her that morning, the one the little lady had instantly loved because it felt so soft. When he'd told her it was white, she'd been in heaven and her many hugs and kisses put the big man there too.

Amelia went to the back door where both dogs waited, tails wagging, happy grins on their faces. She wiped off the snow from their fur with the towel she left there for just that reason and, while doing so, she had a good talk with Grumpy.

"There's a little blind girl in the house who needs you very much, you silly sourpuss. If you don't behave like a true gentleman, you can forget about treats for a month. Have you got that?"

The puppy twisted his head to the side, whined and gave her a cranky sneer. He sniffed as if to say, *you don't scare me.*

She picked him up and tickled his belly where she knew he most liked attention and then she hugged him, wanting so badly to put him in a good mood. Finally, she stepped into the room and made her way to the couch. She sensed when the puppy stiffened and saw a look of horror appear on Harley's face.

The vibration of the growl started even before the rumbling noise came from the pooch's lips. But before she could pull him away, small arms reached and a little girl's voice rang out filled with adoring love. "Gwumpy!"

Two adults held their breath and watched. Right in front of their eyes, the Grumps became a foolish little puppy, wiggling, licking, crying his puppy words of adoration.

Who got in more kisses, they never knew. Grumpy's tongue bathed Katrina's glowing face and her squealing giggles would never be forgotten.

It was as clear as the lights sparkling on the Christmas tree. Both of these little ones had found their home.

Afterword

Thank you so much for reading *Holiday Heartwarmers Trilogy.*

I loved writing this story and I hope you enjoyed reading it. If so, I would ask you for a favor. Wherever you purchased this book, please take a few minutes and leave an honest review. Authors enjoy hearing that readers like their stories, and hopefully, others will read your words and choose to buy the because of your sentiments.

My website at **http://mimibarbour.com** now has all my books listed with links to the various publishers to make it easy for you to return to where you bought the book and to find my other work.

While you're there, I'd really appreciate it if you would sign up for my newsletter so I can keep in touch.

http://mimibarbour.com/contact.html#newsletter

I only send out newsletters approximately once a month and you have my word that your address will never be shared.

Hugs, Mimi

'Tis the Season

Loveable Christmas Angel – This wonderful Christmas story takes place in Waikiki, Honolulu; a magical city where anything is believable. Leilani is about to find out just how angels scheme to make romance happen for those in their care because Angels really do love romance.

Together For Christmas – Just because Abbie's spirit is locked inside Marcus's body, Christmas is coming and there's a thousand chores needing to be done. An orphanage is relying on her to create a special holiday and he's the only one who can make it happen....with her gentle prodding that is!

She's Not You – Sick and widowed, running scared from a man who insists she belongs to him; Belle is forced to let the charmer down the hall help out. Not just for her sake, but its Christmas, she's in trouble and her little girl has decided their sympathetic neighbor is her special hero.

About the author

MIMI BARBOUR: New York Times & USA Today Best-selling romance author has written 5 series and over 30 books. She lives on the beautiful East coast of Vancouver Island and writes her books with tongue-in-cheek and a mad glint in her eye. The fans all agree that it's the fascinating characters she creates which makes her writing so entertaining and brings them back for more of her magic.

"The favorite part of my job is meeting the characters from each new book. Designing them the way I want and having them act however I think they should. It's thrilling, especially when most of my make-believe folks are so very interesting. They're fun and surprising, and in most cases, people I would love to interact with in reality."

Contact Me

My website: http://www.mimibarbour.com/

Or my blogspot: http://mimibarbour.blogspot.com

Or follow me on twitter: https://twitter.com/MimiBar-bour

Or on Facebook: Mimi Barbour Fan page

Please sign up for my fun Newsletter:
http://mimibarbour.com/contact.html#newsletter